Into
The
Pond

Marsha Cornelius

HICKORY FLAT BOOKS

Into The Pond

Copyright 2017 by Marsha Cornelius

First trade paperback edition December 2017

Cover design by aresjun@gmail.com

Manufactured in the United States of America

ISBN: 978-0692982334

Also by Marsha (M. R.) Cornelius

H10N1

The Ups and Downs of Being Dead

Losing It All

Habits Kick Back

A Tale of Moral Corruption

Up To No Good

REVIEWS for The Ups and Downs of Being Dead:

" . . . a psychological and fun read that is hard to put down."

Midwest Book Review

"Just like in life, rules of the dead are meant to be broken."

5 stars - Lisa Brandt, 98.1 Free FM
(London, Ontario)

'. . .makes for an intriguing, oftentimes hilarious, read about life post-death.'

5 stars - Reading For Pleasure

★★★★★ "Amongst the Best Speculative Fiction I have Read."

Book Pleasures

'Great story of personal growth and change that will leave you wondering whether we can actually be preserved and revived in the future.'

Reflections of a Book Addict

'Highly recommend, great characters, believable transitions and an amazing ending.'

5 stars - For Those Who Love Books

"Rich in detail and vivid descriptions, the reader easily gets caught up in the twists and turns . . ."

Jersey Girl Book Reviews

CHAPTER ONE

Here's a tip for anyone in the market for a new home. Don't buy a house where the master bedroom windows face east; not unless you intend to spend some money on curtains to block out the sun instead of the cheap venetian blinds we installed.

I always meant to put in drapes. My friend Sarah has a gorgeous master bedroom with a fancy bedspread and matching window treatments. (That's what you call them when you use a decorator instead of shopping the clearance bin at TJ Maxx.) She even has one of those diamond-tufted headboards. But then, she's a bank officer who knows how to manage her money whereas my husband Brian and I live from paycheck to paycheck. So there's always a water bill or car payment that supersedes accessorizing.

Currently, the sun is blazing between two of the plastic slats that got bent when I was trying to clean the blinds with one of those stupid dusters that looks like fingers. Just squeeze the handle and all six fingers spread so one fits between each slat. The theory is that when I let go of the trigger, the fingers clamp together and all I have to do is slide the gadget across the whole length of the blind, effortlessly cleaning five slats at once. It's so simple, I can even do it while wearing an evening gown. (Hey, that's what the advertisement showed.)

But the day I decided to clean the blinds, I couldn't find the stepstool that's normally in our closet because Brian had it out in the driveway washing the car. Maverick that I am, I decided to use our plastic laundry basket instead. It was full of dirty clothes. I figured I could turn it over and stand on the base.

I was on my second pass with the magic finger wand when the bottom of the basket suddenly collapsed, I lost my balance, yanked on said cleaning marvel, and bent the slats.

BRIAN SPENT one whole morning watching YouTube videos on how to replace the slats but that was months ago. In typical husband fashion, nothing has happened since.

I managed to pop the dent back out of the laundry basket. Now I just have to remember when I pick it up that the one edge of the lip is cracked and sharp. And every bright, clear morning, the sun's rays come slicing through the gaps like particle beams from a phaser. Anyone foolish enough to open their eyes will suffer irreparable cornea damage.

The offending brightness is compounded this morning by the fact that we just got back from New York where we were covering the annual St. Patrick's Day debauchery for *The Good Life,* a magazine that pays Brian and me for a monthly column called 'Off the Beaten Path'. Yeah, I know, New York is not off the beaten path. Our mission on this particular trip was to find out-of-the-way bars and restaurants that weren't crammed with drunks.

St. Paddy's day was Wednesday, so we flew into LaGuardia Tuesday night and stayed at the Flushing Motel. (The name pretty much says it all.) Our travel arrangements are always made by Madeline: the magazine's office manager, financial curator, and money miser who makes Scrooge look like a Rockefeller. Her preference was for us to take an early bird out of Atlanta at 5:30 Wednesday morning, and come home the same day on a midnight red eye.

I convinced her that by the time we landed and caught the train into New York, it would be midmorning and all the good spots along the parade route would be taken. Since Brian is a photographer, it was imperative that we be set up no later than 7 am for the 11:00 start. So what does Madeline do? Books us on a red eye that gets into LaGuardia after midnight Tuesday.

We got about four hours sleep before we had to catch the train to Fifth Avenue. Hardly worth the paltry sum the magazine shelled out for our plush accommodations. The plan was to get as close as we could to the start of the parade at 44th Street because the pubs we wanted to visit were south of there in Kips Bay, the East Village, and Hell's Kitchen. Our final destination was in Woodside over in Queens, then we'd dash back up to LaGuardia for another red eye home.

Don't ask me why the parade ends at 5:00 pm. I always thought the main reason for celebrating St. Patrick's Day was to drink green beer and Irish whiskey. Evidently, some folks are willing to stand out in the blustery March weather for six hours watching bag pipe bands and females of all ages dance a jig in short skirts. We stuck around for a couple hours while Brian got plenty of pictures of people in the crowd with green hair, green cardboard crowns, green top hats, green beards, green glasses, and various parts of the body painted green.

Around two, we started our search for authentic looking bars, thinking we might beat some of the crowd. No such luck. People were spilling out of front doors and into the streets at every stop we made. We couldn't even get a drink much less some stick-to-your-ribs Bangers and Mash. We settled for day old cheese sandwiches at a bodega in Hell's Kitchen and got our first beer when we boarded our plane to come home.

My advice? If you want to sample some good Irish food and whisky, go the week before or the week after March 17. Of course, that's not what I'm going to write in my article for the magazine. I've been googling stories about St. Paddy festivities for months to tantalize my readers into shelling out big bucks to wait in long lines.

Did you know that McSorley's Old Ale House is the oldest Irish pub in NYC? On one episode of *The Golden Girls*, the old bat Sophia

3

claimed she gave birth to her daughter on a table in McSorley's which could not have happened since the pub did not admit women until 1970.

Here's a little comparison on parade crowds. New York's St. Paddy parade draws around 150,000 people. An average of 3.5 million line the streets of Manhattan for the Macy's Thanksgiving spectacle.

There have been years when the temperature was in the 20s. Just thinking of standing outside for hours in that kind of frigid weather makes me shiver. I snuggle deeper under the covers and burrow my head into my pillow, but it's no use. I'm not going to get back to sleep. And now that my brain is awake, it's yapping 'Coffee . . . coffee . . . coffee . . .' like an obnoxious little dog.

I roll out of bed and grab my robe on the way to the bathroom. I'm brushing my teeth when I hear Brian snort and come to life. He rolls onto his back, and while I'm standing in the doorway, he performs a full body stretch that produces—wait for it—*brapf:* the ceremonial morning fart, officially heralding the beginning of a new day.

MY FREEZING fingers wrap around a hot mug of coffee. The thermometer in the kitchen window reads 45 degrees outside. I'm not walking this morning until it hits at least 55. Yes, I know I'm a big baby about the cold, there's no need to ridicule me. One of the reasons we chose to live in Atlanta is because it rarely snows, and when it does we all stay home. That's my kind of town.

"Check this out," Brian says as he scuffs into the kitchen, his Packers moccasins flapping with each step because they're a size too big. He found them in a clearance bin a few years back and couldn't pass them up. How sad is it that I totally understand?

He's wearing his heavy winter fleece pants—a tartan plaid in red and black—a purple and gold jersey from LSU, and a green hoodie with most of the white Green Day logo chipped off.

I am indeed checking him out when he unfolds the local newspaper to the front page. A three column picture shows a tow truck pulling a car out of a small retention pond. I move in closer to read the caption. *Deborah Ann Wiley, 47, drowned after the car she was driving left the road early Wednesday morning.*

"That looks like Arbor Estates," I say.

"It is."

Arbor Estates is a pretentious subdivision I pass every time I go to Target. When it was first built, it included a guardhouse at the entrance, but hard times have hit even the rich because they no longer pay a security guy to man the fancy shack. Instead they put in an electronic gate that requires a code.

The subdivision is set off the road about 100 yards to accommodate the two retention ponds that catch the run-off from storms. The designer added spraying fountains in the middle of each to make them look elegant. The drive into the subdivision passes between the two ponds and acts like sort of a dam to keep the ponds separated.

I read the opening paragraph which tells how Deborah Ann Wiley drove her car off this raised drive and down into the left pond. By the time rescuers arrived, she was a goner.

"How could someone drown in a shallow pond like that?" I ask. "How deep do you think it is?"

"I don't know. Six feet?"

I visualize a woman careening into the subdivision at breakneck speed and either flying nose first, or skidding sideways into the pond. But that doesn't seem right. I look at the picture again. From the angle of the car, it looks like she was leaving the subdivision.

How does someone go from idling while a gate opens, to a high enough speed to lose control and run off the road at five in the morning? The paper doesn't say anything about her alcohol level but I assume it was in the red zone of the breathalyzer.

"So her car was barely submerged in the pond," I mutter as I tap the paper.

"I guess."

5

"But she doesn't try to get out?"

"Maybe she panicked," Brian says. "They say the water pressure against a car door can be pretty powerful until the water seeps in enough to equalize."

"So she can't roll a window down and swim out?"

"If she had power windows, they wouldn't work."

"What about a cell phone?" I skim the rest of the story. "Yeah. It says right here she called 911 but the connection was lost before she could give an address. All she got out was that she'd driven into the pond at Arbor Estates."

"I saw that. But it took the call center a few minutes to determine where that was."

I shake my head. "And she just sits in the car watching the water rise and doesn't do anything."

"Weird, huh?"

Her name sounds so familiar.

Brian pours himself a cup of coffee. "It says she was a newspaper carrier."

"Oh, my God! She's *our* newspaper carrier. She always sticks a Christmas card into our paper in December so we'll give her some money."

"Maybe you can use this for one of your mystery short stories," Brian says, already losing interest.

The call of the refrigerator has lured him away. He opens the door and stands searching.

I'm tempted to tell him there's nothing to eat but that's just a waste of breath. He'll figure it out. Instead, I go back to studying the picture of the car. Maybe the woman was epileptic, or she had some other kind of seizure. The cops won't find that out until the medical examiner does an autopsy. I assume while they were testing her alcohol level they tested for drugs, too.

"I don't know. It sounds a little fishy to me," I say.

Brian snorts because he thinks I'm making a pun. Then he pops a couple refrigerator containers into the microwave.

"We should look into this," I say.

"You don't need to look into anything." He yanks the newspaper away. "Just use your imagination and dream something up."

I get a bit snippy. "I just want to drive by there and see exactly where she was when she ran off the road."

"No."

"I promise I won't even get out of the car."

"NO."

I grab my purse that's hanging off the back of a kitchen chair. "Ten minutes, tops."

"Gladys!" he yells, but I'm already in the garage.

Sometimes when I'm inquisitive, Brian calls me Gladys instead of Rachel. It refers to the nosy neighbor in a TV show called *Bewitched* that was popular before I was even born. We've both seen enough re-runs to know all about that chinless busybody Gladys Kravitz.

I hop into the Chevy Malibu I bought after my Mini Cooper was demolished. If I don't, Brian will want to drive his Jeep and that just won't do. I need to be able to control the situation.

He dashes out a minute later, juggling one of the containers of leftovers and a fork.

* * *

AS I DRIVE up to the entrance of Arbor Estates, I see the muddy tracks that lead from the road into the pond. I pull over to the merging lane and we both take in the whole scene: the short entrance drive between the county road and the gate into the subdivision, the two retention ponds with their fountains spewing water into the air, and the skid marks through carefully groomed grass.

"How did she run off the road?" Brian asks as he scrapes at the last of the leftovers.

"Good question." I open my door and get out.

7

"Hey, I thought you were just going to look."

"I am."

With a growlish sigh, he gets out, too. "Just remember what happened last time you stuck your nose in someone else's business."

I glance at him over my shoulder. "Yeah, I sold a six-part series to a magazine and got a five-figure advance on a book."

"I meant your beat-up face and two wrecked cars." He trots to catch up with me. "And I hardly think ten thousand dollars should be bandied about like it's ninety-five thousand."

Yes, I got myself into a little bit of trouble a couple months ago. And two cars were totaled. And I nearly got stabbed to death. But I tracked down a cold-blooded killer who is now behind bars, so you're welcome.

"You're just mad because you had to eat that leftover mac and cheese."

Brian burps. "It tasted funny."

I shake my head. "I didn't tell you to put the leftover chili on top."

We stand on the drive looking down into the retention pond. "How can someone who's sitting in a car waiting for a gate to open drive forward and veer into a pond ten feet away?"

"It's more like fifty," he says.

"Okay. Fifty feet. How fast can a Porsche go from zero to sixty?"

"She was driving a Ford Escort."

"Yeah, I know. So she guns the car, it sputters, it coughs, it jerks out past the gate. She's streaking along at fifteen miles an hour when she inexplicably goes off the road."

Brian turns back to the gate. "Maybe she was folding newspapers."

"I think a machine does that now."

"Maybe she was depressed," Brian says. "Maybe she was crying because she had no money and no future. I mean, she has to be up at four o'clock in the morning to start her paper route. How great could her life be?"

"That's not a bad idea."

"Can we go home now?" he asks as he shifts from one foot to the other. "It's freezing out here."

As I drive us back home, I wonder if Deborah Wiley was indeed fed up with her life and decided to end it all in the bottom of that pond.

CHAPTER TWO

The cursor blinks on my monitor waiting for me to start typing. I've got a book to write about the capture of the notorious Farouk al Asad. He was robbing jewelry stores and pawn shops, fencing the stolen goods, and sending the money to some terrorist cell in the Middle East. I'm not bragging when I say that I was instrumental in his capture. (Well, maybe I am.)

I also have to write the article on our trip to New York, and finish a short story about a fictionalized al Asad for a magazine. But all I can think about is Deborah Wiley drowning. I turn away from my computer and stare out the window of the extra bedroom I use as a workspace.

This could be another book, with another hefty advance. I know what Brian said, but ten thousand dollars is nothing to turn up my nose over. And if I do a good enough job on the Farouk al Asad book, they might even double the advance. I need to give this drowning some serious thought.

How hard is it really to get out of a sinking car? I understand the power windows won't work, but why didn't she wait until the car had settled at the bottom of the pond and then open the door?

I swivel back to my computer and search YouTube for drownings. Of course, one of the most popular videos shows a man intentionally driving an old car down a boat ramp and into a lake to show how to get out. The main point seems to be that the instant you realize you're heading into the drink, you need to get that window down while there's still power.

A couple other videos show interesting gadgets that will break a window. One even shows how the headrest has two metal spikes that could be used to break the glass.

According to the last video I watch, if the car is in deep water, the pressure is probably too great to get the door open. But the pond is only six feet deep. Did she even try to open the car door?

I glance at the time. I've been on the Internet for almost an hour and still haven't written one word. Okay. I sit up straight and square my shoulders. I'll start with the St. Paddy's story. With my fingers on the keyboard, I wait for an inspiring opening line.

The lead sentence of an article can sabotage a whole morning if my creativity isn't working. Yet I can't very well start writing until I know what these magical few words will be because they will set the theme and tone for the whole story. (At least that's what I tell myself when I'm procrastinating.) I toyed with using an Irish phrase, like 'May the road rise to meet you' but then I found out that it isn't really Irish. It came from some Hollywood movie. Probably with Maureen O'Hara, that fiery redhead. I'll bet she never would have drowned in a little pond.

Maybe Deborah Wiley wasn't depressed; she was being stalked. Some creep that knew she drove through the subdivision everyday was lurking by the gate. When she drove through, he jumped out, scared her and she gunned her car, shot into the pond and bumped her head on the steering wheel. Or he jumped into her car while she was waiting for the gate to open, tried to assault her but she fought him off. The car plunges into the pond and he holds her down so she can't escape . . .

No, no, no. The newspaper article said she called 911 but by the time rescuers arrived, she was dead. If someone had been lurking in the bushes, I'm sure she would have told the 911 operator that. And if someone had actually jumped into her car, I don't think she'd be able to say 'Hang on a sec while I call the cops. Then you can strangle me.'

I walk down the hallway, past Brian's disgusting man-pit/office in the other spare bedroom. I can tell by the way his fingers are hammering the keyboard that he's playing some arcade game instead of going through all the pictures he shot in New York. I'd say something, but if I do, he'll just ask how the article is coming. Best to leave that sleeping dog with his fleas.

Our bedroom offers no inspiration for my article, or a revelation about the drowning. All I see is the pile of dirty clothes in the laundry basket in our closet reminding me that I need to do at least two loads. And I probably should pull the sheets off our bed. I can't remember when I changed them last.

So it's write or do laundry. Do laundry or write? I clearly have no choice. I'll go to the Batesville Police Department and get more information on Deborah Wiley.

* * *

MY SWEAT pants have been replaced with black yoga pants and I've got on my thigh-length sweater that hides a multitude of sins. The boots are a nice touch that I'm sure make me look like a legitimate journalist. I approach the front counter of the police station with my little spiral notebook in hand.

"Good afternoon," I say, channeling my best professional demeanor, "I'm working on a follow up to the Deborah Wiley drowning on March 17th. Could you tell me who was assigned that case?"

The woman behind the glass types on her computer. But while I'm standing there waiting, I see Detective Baker roaming around in the bullpen where all the cops have desks. He and I don't have the best relationship. I mean, I did help solve a crime that involved a murder, but police never take kindly to citizens who try to take the law into their own hands. I duck down and pretend to tie my shoe until he passes by.

"Detective Furilla is handling that case."

"Great! May I speak with her?"

See what I did there? I figure we girls need to stick together, so I assume the detective is a woman. Then when she says, 'I'll see if *he's* available', we can exchange an unspoken acknowledgement of the disparity.

I watch as Detective Furilla answers the phone at his desk, and then turns to look at the front window to decide if he's busy. I stand up a little straighter to let the girls do the talking. I know, it's demeaning to use breasts as a bargaining chip, but I don't make the rules.

He decides I'm worth his time and waves me back. We shake hands and I get down to business.

"I just have a couple questions about the Deborah Wiley drowning."

"I'll help if I can," he says, motioning for me to sit.

"Here's what I can't understand," I say, leaning my elbows on his desk to show how friendly I am. "Why do you think she didn't just open the door and get out? Or roll down a window?"

He leans forward as well, but it isn't to mirror my body language; it's to get a peep at the girls in the V-neck sweater.

"That's the thing," he says. "The passenger window *was* open. She could have climbed out and practically waded to shore."

I tilt my head in confusion. "The window was open?"

"Yeah. She delivered newspapers, so as she drives from house to house, she picks up a paper from the passenger seat and throws it onto a driveway. When the rescuers got there, they found bagged newspapers floating in the pond and in her car."

"Wow! That's bizarre."

I'm jotting down a quick note when a voice bellows, "What the hell are you doing here?"

Without turning around, I know who it is; my asshole brother-in-law Jake. He's also a detective with the Batesville Police

13

Department. And when I first suspected something was going on in our neighborhood way back in November, I told him about it. Okay, at the time I thought some people were using a rental house to make porn videos, but in the end, my basic instincts were right. Something was going on in that house. But Jake refused to even consider the possibility so when Farouk al Asad was finally apprehended, Jake ended up looking like an incompetent boob. Which he is.

Furilla glances up. "She's doing a follow-up on the Wiley drowning."

I shove my pen into my purse. This interview is over.

"A follow-up," Jake says, his voice still loud enough for everyone in the room to hear. "For a travel magazine?"

Furilla's eyes get one more quick glance at my chest before they roll up to my face. He squints and puckers his mouth. "Who did you say you were writing this article for?"

"I'm a freelancer for the AJC," I say, but I'm already getting to my feet. I'm not in the mood for one of Jake's tirades.

But then he scoffs "Freelance," like I'm a stripper who calls herself an interpretive dancer.

I shove a finger into his chest and raise my voice so everyone can hear me. "Remember what happened the last time you thought I was on the wrong track." And just like that, I throw down my invisible gauntlet: I'm going to figure out why she drowned.

On the drive home, I mull over the fact that Deborah Wiley's window was wide open. I know she called 911. So for a few seconds she thinks someone will rescue her before she has to climb out on her own. And what, get her shoes wet? Ruin a new blouse?

But when the water is up to her chin, and she knows the window is open, why didn't she swim to safety?

* * *

BRIAN IS still at his computer but I'll bet fifty bucks he hasn't done anything with his pictures. And there are telltale signs that he's

14

been foraging for food: a balled-up potato chip bag in his wastebasket, crumbs from a packet of cheese and peanut butter crackers on his shirt, and an open can of soda sitting right next to his keyboard. Doesn't he realize how dangerous that is?

Okay, so I'm the one who spilled cranapple juice all over my laptop and had to get a new keyboard, but it could happen to anyone. He should have learned from my mistake.

"How did it go?" he asks.

"Fine until Jake showed up."

He smirks since he's not a big fan of Jake either. I tell him about the open window and he's just as stumped as me. But like most men, he's easily distracted. He glances at his monitor and I see his attention gallop away. I watch him play until his soldier gets killed. He groans and sits back in his chair.

"Hey, you know what I've been thinking about?" he says.

Now a normal woman might guess either food or sex, but we just had lunch before I left, and Brian has never been a very spontaneous guy when it comes to an afternoon delight. Not unless his adrenaline is pumping like when we were breaking into the house we suspected of taping porn flicks.

Instead, I just shrug because I have no idea what he's thinking.

"I'm going to put a fish pond in the back yard."

See? Now I never would have guessed that in a million years.

"A fish pond."

You'd think my deadpan tone of voice would be a clue, but Brian takes off and runs with it. "Yeah. For goldfish." He practically wiggles in his seat. "And water plants. Look at these."

He minimizes his game and waves me over to have a look. I see a fancy pond with flat stones stacked up at one end so water cascades down into the inviting pool. And another pond with gorgeous blooming water lilies and dragonflies perched on lovely purple swamp irises.

I get a vision of Brian's pond. Half-dead plants, their limp leaves decomposing in the stagnant water, and a neighborhood cat sitting patiently at the edge waiting for the last fish to swim by so it can be scooped out and devoured.

"And it's so easy," Brian says. "You don't have to pour concrete or cut heavy-duty plastic. They have pre-formed ponds now."

He clicks on another page that shows an array of black liners in all kinds of shapes and sizes.

"But you still have to dig up the yard, right? This won't be an above-ground fish pond."

"Well, yeah, I've got to dig a hole, but think how cool it will be to have a fish pond. I can put a little fountain in the middle and we can sit out on the patio at night and drink a glass of wine and listen to the water."

"Sounds dreamy," I say.

There's no point in putting the kybosh on his idea. I don't have a clue how long he's been thinking about this. If I poo-poo the idea, he'll only want it more. I'm sure he's been squirreling away money from photographs he's sold. And since I spent part of my advance catching us up on all our bills, he's free to use his mad money however he wants. I mean, I've got big plans for what's left from my advance.

"Have fun," I say as I back out of the pit.

The need for dark chocolate distracts me. I brew myself a cup of tea, unwrap an individual block of chocolate laced with orange zest, and settle in with the newspaper. I check the police blotter for potential magazine stories first.

Besides writing for *The Good Life* which is basically a travel magazine, I also write fictional short stories: romance under the name Lisa LaFlame, and crime under Rex Rogers. I get some of my best ideas from the blotter.

A woman reported to police that sometime between 7am on March 13 and 6pm March 18, someone entered her home and replaced her carpet.

Oh, this has lots of potential. The woman could have been on vacation, or in the hospital. She comes home, sees the carpet is different and calls the cops. They dismiss her with things like 'maybe your husband ordered it and you forgot'; or 'it sure looks nice, I wouldn't complain', but she insists something is amiss. After they leave, she discovers two eggs are missing along with bread and the rest of her provolone. There's some back and forth between her and the cops. She insists they look for fingerprints but they're too busy to take her seriously. A couple days later, she notices an odor in her house. It's particularly bad in her living room. She gets on hands and knees trying to find the source. Finally, she gets a screwdriver and pulls up the carpet. She finds a big black bloody stain on the hardwood floor underneath.

Once I jot down some notes, I move on to the newspaper's rants. These are phoned in complaints by readers who want to bitch about the construction near the high school, or to bash a politician. Every now and then I find a juicy morsel, but not today.

I'm licking the chocolate off my fingers when I happen to notice the obituaries. There's a three-line post about Deborah Wiley's funeral on Friday at 3 pm at Bates and Son Funeral Home.

My brother-in-law's scoff at my being a freelance journalist, plays back in my head. And I remember how Detective Baker was so sure I didn't know what I was doing when I solved the porn house mystery.

I'm going to that funeral.

CHAPTER THREE

Bates Funeral Home is pretty standard: thick carpet to muffle sobs, soft organ music to ease the grief, and the scent of fresh-cut flowers to soothe the soul. After signing the registry, I slip into Viewing Room Three and stand at the doorway for a moment to get my bearings.

There's not much of a crowd. The paper said Deborah was survived by her mother, Janine Taggart, and a daughter, Shannon. I don't see any teenagers or white-haired grannies. I do see a twenty-something woman in a short black skirt and a silky low-cut blouse. From the distraught expression and the tissue she's wringing in her hands, I assume it's Shannon. She's flanked by two other young women who look on with sympathy, totally out of their element and unsure of what to do. A little more to the left is a buxom blonde in tight black jeans and what looks like a bustier, slightly concealed by a jean jacket. Deborah's mother?

I glance to the side and see a funeral guy standing near the back wall, his hands clasped loosely in front as though he's a soldier at ease. I sidle up beside him.

"Poor Shannie," I whisper, shaking my head. (I like to use a familiar 'nickname' so people think I know the person better than I do.) "This is so hard for her."

"The grieving process is always difficult," he says.

I nod as I scan the room again. There is one small floral arrangement. "Have you heard anything about donations to a favorite charity?"

"No ma'am."

He's pretty tight-lipped. But then Deborah was cremated so he might be miffed that he didn't get to sell a casket.

I'm not going to get any dirt from him so I head for Shannon and her two friends. As I take her hand in both of mine to offer my condolences, it suddenly occurs to me that she might ask how I knew her mother. Saying she delivered my newspaper doesn't sound like a very familiar bond.

I turn to the friend on right. "Thanks for being with Shannon during this difficult time." Then I give the friend on her left a watery smile and move on.

The mother tells me her name is Janine when I introduce myself. By now, I've come up with an answer to the inevitable question; or close to it.

"I was so shocked to hear about Deborah," I say. "I haven't heard from her since we exchanged Christmas cards."

"I couldn't hardly believe it myself," she says. "Course, Shannie woke me from a sound sleep when she called all hysterical."

Her brain processes what she just said and she gets a contrite look on her face like she's embarrassed. (And she forgot to add 'Bless her heart.') Instead, she explains, "I work nights and the bar don't close 'til two."

"Yeah, I've been there with those early morning calls," I agree. "And I guess you had to call your boss, make arrangements to be gone."

She bugs her eyes out as she nods at me. "I had to take off Friday and Saturday. Those are my biggest tip nights."

"Bummer."

"Then I had to drive all the way over here from Eufala." She catches herself nagging again and switches gears. "At least I don't have to pay for no motel. I'm staying in Deborah's room at their apartment."

That sizzles through my mind for a second. "With Shannon."

Janine steps in close like she doesn't want Shannon to hear. "Don't know how they can afford that place. Not with Deborah's shitty pay. And Shannon workin' part-time at Dollar General."

"I know that's right."

"Those sons-a-bitches didn't even send flowers."

I wobble my head. "I suppose the newspaper didn't either."

"Hell, no. Sent a stupid sympathy card, the cheapskates."

"How long you staying?"

"I figured I'd stay through Sunday. I told Shannon I'd help go through Deborah's stuff. Clean out her closet and such."

Oh, yeah. I'm guessing the fashion statement is generational and Janine is about to inherit at least three pairs of boots, a ton of tank tops, and maybe even a leather jacket. If Deborah had a boyfriend, there could be a drawer full of Victoria's Secret knock-offs.

"Are donations being made to any charities?"

She scrunches her nose up like she doesn't understand.

"The lack of flowers," I say as I nod to the lone arrangement. "I thought maybe you had asked people to donate to the Cancer Association or something."

She snorts. "If anybody wants to donate money, they can send it to me. I paid big bucks to get her cremated. And that didn't include the urn."

"I guess you bought the flowers, too?"

"Nah, they're from Deborah's church."

Two women come into the room dressed in nearly identical black yoga pants and black knit, zip-front athletic jackets. They're too far away for me to make out the logo.

"You just give me a great idea," Janine says. "I'm gonna call the newspaper and Dollar General both, see if they'd like to donate some money towards Deb's funeral expenses."

"That's a good idea. Maybe pay them a visit so they can give you the check right then instead of having to mail it."

"Damn, Girl!" she practically shouts. "No wonder you and Deb was such good friends."

I give her a friendly pat on the shoulder and move away before she wants to hear about the drunken escapades of Deb and Rachel, best buds.

The Yoga Twins hurry through the receiving line and then set up camp at the back of the room like they're waiting for someone. They're my last hope for a scoop.

When I get closer, I see that the logo is for Now's the Time Fitness. Brian checked them out once, but their monthly membership was too high and they didn't have a pool for laps.

One of the women has her hair pulled back in a ponytail. The other has one of those new cuts where one side is shaved and the hair on the crown swoops over to the other side.

I nod at Ponytail. "My husband keeps telling me I need to check out Now's the Time."

"Oh, you should. It's a wonderful facility."

While she's priming me, Buzz Cut snatches a business card out of her shoulder bag. "I'm a personal trainer there."

She shoves the card into my hand.

"We both are," Ponytail adds, but she wasn't quick enough on the draw.

I glance at the card. "Is that how you knew Deborah?"

"Yeah," Ponytail says. "She was a personal trainer, too."

"I'd be happy to work with you," Buzz Cut says. "You've got a lot of potential. The long legs, the trim waist. You just need to tighten it up a little."

Trim waist? Isn't she kind.

"So I guess you were all good friends."

"Not really," Ponytail says. "We all had different clients."

I let my eyebrows bump just slightly in confusion.

"We thought her boyfriend might be here," Buzz Cut says.

Ponytail's ponytail swishes as she nods. "They must have been serious the way he spent money on her."

I give them a knowing nod. "Jewelry?"

"Hell, yeah," Buzzcut says. "Necklaces, and bracelets. And the clothes!"

Oh, Janine, have you hit the motherlode. Although I've got to think Shannon has beat her to the jewelry.

Buzz Cut drops the real bomb though. "He pays the rent on her apartment."

Holy Crapoly. A real sugar daddy.

Right on cue, a man in an expensive suit strolls into the room. His grey hair is combed to the side in a wave, and when he smiles at Funeral Guy, his pearly white veneers nearly blind us all. He's got Sugar Daddy written all over him.

He moves quickly to the front of the room, pausing for just a moment to get a glimpse of the portrait of Deborah on an easel. Then he shakes Shannon's hand while putting his other hand on her shoulder. Funny that she doesn't seem to recognize him. Instead, she kind of bows her head and nods. Janine wrinkles her nose in a smirk.

He turns to face everyone in the room. "May we all bow our heads for a prayer before we send our sister, Deborah Wiley, to her final resting place with God the Father."

What? He's a preacher?

He runs through the usual platitudes of her leaving her Earthly home so soon, and being in a better place now. But there isn't one word that sounds at all personal. I swear, if he hadn't looked at her picture, he wouldn't know her if she walked into the room.

Once she's been sent through the pearly gates, he asks if anyone would like to share a few words about Deborah. He looks right at Janine. She glares back but he apparently won't take no for an answer. She steps over to the picture of Deborah.

"Well," she says. "I'm Deb's mama."

Before she can start on her first memory of Deborah as a young toddler, shedding her wet diaper and playing in the sandbox naked, the preacher is out the door and gone.

* * *

BRIAN IS sitting on our back patio when I get home. Next to his lawn chair is a small cooler. Beers in the afternoon?

I open the screen door and it screeches on the track that's been out of alignment ever since Brian backed into it while we were moving the sofa.

He turns and smiles. "How was the funeral?"

I grab the only other chair that doesn't have torn webbing in the seat and the aluminum legs aren't bent, and slide it over next to him. "Not bad."

I reach down to the cooler between us, get out a long-neck and hand it to Brian to twist off the top. "What's the occasion?"

"I'm trying to decide where to put the fish pond."

"Well that certainly calls for a couple beers."

I give him a recap on Shannon, Janine, and the preacher—the trailer trash clothes, sharing an apartment, the mother hoping to extort money for the cremation. And the two-minute ceremony.

"Not that I'm complaining," I say. "The shorter the better."

"What church did she go to?"

"I didn't catch the name. All I know is it was Baptist. And I think the preacher's name was Jimmy or Johnny."

"Local?"

"I doubt if she drove to Marietta for services."

23

Brian pulls out his phone for a quick search. I take a long pull on my beer and breathe out a sigh. A warm afternoon, the sun on my face, a cold beer, and my husband, who's about to wreak havoc on our backyard. Can't get better than this.

"I got a Johnny Daniels," he says.

"That sounds like it."

Brian taps a couple more times. "Ha! It's Six Flags Over Jesus."

"No kidding."

This is a mega-church not too far from us, with jumbo-tron screens hanging from the rafters so all the parishioners can see the anguish in the preacher's face when he says he needs more money. They've got a giant cross in the middle of a fountain out front, and flags in a circle with pictures of doves on them.

I've never been there for a service, but the place is so big that the area schools use the sanctuary for high school graduations. It looks more like a big city theatre with the half-circle of seats that start on the floor and rise all the way up to a nosebleed section. It's got to be big to accommodate the 6,000 people who come to services on Sunday.

We were at the church when my sister Gwen's older son Sam graduated. And trust me, it's a whole lot nicer than sitting outside on a football field. Unfortunately, we got to the church late and had to sit in one of the balconies so Sam wasn't much more than a speck on the stage. But we got some nice pictures of him on the Jumbo-tron screen.

"We should go to church Sunday," I say. "I'll bet someone will be talking about the drowning."

He shakes his head. "Not a snowball's chance."

That's fine. It's probably better if I go alone.

"Guess what else I found out," I say. "Deborah was a personal trainer at Now's the Time Fitness."

"No kidding."

"Yeah, you should have seen the two women who came to the funeral. They must have come straight from the gym. Yoga pants, skimpy sports tops that push your tits up and out."

I notice a little jump in Brian's ratty gym shorts. Evidently, he's going commando so he's roaming free. That reminds me that I still need to do laundry. He probably doesn't have any clean underwear.

He fluffs his raggedy AC/DC tee shirt to cover the indiscretion.

"One of the women had a punk haircut. You know how they shave one side and let the other side grow long. I bet when she works with a client she threatens them with a spanking if they don't work hard enough."

Another jump in his shorts that makes his shirt rise.

"The other woman had a perky ponytail. And legs . . . ?" I click my tongue. "She wraps those around a man, I bet she could squeeze him in two."

Is it sick that I draw his attention to attractive women? I know he looks, why should I pretend he doesn't? And I'm definitely not the jealous type who snarls when he turns to watch a woman walk away. He knows my Top Five Hot Men list. When Prince died, he drew me a hot bath with lots of candles and brought me a big glass of wine. And he thought it was cool that I had a massive crush on Aaron Rodgers from the Packers.

Besides, I asked Brian to go with me to the funeral and he refused. So I want him to regret that decision just a little.

"I think I'll mosey over to the fitness center tomorrow and see if I can find out anything else," I say.

"I'll go with you," he says in a rush.

Of course he will.

We stare out at the small backyard in silence. He's envisioning an afternoon of digging and a finished pond. I see weeks of a big hole catching rainwater, and muddy footprints all through the house.

"Hey, Sarah called," he says. "She wanted to know if you'd heard about the drowning yet."

We both chuckle and clink our beer bottles together.

CHAPTER FOUR

Most Saturdays, Sarah, Ellie and I walk our neighborhood. It's usually girl talk and gossip; who needs to mow their lawn, who got a hideous haircut.

As we swing our arms and puff along Abernathy Way, I rib Sarah a little for thinking I'd miss the biggest story of the month: a drowning just a mile away.

"You were in New York," she says as an excuse.

"I know. And I appreciate the tip. But just so you know, you're going to have to be quicker than that if you want to be the first. Thursday when I took my walk, Linda Peck told me when she came out to her mailbox. And Frank Nelson was spraying weeds when he saw me and called me over."

"Yeah, really," Ellie says. "Everyone in this neighborhood knows Gladys. If you want to scoop a story, you can't wait two days."

"Next time, I'm texting you. I don't care where you are," Sarah says and we all laugh.

Then as we walk, I regale them with what I've learned so far. And they've got their own questions. 'Which Dollar General?' 'What's the name of the apartment complex?' And of course, my favorite. 'Don't you think you should just let it go?'

ONCE I'VE walked off my breakfast, Brian and I head to the fitness center. He's wearing the same shorts he had on yesterday. (I hope he's wearing under garments today. I did a load of wash last night just so he'd have some briefs.) He was thoughtful enough to change his shirt. Today it's an Eagles tee shirt that is so old, the logo is perforated with holes. Someday I'll take it out of the wash and that creepy bird head will be gone.

I'm wearing a pair of yoga pants Sarah talked me into buying when we were going to exercise together every Thursday evening. And it wasn't just yoga—it was hot yoga. I went once and thought I was going to suffocate.

Enthusiasts gather in these small rooms like saunas, roll out their mats, and stretch to Indian music. The air was so dry, it hurt my sinuses. And I couldn't take little shallow breathes because the instructor was constantly telling us to inhale deeply. I swear the hairs in my nose curled up and fell out.

At the front desk of Now's the Time, I tell the young man that we're new to the area and looking to join a fitness center. They always let you come the first time for free. It's a standard marketing ploy.

His name tag says Alec. He looks about twenty, and has a Bruno Mars pompadour. The black tee he's wearing must be a child's medium, it's so tight.

Alec gives me a big smile and says he'd be happy to show us around. (He totally ignores Brian.) Now if I was delusional, I'd think he finds me attractive, maybe imagines a torrid weekend with a hot older woman. But being the realist I am, I know that selling a membership means closing the wife. Husbands who come with their wives don't get to decide.

Brian understands this. "I know the equipment. I'll just have a look around if that's okay."

Alec gives him a fakey smile, trying his best not to look at his dirty Asics. Then he escorts me into this huge room of glistening torture machines. Pounding music inspires everyone to pump faster, sweat harder. And everywhere I look are mirrors. It's a nightmare.

I step closer to one of the mirrors and pretend to check my hair. Really, I want to make sure I'm not sporting a camel toe. I glance over to see if Alec is checking, too. But he's busy admiring his physique.

Our first stop is the cinema room. This is a darkened enclosure with several rows of stationary bikes, elliptical machines, and treadmills. Plus a huge screen on the wall that shows movies all day long. There are even a couple of arm chairs for folks who get so exhausted walking at two miles an hour that they have to sit down to watch the ending. This is where I would spend my time—if I was a member.

"That was so sad about Deborah Wiley, wasn't it?" I say.

"Who?"

"The woman who drowned."

"Oh, yeah. I didn't really know her."

I give him a coquettish head twist. "Didn't she work here every day?"

"Yeah, but we're usually working with clients. There's not a lot of hanging around shooting the breeze."

Swell. I stuffed myself into these pants and I'm not going to learn anything new. I should have known it was a long shot. If Ponytail and Buzz Cut didn't know the boyfriend, neither would Alec.

He shows me the group exercise room, the cycle room, the pool, even an area set up for an express 30-minute workout at different stations. Once we've circled around, he leads me to the dreaded 'closing' table where we'll sit and he'll do his best to get me to join.

"I really can't make that decision without asking Brian," I tell him.

I can see that he doesn't believe me, but he's still too young to pour on the bullshit. Something like, 'A strong, independent woman like you? I would have guessed you make all the important decisions.'

He'll learn.

Once he gives up, I wander around looking for Brian. He's standing in front of a mirror holding two weights and squatting. He sees me in the mirror.

"How was the tour?"

"A bust. Alec barely knew her. I'm going to see if any of the members know anything."

Brian sets his weights on a rack and pulls the front of his shirt up to wipe the sweat off his face. "Start with that guy on the overhead press." He nods at a middle-aged guy whose shirt is soaked with sweat. Ick. "He says Deborah was his personal trainer and he thought she was getting married."

"What?"

"Yeah, I guess she and her boyfriend were pretty close to tying the knot."

No way the guy knows something Ponytail didn't. My guess is Deborah told all of her male clients she had a steady boyfriend to keep them from hitting on her.

Brian shrugs at my disbelieving head bobble. "He says she was looking at dresses."

Okay, so I'm pissed that Brian got a scoop. He's really starting to take this sleuthing business seriously. But I reassure myself that he'll never be as good as me.

I drape myself on a corner of Sweaty Man's machine and smile. "I understand Deborah was your personal trainer."

Sweaty lets go of the steel bar he's been pulling down behind his back, and sucks in his gut.

"She was," he says, then swipes a wet arm across his dripping forehead.

"A woman that fit? I can't believe she didn't swim to shore."

"Me, too." This guy's a real fire ball.

I flex my arms. "I mean, she could probably bench press the dang car!"

Sweaty gazes into the beyond as he nods at some vision of Deborah, scantily clad no doubt, and glistening from exertion.

"Did you ever see her boyfriend?" I ask.

"Nah. At first I thought it was a ruse, like wearing a wedding ring. But she was always showing me something he bought. She had this pair of yoga pants that looked all steampunk with gears and hinges. God they were hot."

"My guess is he was older," I say. "Pulling in big bucks. No wife spending his dough."

"That makes sense. Or he sure had her fooled. I know those diamonds looked real to me."

"Do you have any idea where she lived?"

"Oh, hell no. Do you know how many guys would be knocking on her door if they knew where she lived?"

* * *

SUNDAY MORNING, I hobble to the bathroom on sore legs. I don't know why I felt compelled to try all the different equipment at the fitness center. Especially the machine that pulls your thighs apart and you have to strain to pull your knees back together.

I ease myself over the toilet but the muscles in my legs give out and I drop like a stone. When I try to stand again, my quads scream in agony. I'll have to sit here until Brian comes to my rescue. He'll have to use the paraplegic arm wrap to lift me off the toilet. How embarrassing.

I decide to try something else first. With my left big toe, I reach out and drag the bathmat over, then I kind of roll off the seat and onto the floor. From there, I get my elbows on the toilet lid and hoist myself up.

A nice hot shower helps ease the pain. I'm going to Deborah's church this morning no matter what. This morning's paper had a follow up on the funeral and the mystery surrounding her death. In this article, the church was named. I'm guessing any parishioners who read the

31

story are wondering if they'd met her. I've got to get to services early so I can comb the crowd for clues.

JUST LIKE I remembered, the main entrance has a big fountain out front with a cross in the middle. Instead of a quaint steeple and stained glass windows, this place looks like a corporate headquarters. I guess it's God's headquarters.

Inside, a huge lobby extends all across the front of the building. Enormous windows rise up a couple floors, and there are wide stairwells at both ends for folks to climb to the balconies. I count at least six doors that lead to the main sanctuary, like in a sports arena. The only thing missing is the smell of hotdogs and popcorn.

I do smell coffee. Tucked under one of the massive stairways is a table with a 30-gallon urn and trays of cookies and pastries. I'm drawn by the promise of a cheese Danish.

A cluster of people blocks my access to the goodies but while I wait for a shift, I can listen in on conversations. Two men are talking about the Braves chances this season. A woman wearing a Kelly green sweater tells a friend about the corned beef and cabbage she made on Wednesday.

Then I hear: "My cousin said a deer ran into the side of her car so she couldn't get her door open."

I rise up on my toes to see who said it. There's a small huddle of women at the end of the table near a tray of pastries.

"I heard she hit a tree first and was knocked unconscious," someone else says.

A sourpuss with red lipstick oozing into the wrinkles around her mouth says, "She may have been drinking."

I insinuate myself into the group. "Deborah Wiley."

The women nearest turn to look at me, a blank expression on their faces.

"That was her name," I say. "Deborah Wiley."

I've been in the middle of this kind of mob action before. No one really knew her but since she was a member of the church, they have a connection. And they all want to appear to know more about her than they do. Even if it's someone really famous, people grasp at any link to them. 'My brother-in-law used to fly to Chicago all the time and that's where Robin Williams was born.' Stuff like that. And I ought to know because I'm a master at misconception.

When no one takes my challenge, I add another morsel. "She was our newspaper carrier."

I get an eyebrow raise on that. A few heads bob in admiration; but I also get a doubtful smirk from Lipstick Lady. I think about tossing in the fact that we gave her $25 every Christmas but some of these folks might think I'm a cheapskate. At least I've upped the ante. Someone will have to do better than the fact that Deborah Wiley touched the newspaper I read.

"She worked at a fitness center, too," a woman off to the side says.

Bingo. We have a contender.

"Yeah, a personal trainer," I say. "She was really buff, wasn't she?"

Now we're in a championship match, battling it to see who comes up with a stumper. The rest of the huddle become onlookers who follow our volleys back and forth.

"No kidding," the woman says. "I wish I could wear a size 2."

Oh, nice return. It's a high lob that goes over my head. The crowd gasps at this intimate detail, but I've got it. With a strong backhand, I come up with a doozy. "I wonder how her boyfriend is handling the loss."

By the expression on the woman's face, she had no idea Deborah was in a relationship. Point – Rachel!

As much as I enjoy the game, I'm not getting any closer to my goal: new information. I snatch a sliver of raspberry Danish and move on to the next gathering.

This group is perusing Jesus tee shirts being sold by the youth choir and the conversation seems to be about some Christian rock band called Double Dub. A girl behind the table has a shirt with their logo and then in smaller lettering—WWJD. Definitely not the demographic I'm looking for.

The next table has hand-crocheted bookmarks, for those who don't have the fancy Bible with that little ribbon in the seam. The women's auxiliary has drawn quite a crowd. My ears perk up when I hear 'boyfriend'. So either the wildfire has already spread over here from the coffee klatch or this is someone with new information. I squeeze in between an old woman tottering on a cane and a fifty-ish woman wearing a felt Fedora.

Someone says, 'He must be heartbroken'; and another says, 'I heard they broke up and that's why she drove into the pond.'

"Was he a member, too?" I ask.

Bird heads jerk as everyone glances around for an answer.

"I don't think he was," a woman says who looks about my age. "She always came alone."

Now we're getting somewhere. "Shannon never came with her?"

Damn, I'm good. Not only do I know about the boyfriend, I also know her daughter's name. The woman is struggling for a response when a bell rings, just like at the theater when the curtain is about to go up. Like zombies, everyone turns and heads for the main doors, tossing their coffee cups into conveniently located trash receptacles.

I scurry to catch up with the woman. "Do you remember when Deborah joined the church?"

"I'm not sure she did," she says as she holds the door for me to walk in.

34

The magnitude of the building stuns me again. Rows and rows of seats curve in a massive half circle around a stage that rivals the Dolby Theatre in LA. Giant screens are mounted on the wall so we can all see the pastor's sincerity. (I'd be speculating on how much he paid for his suit.)

Organ music plays as I walk down the aisle beside the woman. "How did you meet her?"

"I sat next to her once," she says. "I told her about our Sunday school class but she never came."

A man about halfway down the aisle stands and waves an arm our way. The woman squeezed past knees and over purses to take the only empty seat next to him. I glance around and realize the place is packed. I go back out and up the stairs to the balcony.

I finally find a seat in the nosebleed section. This is where all the sinners and outcasts come. Women with babies sit rocking, ready to jump up at the first sign of a whimper. I see teenagers who have escaped the embarrassment of sitting with family. A couple kids off to my right look like they might go at it as soon as the house lights come down. Do they actually dim the lights in church?

The service starts with a huge choir singing a rousing tune while parading down the two main aisles and up the stairs onto the stage. We all stand and sing along.

The preacher follows one of the lines but it isn't until he reaches the pulpit and turns to smile at the masses that I'm sure he's the same one from the funeral. I'd recognize those teeth anywhere.

After a few welcoming remarks, Preacher Johnny invites us all to turn and greet our neighbors. I look around briefly, but nearly everyone in my section has their nose buried in their phone. Below, the masses are reaching over the backs of pews and across the aisle to show how friendly they are. I imagine there are women down their hoping they didn't forget to switch their hand sanitizer to the purse they're carrying this morning.

35

Preacher Johnny comes down from the stage to glad-hand folks in the front row. He looks more like a politician. Maybe the first row is reserved for big donors.

There is movement in the aisle down to my left. It's Shannon Wiley and she's boogyin' towards the front like she's got the devil after her.

Now if I'd put money on it, I'd have said that Shannon hadn't seen the inside of a church in years, if ever. And the same with Grandma Janine. Neither one seems the type. In fact, I'm surprised Deborah came to church, but then maybe her new beau was a good Christian and she was coming here to practice. He couldn't be a member or she'd have sat with him. The general consensus is she came alone.

Shannon is making good time in her dash to the front. Is she trying to get to Preacher Johnny to bless him out for leaving the funeral so fast? Was Deborah having an affair with the holy man and Shannon wants to expose him? If that's the case, why didn't she confront him at the funeral? Will there be a big scene with Shannon screaming and crying, and the preacher dropping to his knees to beg for forgiveness in front of six thousand believers? I hope so.

She's getting close when a man in a black suit and white shirt steps into the aisle and intercepts her.

Dang! I wish I'd brought some binoculars. I can't tell what's going on, but it looks like the man is trying to gently herd her back up the aisle. He nods and grins to folks along the way but he looks like he'll break her arm if she doesn't comply. I scurry to the railing to lean over and see where she's sitting.

But she doesn't sit. She heads for the nearest exit. I guess if she can't make a scene, she's not interested in being saved this morning. I nearly break my neck running down the stairs. Why did I wear high heels when I knew I was on a mission?

I catch sight of her through the huge windows. She's heading for the blue parking lot. Thank goodness, she's moving pretty slow. If I didn't know better, I'd say she was crying.

I've almost caught up to her when I have to stop to take a deep breath and dig a thumb into the stitch in my side. I call her name. "Shannon?"

She turns around; and she *is* crying.

I dig in my purse for a clean tissue. I'm too winded to speak so I just hand it to her. While she dabs, I gulp another breath.

"I'm Rachel Sanders," I say. "I met you at your mother's funeral Friday."

"Oh, yeah."

"I saw you were hoping to shake Preacher Daniel's hand this morning."

Confusion grips her for a moment, then she snorts.

"I wasn't trying to see the preacher," she says. Then she looks around like someone might be listening. She opens her mouth to say something else, but then she shakes her head. "It don't matter."

I wait patiently, hoping she'll say something else, but all she does is blow her nose.

"Listen," I say, "I was going to Cracker Barrel. Can I buy you lunch?"

CHAPTER FIVE

We drive to Cracker Barrel in separate cars. I can't help noticing that Shannon drives a nicer car than me. I guess since mama's boyfriend pays the rent, she can pour her wealth into a Toyota Camry.

The church crowd has descended upon the restaurant which means we have to wait for a table. It gives me time to run through the boring get-acquainted questions, such as 'How do you like working at Dollar General?' (The pay sucks and she doesn't work enough hours.) 'Have you lived in Atlanta your whole life?' (She makes a vague reference to a boyfriend with Nazi tattoos, including one on his throat, that drove both her and her mother out of Eufala, but I don't quite get whose boyfriend he was, grandma's, mama's, or Shannon's.)

Once we're seated, Shannon jumps on the menu. I'm thinking of getting the turkey breast sandwich. Since New Year's, I've been trying to eat healthy. Sarah is coaching me.

"It's not a diet," Sarah says. "Diet means you lose some weight and then you go back to eating the way you used to. You're never going back. You're starting a new eating lifestyle and it won't end until you die."

At the time, I was eating a sandwich on whole grain bread with tomato, lettuce, bean sprouts, and one eensy weensy slice of turkey. I thought if I died right then, it would put me out of my misery. She had the decency to let me smear some mayo on it and thankfully, I survived.

Shannon orders the country-fried steak with mashed potatoes, fried okra, and macaroni and cheese. How can she be skinny eating like that? I don't want her to feel bad so I order the fish platter. At least I go for the hash brown casserole instead of the mac and cheese. Hey, hash browns are a vegetable, and the fish is *lightly* battered. A vision of Sarah's snarling face pops into my head so I get the steamed broccoli instead of the bacon-riddled green beans.

Once the waitress is gone, I ask Shannon if her father is still alive. I didn't see him at Deborah's funeral.

"Nah," she says. "He died in a motorcycle wreck when I was five."

I tell her I'm sorry but she looks baffled, like she doesn't understand why I'm apologizing. Then she asks if I'm married.

I nod. "Brian and I have been married for fifteen years. No kids." I just throw that in now since it always seems to come up. And of course, the next question is always why so I cover that, too. "Female problems."

Shannon gives me a knowing nod. The sisterhood has been established.

"So where's your apartment?" I ask.

"Westbrook."

"In Fulton County?" Dang, that's one of the new exclusive communities in the burbs. High-brow shops take the first floor, then the second and third floors are apartments with all kinds of amenities, not the least of which is a balcony that overlooks the shopping boulevards below. And of course there are tons of restaurants, a movie theater, a skating rink. They even have their own Whole Foods, and a big home furnishings store. Brian and I checked it out when the complex first opened. I couldn't afford the placemats, much less the $3800 dining table. And that didn't include the chairs! The clothing stores are all fancy boutiques, and the shoe store doesn't even sell sneakers.

"Isn't your mom's fitness center right across the street?"

Shannon gets teary-eyed as she nods.

"I'm sorry," I say. "I shouldn't have said that."

"It's okay," she says. "I just don't know how I'm gonna get along without her."

"I've never lost a parent. I can't imagine what that must be like."

I *have* imagined my parents careening off a snow-covered mountain road in the dead of night because they think they can go anywhere with that humongous RV they bought a couple years ago.

"And the way she died!" she says, her voice cracking.

The tears are gushing now. She blots them with her napkin, hoping to preserve her makeup.

"Maybe this was a bad idea," I say. "Would you like me to see if they'll pack our lunches to go?"

"No," she sniffles, "I'll be all right." More dabbing. "The man at the funeral parlor said it's good to talk about it."

"So I've heard."

She inhales a deep, shaky breath and blows it out slowly. Then she squares her shoulders like she's ready to take on the world again.

I click my tongue as I shake my head slowly, like I'm thinking to myself. "The thing I don't understand is why she didn't just get out of the car."

"Oh, no way! That's why it's so sad. She was scared to death of the water."

"She was?"

"Yeah. I guess some cousin of hers tried to drown her when she was a kid."

"Oh, my God!"

"They was all at some lake. She was paddling along and he swam under her and grabbed her leg and pulled her under."

"What a jerk!"

40

"She never would go near the water after that. Not even in a boat."

So Deborah Wiley drives her car into the pond, she sees the water rushing in through the passenger window, she calls 911 but she absolutely will not swim out. Crap! My story has ended before it really got started.

The waitress arrives with our lunch. And now I've got to pay for two meals and I won't even get a story out of it. I'm just glad I didn't order the Weight Watcher Special.

Shannon's country-fried steak looks and smells delicious. My fried fish is pretty tantalizing too, even without the mac and cheese.

I'm glad neither Brian or Sarah is here to badger me when I cut my first bite of fish and plunge it into the tartar sauce. I even close my eyes as I chew. It's been a while since I had some fried food goodness.

Shannon shovels a huge forkful of steak and gravy into her mouth. She chews for a second but then hesitates like she doesn't want to swallow.

"Does it taste funny?" I ask. "Should I call the waitress?"

She shakes her head and finishes chewing but her eyes fill with tears again. "My mama would kill me if she saw me eatin' all this."

I give her a sympathetic frown. "She was a personal trainer. I guess she wanted people to eat healthy."

Her pain quickly turns to anger. She saws away at her meat and jabs a piece with her fork. "Yeah, well I'll eat healthy when I can afford it. Right now I need something that'll tide me over until my shift at Taco Bell tomorrow."

"I thought you worked at Dollar General."

"I do, but I applied at Taco Bell yesterday. I need a second job." She's getting better at controlling the tears now and just blinks them away. "I gotta move out of Westbrook. There's no way I can afford it."

And with Deborah gone, there's no way Sugar Daddy is going to keep paying.

"I don't see how I'm going to afford any apartment," she says. "They're all over a thousand dollars, and that's for a one bedroom. I've got a car payment, and insurance."

"I can't imagine how much the rent is at Westbrook. The only thing Brian and I can afford there is the movie theater; and that's for the matinee."

"Oh, it's expensive," she says as she shakes a bunch of salt on her fried okra. "At first I thought it was cool livin' there. We moved in last summer so I figured I'd meet some rich guys out at the pool. I seen this gorgeous bathin' suit at TJ Maxx." She waves her fork at me. "Spent fifty bucks on it! Every now and then I'd meet some guy at the pool but it never lasted long."

This doesn't surprise me in the least. Sure, she's a beautiful girl, but her accent is what I call Georgia Cracker. It's white trash Southern spoken real fast, as opposed to Savannah Genteel which is a slow, sophisticated drawl. I'm sure as soon as the bad grammar comes out of her mouth, those guys shy away.

"I'm not sure I'd want a rich guy," I say. "They're so full of themselves."

"No kidding." She washes down some mashed potatoes and gravy with her sweet tea. "Here's a good one. I walk up to a guy in one of them pool chairs. He looks up and I know he likes what he sees. We talk for a couple minutes and then he picks up his glass and shakes the ice. 'I was just goin' up to my room to get another cocktail. You want one?' he says. So I say sure. Then he says, 'Why don't you come up with me, tell me what you want?' So I go up to his apartment."

At this point in the story, she starts playing with her food, drilling one tine of her fork into the end of a piece of macaroni.

"One thing leads to another," she says without looking at me. "We get carried away." Suddenly she looks up at me. "You shoulda seen his bedroom furniture. It was right out of Southern Living."

42

But now she's back trying to impale the piece of macaroni. "Next time I see him is at Marlow's Tavern downstairs. And he acts like he don't know who I am. I mean, he was as frosty as a cold beer mug."

I click my tongue in disgust. "That's a man for you. Once they get a nut off, they're on to the next one." I notice that I've started talking in a deep southern accent like hers. I hope she doesn't think I'm mocking her.

"I sure woulda liked living there. He had a leather sofa, and a one of them fancy mini-bars."

"Maybe you can find someone who's looking for a roommate."

She kind of growls and clenches her teeth. "That son-of-a-bitch. I wish he'd never talked Mama into moving in to that place. I told her it wasn't our style."

"Who's that?"

"Oh, her on-again, off-again boyfriend."

"He pays the rent?"

"Yeah, but I told her it was stupid. 'Specially since he's married."

"Oh, boy."

I try to sound disappointed, but my heart zings. My fingers are all tingly. I'm back on the case. Was Deborah getting it on with the preacher and his wife found out?

"See? You know it was a bad idea. Why couldn't she get it in her head that he was just playin' her?"

"I've never understood why women get mixed up with married men."

"It's a losin' proposition," she says as she picks up a piece of fried okra with her fingers and pops it into her mouth.

"I was talking to this guy at the gym where your mom worked. He said she was looking at wedding dresses."

43

"A wedding dress!" Shannon blows out such a gust of air that some snot comes with it. She wipes it away with her napkin. "There's no way that prick was going to leave his wife and marry my mom. At least she knew that."

I casually cut another bite of fish and dab it nonchalantly into my tartar sauce. "So who is Mr. Money Bags?"

She snorts. "Darrell Pressley."

My mind hiccups for a second. "That's weird. We have a Georgia Senator named Darrell Pressley."

She stops cutting to point her knife at me. "That's the one."

CHAPTER SIX

I know it sounds like a cliché, but I actually choke on my bite of fish. And I'm not talking about a little 'cough, cough' and a dab with a napkin. I'm a full-blown choker. I can be in the middle of swallowing, think of something to say, and inhale my own spit. Don't get me started on the number of times I've choked on hot salsa, tequila, fresh-ground pepper—the list is endless.

This kind of choking requires deep-lung wretches and hacks. My eyes water. My nose runs. I'm making more of a scene than when Shannon was crying.

Finally, I manage to guzzle a bunch of water and get the spasm stopped. I snatch a tissue out of my purse and ask her in a wavering voice to tell me more about this affair with Darrell Pressley.

"She met him on her paper route, can you believe that?" She stabs her last bite of country-fried steak and uses it to wipe the last smears of mashed potato off her plate. "She was running late and he was standing on his porch waiting for his paper."

I have a vision of Senator Pressley standing on his porch, arms crossed, impatiently waiting to see what The Atlanta Journal-Constitution has to say about him.

"She sees him waitin' so she parks the car, grabs his paper and trots up to the porch to hand-deliver it."

"And I imagine if she looked half as gorgeous as you, he was smitten."

"I don't know what smitten is, but I'm sure he had a boner pokin' out of his bathrobe."

She gathers up five or six pieces of fried okra and starts popping them into her mouth one at a time.

"Next thing she knows, he's waitin' on his porch lots of mornings. She starts dressing nicer and they get all flirty. He wants to know all about her, where she lives, how come she don't have a boyfriend, that kind of bullshit. One day he tells her his wife has to go to some convention. He hates to eat alone. Would Mama join him for dinner? Says he'll grill some steaks."

"Men think they're so smooth."

"Ain't that the truth? At least he didn't lie about being married."

It sounds like Shannon is following in her mother's footsteps, falling for men's nonsense. Interesting that she doesn't see it.

I encourage her to continue. "So she goes to dinner . . ."

"Yep. And ends up in bed with him. I guess she gave him a good ride because not two weeks later, he's pushing for her to move to an apartment in Westbrook. I tried to tell her he was just interested in some poontang but she insisted it was more than that. 'He wouldn't pay for an apartment if it was just a booty call,' she says. She was sure he'd fallen head over heels for her and now he wanted to support her."

I can't eat another bite so I push my plate away. "What a slug."

"I told her he just didn't want to come to our shithole apartment."

"And now that everyone has a camera on their cellphone, he couldn't take her to a hotel."

She points a finger at me. "Exactly."

If she thought she could get away with it, I swear Shannon would pick up her plate and lick the last of the gravy off.

"You know what's kinda strange?" she says. "I swear someone else had been living in the apartment. You know how when you rent an apartment, it smells like fresh paint, and the carpet has been shampooed. But I found mustard and ketchup packets in a kitchen drawer, and a towel in the closet on the balcony."

"Do you think he had another woman living there before?"

Shannon tilts her head and gives me a smirk. "Don't you?"

* * *

I LITERALLY trip running up the stairs to Brian's bedroom office.

"You are not going to believe this," I say, panting from the run. "Deborah Wiley was having an affair with Senator Darrell Pressley."

"No way!"

I hold my hand up in scout's honor. "Shannon told me herself."

"The Senator was porking her mother right in front of her?"

"Well not exactly. Deborah had Shannon's work schedule so he came over while her daughter was at work. And guess where the apartment is—at Westbrook!"

"Damn, she must have been one fine piece to warrant paying for an apartment there."

"No kidding. Seems like it would have been cheaper to pay a hooker."

Brian swivels back and forth in his chair, thinking. "That probably wouldn't be safe. Someone would see them. Besides, a lot of men don't like using prostitutes because they know they're faking it."

"And you would know this how?"

He doesn't bat an eye. "Do you really think hookers have an orgasm every time they're with some stranger?"

"Good point. Anyway, Shannon tried to talk her mom out of it, her mom would break it off, and Pressley would swear he was working on dissolving his marriage."

Brian googles Pressley. "He's fifty-two. So why would he go for a woman in her forties instead of some young babe?"

47

"Young babes are too prone to blabbing, or wanting to take selfies. If I had to guess, he picked Deborah because she was menopausal."

His eyebrows scrunch up like he thinks I've got a screw loose.

"She couldn't get pregnant," I clarify.

The lightbulb goes on but he still thinks I'm wrong. "Come on, Rachel. Aren't all women on birth control?"

"Yeah, but what if she decides not to take it? What if she believes the slime ball really wants to leave his wife, he just needs a good reason. What's better than a kiddo on the way?"

"So he puts both her and her daughter up in an expensive apartment in Alpharetta."

"Yeah, and Shannon swears someone was living there before them. I bet he's rented the apartment under a company name. If anyone sees him coming or going, he can say the apartment is used for out-of-town businessmen, just like corporations do."

Brian reads more on his computer. "It says here he's running for the U.S. Senate next year." He leans back and rubs his hands together. "A U.S. Senator boinking our newspaper carrier. This could be fun."

As he whirls back in his chair to face me, I catch that bad-boy gleam in his eye. That can only mean one thing. I just wish I'd shaved my legs this week.

It's interesting how Brian's sex drive has perked up lately. After fifteen years of marriage, his desire seemed to slow down. I thought he'd exhausted his supply so to speak. But then we got caught up tracking a couple thieves we called Bonnie and Clyde and the next thing I knew, he was as frisky as a teenage boy again.

Have you seen the commercial where it shows a clogged drain pipe? They pour in a little drain cleaner, the sludge slowly inches its way for a moment before woosh! The pipe is clear again. That's what happened to Brian only I think it was adrenaline instead of caustic acid in his pipes. Now any hint of adventure has Little Brian up and at 'em.

But here's the thing about an afternoon delight. There's no way to dim the lights and hide the flaws.

Other factors to consider:

I just ate a big lunch, so if I'm on the bottom, and Brian starts really rockin' and rollin', he's going to shake up all that fried fish and tartar sauce.

Also, my lunch included broccoli. The question is how much gas will that portion produce, and when?

My solution is to go with the darling shorty robe I found at Goodwill. It's a genuine Victoria's Secret and it only cost me six bucks. The satin feels great on my skin, and the sexy red fabric covers most of my thighs. If I get on top, my lunch won't get too jiggled.

Brian has this sexy thatch of dark hair that starts at his belly button and heads south. I call it the happy trail. When he's lying on his back, his beer gut isn't as pronounced and it doesn't take long for me to get turned on by this pathway to heaven.

Add in some neck kisses and nipple flicks and he's got my motor running. I climb aboard and let my red robe drape over my legs. He's got free access to the girls, and I can either speed up or slow down depending on the grimace on his face.

He works his magic massaging finger while I ride him like a rodeo star and moments later, we're both screaming.

I slump onto his chest and enjoy a couple minor aftershocks before rolling over onto my pillow. Brian tucks an arm behind his head and stares at the ceiling. Man, he looks good with his biceps bulging and his belly flat.

Then out of the clear blue, he says, "Do you think we could tie him to her death?"

"What? Who?"

"Senator Pressley. Do you think he had anything to do with Deborah Wiley's death?"

"You mean like murder?"

"I don't know what I mean. But it sure seems like more than a coincidence that she ran off the road right outside of his subdivision."

"What?!"

"Yeah, he lives in Arbor Estates."

It occurs to me that while we were bumping and grinding, Brian was thinking about a crime while I was thinking about Matthew McConaughey. In hindsight, he did seem to hang on for a lot of bouncing on my part. Perhaps solving crimes can be as distracting as baseball stats.

I roll to the side and prop my head up on my hand. "Murder is quite a leap, you know."

"All I'm saying is we need to see the ME's report."

"And how do you propose we do that?"

"We should talk to Detective Baker."

"It's not his case," I say. "And he doesn't like me, remember? He even insinuated that if I ever got involved with bad guys again, he'd let them shoot me."

"Yeah, I know," Brian says, a little too quickly. He doesn't seem too concerned about my possible death. "But he likes me. And I'm sure other detectives overhear conversations. All we want to know is if the medical examiner found anything suspicious."

He reaches down to the floor to haul up his jeans, and gets his cell phone. I can't believe he's got Baker's private number. When Baker answers, Brian talks to him like they're best buds. He invites him out for a couple beers but I guess the detective balks at the idea because Brian quickly adds that it's the least he can do after all Baker did for us. After a few 'yeahs' and a 'where's that?' Brian ends the call.

"It's all set," he tells me. "I'm meeting him at some place called Stan's."

"I've never heard of it."

"Baker says that's the whole point. No one knows about it. He's going over there to watch basketball."

"I just need to get a shower and I'll be ready to go."

"No! He won't talk if you're there."

I'd be offended if it wasn't the truth. But I have lots of questions and I can't depend on Brian remembering them all. If he writes them down, Baker will know I'm fishing for information.

The wheels turn in my head. "How about this. I'll call your cell just before we go into the restaurant. You put it on speaker and tuck it into your breast pocket. I'll sit way across the room, but I'll be able to hear the conversation. We'll meet outside the bathrooms and I'll remind you of anything you may have missed."

I get the evil eye glare; and so soon after the post-coital bliss.

"I'll tell you this," he says. "I'm not going to even mention Senator Pressley. Politicians always have informants. I don't want the FBI or the CIA coming after me."

"Yeah, let's not get ahead of ourselves."

I duck into the bathroom before he can stop me.

CHAPTER SEVEN

We get to Stan's around five. The game has already started but I had to change my clothes because the pants I wanted to wear only go with one shirt and it was dirty.

We sync up our phones and Brian goes in first. I figure Baker will be watching for him, so if I try to sneak in, he'll see me. Once he and Brian are gabbing, I'll slip in and find a table in the far corner.

Like Baker said, the place isn't very crowded. What he didn't say was that it was a total dive. I smell old grease and stale beer as soon as I walk in. I'm not ordering anything to eat until I get a look at their health inspection.

I've got my phone to my ear which helps disguise me as I search for a good spot. There's a small high-top in the back. I listen to Brian order a beer and offer to buy Baker's next round. They sit across from each other but their chairs are turned so they can both see the TV screen hanging from the wall.

"How's Rachel doing?" Baker asks. "Her face all healed up?"

"Yeah, she's doing fine. In fact, she's writing a book about the Al-Asad case. I'm pretty sure you'll be an integral part of the story."

Baker blurts out a laugh. "I'll bet."

"No really."

Isn't he sweet? Putting in a good word for me.

"So is she staying out of trouble?"

Oh, great. I can sense Brian veering off the track already.

"Well," he says, drawing it out. "She's become intrigued with the woman who drowned in her car at Arbor Estates."

"Intrigued. That's funny. You mean she's sticking her nose in someplace where it doesn't belong."

I watch Brian's reaction. His mouth gapes open like a fish on a hook because he knows I'm listening to the conversation. He doesn't know if he should commiserate with the cop and gain his trust, or defend his wife, whom he hopes to have sex with again sometime in the next five years.

Baker's no fool. He's wondering why Brian is suddenly stunned into silence.

"Are you taping our conversation?" he asks.

And just like that, Brian's hand jerks up toward his breast pocket. I want to smack my head. I know all about knee-jerk reactions but this is ridiculous.

Baker swivels around in his chair and scans the restaurant. I quickly snatch up my menu and hold it in front of my face.

The waitress comes up to see if I'm ready to order. I glance up from the menu, but it isn't the waitress, it's Baker.

"Why don't you just join us?" he says.

I HAVE TO listen to a big long lecture about leaving police work to the police. And if I want to investigate a crime, I need to go through the police academy and work my way up the ranks like everybody else.

My beer is nearly gone by the time he finishes his harangue. And my neck has a catch in it from all the nodding. I signal the waitress for another round. Brian is surveying the menu. Ick. I don't want to die of ptomaine poisoning during the night, but I'm starving.

"Has anyone been hospitalized after eating here?" I ask Baker.

"The food is pretty good."

"Sure, a guy would say that. But what about their health inspection?"

Baker nods at the bar. "It's right over there. Looks like a 95 to me."

Okay, so he's got me there, but I still don't see a lot of choices on the small menu. As I debate between nachos and hot wings, I casually let a little info slip.

"She was deathly afraid of the water."

I can sense Baker staring at me, but I don't look up from the menu.

"Who?" he asks.

"Deborah Wiley."

He blows out a harsh breath. "And how would you know that?"

Finally, I look up. "Her daughter Shannon told me. Some near-drowning when Deb was a kid. Shannon says there's no way her mother would try to swim to safety."

He lets that percolate in his mind for a few seconds, mulling over how it fits in the whole picture. Then he says, "If you know why she drowned, what are you poking around for?"

Oops. I guess I wasn't thinking it through. We can't tell him about Pressley. Not yet anyway. I'll have to go with an old idea.

"What if someone was stalking her? He knows her route, he waits in hiding, when she stops at the gate, he either scares her or jumps into the car with her. She runs off the road and into the pond."

Even as I'm talking, Baker is shaking his head 'no'.

"Look," he says, the muscles in his neck clenching to stay calm, "I understand that you're a writer and you enjoy making stuff up—"

"I don't make stuff up!"

"—but there is absolutely no corroborating evidence to suggest that this was anything but a tragic accident."

"How can you be so sure? You didn't know about her fear of water."

He takes a deep breath and slowly blows it through his nose. It's a calming technique I've learned after being married to Brian for fifteen years. It also gives him time to make a decision.

"Okay, listen. I'm going to tell you this so that you will stop wasting your time, and mine. You seem to think that just because the daughter was too distraught to tell me about her mom's phobia, we didn't do our job. But we did. There was absolutely nothing in the ME's report to indicate foul play. And for your information, Shannon Wiley is coming down to the station tomorrow morning. I'm sure she would have told me all about it then."

The waitress shows up with our next round, interrupting Baker. I order hot wings and fries. I figure the boiling oil will kill any germs on the chicken, and the hot sauce will destroy any bacteria that still manages to make its way into my stomach. The fries are to soak up the beer. Brian orders the nachos *and* a burger with fries. (He knows I won't embarrass him in front of Baker by telling him he can't eat all that.)

Baker orders a chef salad with chicken tenders. I'd point out how he's putting his life in danger by ordering possibly unwashed lettuce but I want to get back to the medical report. I'm sure I'll get all the information he's got before he croaks.

Once the waitress leaves, Baker purposely turns away from me to watch the game. North Carolina is playing Kentucky. Boring. I've never been a big fan of basketball. It requires paying attention. Now with football, I can go to the kitchen for more chips and if I hear a sudden cheer, I can get back in time to see the replay at least twice. And with baseball, I can start the dishwasher and take the clothes out of the dryer, and when I get back, the score is still three to nothing. If I want to watch basketball, I just wait for the last two minutes. It all comes down to like the final 30 seconds anyway.

I let Baker watch. If I piss him off, he may just move to another table. Finally some guy fouls another guy and there's a break in the action.

"So you were saying about the ME's report?"

He must be married because he gets that slump in his shoulders that means he might as well tell me everything and get it over with.

"The lab didn't find any traces of alcohol, drugs, or poison. We checked out her car. It was a piece of shit but the brakes were fine. No one had tampered with anything. The doors were locked which is appropriate for a woman driving alone early in the morning. The passenger window was open because she tossed the papers out."

He waits just a second for me to process all this, then he continues. "The water comes rushing in through the open window. Maybe she tries to swim out, maybe not. I'm sure she's scared. The foot wells fill quickly. She calls 911 and the operator is trying to get information about her location. But Wiley panics. She doesn't know the name of the street, just the name of the subdivision. The operator gets a ping off the cell phone, but the tower is in Fulton County and Wiley was in Mansell County, so that slows things a bit.

"It's a small car so the water is rising. But at no time does Ms. Wiley say she saw a stalker or that someone had threatened her. At about 30 seconds, the water is causing the front of the car to tip further into the pond. We think she climbed over the front seat to the back, which was still sticking out. But she's hysterical, choking, crying. Then we think she dropped her phone. We found it on the floor of the back seat. There is no more conversation. The car slides all the way into the water. At 45 seconds, any air pocket in the back is now filled with water."

I'm nodding, thinking through Deborah Wiley's torturous ending. "And she drowns."

Baker gives his head a little tip to the side. "EMS tried to resuscitate but she was unresponsive. The ER continued to try, but they got no brain activity. She was pronounced at the hospital."

CHAPTER EIGHT

Brian wakes up starving. I'm not surprised after eating all that food last night. His nachos were delivered first so naturally I wasn't going to just sit there and watch him shovel in chips loaded with beef and guacamole and strings of cheese. Baker ate a couple just to be sociable, but Brian managed to finish the bulk of the order before his burger arrived.

Even after the nachos, he managed to put away everything in his little wax paper-lined basket. I can't believe he could drink two more beers with all that food in his stomach, but then I'm not a guy.

So after he spent an evening gorging, his belly is in a 'bulking' state, demanding more food. It happens to me every time we go on a trip. That first day back home is a killer. My stomach growls and gets these sharp pangs that I do my best to ignore.

I try to talk him into a cup of yogurt and some oatmeal but he insists on bacon and eggs. His excuse is that he's going to start digging the fish pond and he needs lots of protein.

As soon as he's done eating, he gets up and heads for the garage.

"Aren't those the jeans you wore to the bar last night?" I ask.

"Yeah."

"You're going to dig in the best pair of jeans you own?"

He makes a little smacking sound with his mouth and turns toward the stairway. A moment later, he reappears wearing an gnarled old pair of jeans, a torn tee shirt—which doesn't look much different from nearly all his tee shirts except that this one is for Death Cab for Cutie and he was never a big fan of their music—and a pair of old sneakers. He dons a ripped flannel shirt and passes my inspection.

While I'm washing up breakfast dishes, I watch him carry a shovel out to the designated fish pond area which he marked off with four stakes. (That would be tragic if he forgot where he decided to put it after all the analyzing on Saturday.) He lines up the shovel for the perfect ceremonial first dig, stomps on the blade and stops.

Now what? Is he having the 'kid in a snowsuit' moment? That's where you get your kid all bundled up to go play in the snow and they decide they have to go to the bathroom. But Brian just stands there, leaning on his shovel and thinking.

I decide to wander outside. "What's up?"

He looks down at the shovelful of dirt. "I don't know where I'm going to dump all this."

Good point. There is no ditch in our backyard, no low spot to be filled, no stand of trees he can pile it in, just our yard and the next yard and the yard after that. There isn't a vacant lot across the street that he can wheelbarrow the dirt and dump it.

What am I thinking? We don't even have a wheelbarrow.

We both study the problem. He's probably thinking he needs a beer. I'm wishing I hadn't come out here.

I look around our barren yard. It's nothing but grass and the few bushes around the house.

"Don't fish need some shade?" I ask. "Especially in the summer when it's really hot?"

"I remember reading something about that."

"So what if you put all the dirt on the west end; one of those humps like you see in the new developments. Then you could plant a small tree or some bushes."

"Great!"

He doesn't really think it's a great idea. He's just happy that he doesn't have to haul away the dirt. And he doesn't have to stop the project he just started. I let him get a rhythm going—stomp, lift, dump—before I move on to the real reason I'm out here.

"You know, I've been thinking about what you said. It can't be a coincidence that Deborah Wiley drowned at the subdivision where Darrell Pressley lives."

Stomp, lift, dump.

"What if something happened at his house that morning? Shannon said Pressley would wait on his front porch for his paper. Maybe she carried the paper to him and they got into an argument?"

Stomp, lift, dump.

"Maybe he told her it was over, for good this time. Or she got tired of waiting for him to leave his wife and she called it off. So she's got that on her mind, she drives up to the gate, but then she has a change of heart. She grabs her phone to call him but instead she goes off the road."

Brian stops and rubs his sweaty face on the sleeve of his flannel shirt. "I thought you told Detective Baker you weren't going to take this any further."

I blow a puff of air through my lips. "I did, but I didn't expect you to believe it, too."

Stomp, lift, dump.

"What if her heart was broken?" I continue. "If he called it off, maybe she was so crushed, she was crying and drove off the road."

He stops and wipes again. "Would she really be that broken up? I mean, he was a senator. Why would she think he'd leave his wife for her?"

"Who knows? Women do crazy things."

His mouth opens but he quickly shuts it. That thought is better left unsaid.

"I wonder if she's ever suffered from depression," I say. "Shannon told me her dad died in a motorcycle accident. Maybe Deborah had a history."

"And what? She was so depressed she drove into the pond knowing she wouldn't be able to get out?"

"Maybe it was all subconscious. Maybe she's been analyzing her life for a while. Single, in a dead-end relationship with a married man who doesn't even want to be seen with her, she's in her mid-forties."

I remember how depressed I got when I hit forty a few months back. It was awful. Of course, the worst part was that no one had a surprise birthday party for me. That was pretty hard to take. So yes, I think Deborah Wiley could have been depressed and just decided to end it all.

I've got to call Shannon.

SHE PICKS UP after two rings. But I can't just jump right into asking if her mom suffered from depression. I ask if she can talk and she says she's driving to work. Then I ask how she's doing and she tells me she's fine. I'm running out of mundane things to say but thank goodness Shannon comes to the rescue.

"My grandmother finally left this morning."

"You sound glad."

"Hell, yeah. She cleaned out my mom's closet. Even took her suitcase to pack all the clothes in."

"Damn!"

"I'm glad I hid all the jewelry. I didn't really get into mom's clothes that much, but she had some gorgeous necklaces and bracelets."

"I can imagine."

"Nana was pissed she couldn't find anything. She even came right out and asked me where all the stuff was! Can you believe that?"

"What did you tell her?"

"I said I was keepin' it all. Then I told her I had to go to work and she needed to get out."

Wow, that was harsh. Bootin' out granny. But then I thought of my own mother. If she was on the hunt for something, she'd probably wait until I was gone and then tear my house apart. But I'm pretty sure she'd at least clean while she was snooping.

"Where did you hide the stuff?"

Shannon chuckled. "I got it in my car."

"That was smart." If she remembers to lock her car at work.

The chitchat has warmed us up again, so I dive into my reason for calling.

"Was there a problem between your mom and Pressley? Do you think he might have wanted to break it off with her?"

"No way. With all the sex he was getting? He was in high cotton. Never even had to take her out for dinner. He'd just pop in and pop out."

I snicker at the innuendo.

"What about your mom?" I ask. "Was she rethinking their relationship?"

"Nah. She was pretty much convinced that nothing was going to change. But she loved the apartment and all the stuff he gave her. She wouldn't want to give that up."

I hear a horn honk through Shannon's phone. "Are you okay?" I ask.

"Yeah, some dumb ass tried to cut me off."

I should probably let her concentrate on driving, but I've got more questions. "What about when your dad died? Was she upset about that?"

"I guess a little. But I don't remember her gettin' all depressed like you see in the movies. I guess she coulda been hidin' it. I was only five. What I do remember is quite a parade of men coming to the house after Daddy died. Mama'd drop me off at Nana's and sometimes they'd git into an argument. Then she'd pick me up the next day and she'd be singing to the radio."

"Did she stay in any of the relationships for long?"

"Not at all. In fact, when I was in high school, I started thinkin' back, wondering if she was whoring for money. We was pretty poor when I was small. I asked Nana but she never would tell me. I know we moved in with her when I was in the third or fourth grade so maybe Mama was turning tricks and Nana put a stop to it."

"This was in Eufaula?"

"Yeah. But those two couldn't git along for nothing. Mama finally packed us up and we moved to Atlanta. She hooked up with some guy that was into fitness. That's how she got started as a personal trainer. But their relationship didn't last too long."

"Was she sad when they broke up?"

"Nah. She'd met Ricco by then. He was a trip. Had an adult store in Roswell that sold all kinds of kinky sex toys. She was with him for a long time."

"And what happened to her and Ricco?"

"I don't really remember. I was out of high school by then and tired of all that sicko shit. I mean he had whips and handcuffs. They even had some kind of harness hangin' from the ceiling. I'd bang on the wall for them to shut up but they never did."

"Wow!"

"Yeah. I finally decided to leave but I couldn't afford an apartment on my own so I moved in with this guy Ronnie. He was kind of a jerk but at least he had a job. We managed. But then when Mama met Darrell, and moved into that apartment, I told Ronnie to shove it and moved back in with her."

CHAPTER NINE

So Deborah was living with Mr. Kinky. And he owns a store that sells sex stuff to other kinky people. I'm no prude; I know all about the handcuffs and vibrators and nipple clamps. But I've never been inside an adult store. This might be a fun excursion for Brian and me.

I look up Ricco's business in Roswell. I know, I still haven't written the St. Paddy's piece, but I've got another week before I have to turn it in and still get a paycheck in April. And I've started on the book about al Asad—sort of.

Browsing through a sex toy store could give me some ideas for a piece in one of the romance magazines I submit to. Or I might try my hand at writing erotica again. I've attempted it a couple times; I even keep an extensive list of verbs like throbbing, pulsing, pounding. One of my favs is thrumming. If I try the BDSM route though, I'll need a new pen name; something like Meena Balzer.

Whatever the outcome, I'm dying to meet Ricco.

Brian is all for the visit. Now that I've opened the door to adventure, his sexual appetite is on the rise. And he's been digging that goofy fish pond all morning. He's ready for a break.

Neither of us is prepared for the size of the store. I had visions of a small bodega with a few shrink-wrapped dildos and maybe some edible panties. This place is huge.

The lingerie section is mind-boggling: bras with cut-outs, crotchless panties, garter belts and stockings, lacy cover-ups, and of course some leather for the dominatrix. Lots of this stuff comes in plus sizes which pleases me.

There's a whole separate alcove for dildos and vibrators. A wall of porn videos. Lotions and creams for everything.

"Check this out," Brian says, handing me a box with a picture of a woman on her knees. She's bent over a chair with her thighs bound to two of the chair legs, and her arms tied to the other two.

That looks dangerous. Once a guy got going, she'd have no way of stopping him. I understand people into this stuff have a safe word but I'm not convinced it works. My safe word would have to be something like 'divorce' or a threatening string of words, like 'you'll have to sleep some time.'

I glance at the price tag. Holy crap! How do people afford this stuff? An idea for a story pops into my head: *Managing the High Cost of Sex Toys.*

A little further on, I come across a hanging contraption that can be suspended from the ceiling. The pictures on the box show people in all kinds of positions.

I envision myself hanging weightless in this 'chair', my calves, thighs, and arms harnessed in slings that have me pretty much spread wide open. Do those straps get tight? If I hung there long enough, would my weight start to cut off the circulation to my extremities? Of course, knowing Brian, his performance wouldn't take long to complete so I guess I wouldn't get a deep vein thrombosis in under five minutes.

But what if I got a Charley horse in my inner thigh? Or muscle cramps in my toes? How long would it take to get me out of that torture device so I could walk it off? I just don't think I'm a harness kind of girl.

We move on to peruse the wide assortment of nipple clamps. Some of them look like jewelry, others resemble mini jumper cables.

"These are funky," Brian says, showing me two bejeweled butterflies with loops at the top and bottom. Evidently, once you lasso your nipple in the loop, the butterfly slides up to cinch it tight.

"No thanks."

"You know, we've got those tiny chip clips at home," he says. "We could experiment with them sometime."

"On you?" I ask.

A clerk comes up and asks if he can help. He has piercings all over his face, and I must assume in other places. His arms are tattooed.

"Those pinchers look really painful," I say.

"It's all in your perspective. I think high heels with pointed toes look painful but women wear them all the time. They even run, and dance in them."

He's got a point, but I'm still not going to let anyone pinch my nipples with tiny metal jaws. And I certainly wouldn't allow those little snappers on my Va J-J.

I glance at his name badge. *Ricco*. Mr. Kinky! I give him a more thorough once-over. Dark slicked-back hair, sexy beard stubble, buff body; he probably has strong leg muscles perfect for picking up a woman, impaling her on his tool, and bouncing her vigorously.

A sheen of sweat breaks out on my chest. And I have a feeling my face has turned a brilliant shade of red.

"You look familiar," I say. "Didn't you go with Deb Wiley for a while?"

"Yeah," he says. By the look on his face, I can tell he's heard about the drowning. "We lived together for a couple years."

"I was so sorry to hear about her accident," I say.

"Me, too." He bows his head slightly and stares at the floor. "She was a vibrant woman."

The way his voice gets all husky makes a little tingle run up my back. I let him relive some memory of her before I move on.

"And then to drown like that—"

"I know!" He stares at me with wide, expressive eyes. "She hated the water."

I nod in agreement but keep quiet. It looks like he's got a story to tell.

"One time we were taking a bath together. She was on my lap, facing me. I was getting really turned on. Then I made the mistake of sliding down into the water. I asked her to hold me under until I came."

"Shit!" Brian gasps.

Ricco held up a hand. "It's not like she could really hold me down. If I needed to get up I totally could have. It's just the rush, you know?"

Brian and I both nod like we get it—which we don't.

"Anyway, she freaked out, jumped out of the tub. After that, she'd never take a bath with me. I think she was afraid I might try and hold her under the water." He turns to Brian again. "Which I would never have done."

"Did she break up with you because of that?" I ask.

"No." He shakes his head and looks away. His mouth curls down. "I moved out of her place. It all came down to the fact that she couldn't trust me, and that's a huge part of the agreement. Plus, I got the feeling she was just experimenting and I'd been into the lifestyle for years. I knew sooner or later she'd get tired of it. I didn't want her pushing me to give it up."

"Did she take it hard? When you left?"

"Not really."

"She didn't ask you to stay. Promise to try harder, anything like that?"

"No, she was fine with it." He takes a deep breath and his shoulders rise. "You had to understand Deb. She had that wanderer's spirit. Even when we were at our best, I'd still catch her checking out other guys. I think she was always wondering if she could find someone better."

And was Darrell Pressley the top of the line for Deborah Wiley?

* * *

SINCE WE'RE OUT running errands, Brian wants to stop at Lowe's and pick up the fish pond liner. They have all styles, from a plain round pool to curvy-shapes that even have different depths. This will be interesting to watch him dig out the exact shape of this thing.

I balk at the price but he assures me they're more expensive at Rural King and on Amazon, even with the free shipping. He's ignoring the fact that this is just the beginning of a money drain; there will be pumps and filters and plants and fish to buy. But it's his stash from selling photos so I just bite my tongue.

Lashing the stupid thing to the top of my car takes two employees. I'm convinced the first gust of wind will destroy the plastic even though they all insist it's high density polyurethane. Whatever.

At least I don't have to drive on the expressway. And Brian has the good sense not to bug me when I drive 35 the whole way home. By the time I get out of the car, my back and shoulders ache from gripping the steering wheel.

He unties the liner and we carry it to the back yard. There are no instructions, no template to lay on the ground to get the approximate size for digging. I don't even want to get started on making sure it's level.

I head for the kitchen to start dinner. As I brown hamburger, I glance out the window. Brian has wrangled the liner halfway into the hole he dug, but it isn't close to fitting. He pulls out the liner and digs some more.

I dump tomatoes, and onions, and red beans into the pot and add a packet of chili seasoning. Brian has wedged the liner back into the hole. Still doesn't fit.

By the time he gives up for the day, the chili is on the stove staying warm, and he is covered with dirt.

"Why don't you take all your clothes off in the utility room," I say. "The chili can keep until you get a shower." (See? I can be diplomatic if I want.)

Being the good husband that he is, he takes off his shoes and leaves them on the rug by the sliding glass door. But dirt has sifted into his shoes all afternoon so his socks are red with Georgia clay. I cry out and he hops back onto the rug to shed the offending apparel.

On his short walk through the kitchen, I see dirt flaking off him. He's like that kid in the Peanuts cartoon that lives in a cloud of dust.

After dinner, Brian settles in to watch the latest match-up in March Madness. (For others who find basketball unwatchable, this is the time of year when college teams battle it out for the national championship.) I decide to get a shower and shave my legs. I know, we just enjoyed a romp yesterday, but after our visit to the sex store, I wouldn't be at all surprised if Brian has plans for later. My motor has been idling a bit higher than usual, too. I just hope whatever he has in mind doesn't include rope.

I'm all snug under the covers in my favorite flannel pants and tee shirt, reading Linda Sand's latest book, when Brian finally comes upstairs. But instead of brushing his teeth, he stands at the foot of the bed with his hands on his hips and a stern expression on his face.

"You forgot to start the dishwasher," he says.

A nasty comment is about to erupt from me when he climbs on the bed and crawls toward me, his face menacing. "You're a bad girl. A bad, bad girl."

Dear Jesus, my body ignites like a string of cheap firecrackers. I pucker my lips like women do in the porn movies; I even press a finger to my lips and whimper.

Evidently, that sparks his own incendiary device because he rakes off the covers and pounces on me. I squeal.

"I think you need a spanking," he growls and rolls me over.

He proceeds to smack me a couple times on my butt while I kick my legs and wail. "I didn't mean it. I'll never forget again. Please let me go!"

My helpless position brings out a side of Brian I've never seen before. "So you say," he says, keeping his voice deep. "But let's make sure you've learned your lesson."

He wraps his arms around my waist, pulls my butt up into the air, and jerks my pants to my knees. I gasp and nearly have an orgasm right then and there. With bare hand to bare butt, he spanks.

"You. Are. A. Bad. Girl," he says with each smack. But each strike gets harder. I stop laughing. This isn't fun anymore.

"That hurts," I yell as I wriggle away, kicking at him.

He rocks back on his haunches, panting. I swear he's turned into some primal beast. What's even more surprising is that I'm still turned on as well. My first thought is to get out of these pajamas and go to town with Brian. But am I opening the door to a new kind of craziness?

I roll off the bed leaving my pants where they lie. I need a glass of wine while I process all this.

MY HAND SHAKES as I pour myself some moscato. Where did all that come from? Neither Brian or I has ever been the violent type. And to get aroused by the idea of him taking me against my will is disturbing. Is this what BDSM is all about?

Brian pads into the kitchen on bare feet, wearing only his boxers. He comes right up to me, takes my wine glass and sets it on the counter. Then he wraps his arms around me and pulls me close.

"I'm so sorry, Rach," he says. "I didn't mean for that to get out of hand."

I bury my face in his shoulder. "It just scared me, that's all."

"Yeah, me too."

I kiss his neck. It feels great being in his arms, safe and no longer confused.

He slips his hands under the tail of my tee shirt and gently rubs my stinging skin. I moan, letting my lips vibrate on his neck.

"Let's make a deal," I say. "No more pain."

"Agreed."

He slowly brings one hand to the front. "How about a little pleasure?" he asks and he slips a finger between my thighs. His back hand pulls me close as he rubs.

"Oh, yeah," I groan.

I slip a hand into the front of his boxers, and the next thing I know, he picks me up and sets me on the counter. I gasp as the cold granite cools my spanked bottom. This whole situation is such a turn-on, I wrap my legs around him and pull him into me. It's the most erotic thing we've ever done.

Once the last of our grinding and groaning fades, he helps me back down off the counter. My butt feels wet and I realize he set me right in the moscato I spilled while pouring. Now I'm all sticky, in more ways than one.

CHAPTER TEN

Brian spent all day Tuesday getting his hole dug. He'd drag the black plastic pond into the hole, it wouldn't fit, and he'd drag it out again. Then he'd shave a little dirt off the side, drag the pond back into the hole, and it still wouldn't fit. It was exhausting just watching him from the kitchen window.

At least it's in the ground now. It looks a little wonky but I'm not saying anything. I'm tired of the tracked-in dirt and the dust that's blowing into my kitchen window. It's supposed to rain tomorrow and then he'd be digging in mud. Or worse, the project would get postponed a day, then two days, then a week and I'd be looking at that hole in the yard all summer.

Plus, I finally got the article on St. Paddy's written yesterday, so I'm ready to look at pictures. He needs to wrap up this project. I watch as he drags the hose out and throws it into the fish pond to fill it.

The phone rings and I check the caller ID. It's Shannon. "You won't believe what happened this morning!"

"Probably not," I say. I'm not really paying attention because as soon as Brian turns on the spigot, the hose jumps out of the pool and the water runs down the outside of the liner and into the hole. I tap on the window to get Brian's attention and point at the hose.

" . . . and the shithead won't take my calls," Shannon says.

"Wait a second. Who won't take your calls?"

"That jerk Darrell Pressley."

"You tried to call him?"

"I been trying since Friday. And I couldn't get to him at church on Sunday so I started right in again calling Monday."

"Why do you want to talk to him?"

"To tell him he's a son-of-a-bitch for using my momma like that."

"And you thought calling him out in front of God and the whole church was the way to go?" My voice gives away my disbelief.

"Yeah, I guess I wasn't thinkin' straight. I was just hopin' he'd feel guilty enough to pay for some of the expenses."

"That's not a good idea. The man is running for the U.S. Senate. Sometimes those guys have clout. Or they have someone pouring money into their campaign and they don't want it to blow up in their face."

"Yeah, yeah. That's what Nana said."

"Well, you should listen to her," I say. "Politicians are backed by big money now. And even if they act like they care, there are people in the background who might come after you. They could be dangerous."

"Oh, yeah? Then explain this. I got an email from the apartment rental office. Well, it wasn't to me, it was to my mom on her iPad. It said 'thank you for paying your rent up through September'!"

"What?" I screech. Holy crap. Pressley is paying for her silence.

"That's kinda what I said when I read the note."

"Did you call the rental office to confirm?"

"Are you kidding? What if it's a mistake? I don't want 'em to throw me out next week."

Brian wanders in from the backyard and starts undressing on the rug in front of the sliding door. I turn away. I don't want him to think I'm ogling his body. He's had his share of high-jinx this week.

"Does the notice have an apartment number on it?"

73

"Yep," she says. "Twelve fifty-five. It's our apartment." She catches herself and I'd swear she's smiling. "I guess it's my apartment now."

"Yikes! Do you think he'll be coming to you for sexual favors?"

"He better not. I know too much."

"Well, I'd keep looking for another apartment just in case." I roll my eyes when I hear what I'm saying. I sound just like my mother.

Shannon confirms my horror.

"Whatever," she snips and then says she's got to go just like I do when I'm tired of listening to my mom.

As soon as she hangs up on me, I google Westbrook Apartments and call the number. The receptionist has a sultry, rich-bitch lilt when she answers and gives her name.

I decide to go with the spoiled brat ruse. "Hello Tanya. This is Shannon Wiley in apartment twelve fifty-five. My stepfather promised to get my rent paid today. Would you please check to see if he has?"

You see how that's done? You don't ask them to do it because you give them an option to refuse. You just make a polite but firm demand.

I hear typing and she comes back quickly. "Yes, Ms. Wiley, the lease on your unit has been paid through September."

"By Arthur McMurray Doyle?"

The receptionist hesitates. Probably isn't supposed to give out that kind of information.

I up the snooty factor a bit. "I just want to make sure my mother didn't have to cover for his negligence."

"I wouldn't know that," she says. "It was an electronic transmission from JGP Enterprises."

"That's him. Thanks so much for your help."

I'm feeling very cocky when I hang up, but when I turn around Brian is glaring at me. "What are you doing?"

"You won't believe this!"

74

I tell him all about Darrell Pressley paying Shannon's rent . . . excuse me, her lease.

"It's interesting," I say. "Even though the police insist it was an accidental drowning, Pressley feels guilty enough about something to pay six more months on the lease."

I snicker when I tell him Shannon was afraid to call the leasing office to confirm.

"What if she'd been right?" Brian says. "What if it was a mistake? You could have messed everything up."

"Oh, come on. If they credited the wrong apartment, don't you think the guy who *paid* his rent six months ahead would notice when he got a delinquent letter?"

Brian gives me the pucker-puss; that's where he can't come up with a good retort but he still wants to go on record for pointing out that I did something bad.

When I get to the part where the lease was paid by JGP Enterprises, he perks up.

"That's a shell corporation if I ever heard of one," he says.

I wag my eyebrows and give him an encouraging nod. "Maybe we should look into it."

"I'm on it." He grabs a bag of Funyuns out of the cupboard.

"Hey!" I yell as he dashes for the stairs. "I'm fixing dinner here."

"Don't worry."

"And I need your New York pictures," I add but he's already upstairs. I hear him close his door.

I fume as I stare into the refrigerator. Now that I've told him I'm fixing dinner I guess I'll have to find something. Thankfully, I've got cheese. I can fix anything as long as I have cheese. Although I made the mistake of revealing this philosophy to Sarah once and she blasted me about why cheese is bad for us: like how it's high in calories, and it's mostly saturated fat, and it has a lot of salt. I don't care. I'm never giving up that creamy goodness.

While I wait for water to boil for macaroni, I boot up the new iPad Brian got me. Well, it's not new. I'm pretty sure he got it used on eBay. Either that or his friend Randy is selling hot iPads. Randy is a photographer friend of Brian's who has more equipment than anyone I've ever known. We borrowed a surveillance camera from him back in November. It was a piece of crap but it did the trick.

I have a desktop computer up in my office but I wanted something I could use while traveling so Brian got me the iPad. He even downloaded a Solitaire game so now we can ignore each other for hours.

If he's looking into this bogus corporation, I'll see what else I can find on Darrell Pressley.

Over Italian casserole, we discuss our findings. (It's Italian because I used a can of tomatoes and threw in the last few slices of pepperoni that were turning grey.)

Brian found one small reference to JGP Enterprises. "It's a subsidiary of a larger corporation. I went to the website but it's totally inactive. It listed a nominee director but when I googled the name I got a school teacher in Iowa, and a hockey player who died in 1994. It also claimed to be a subsidiary of a larger corporation . . . in Croatia."

"So basically, we're nowhere."

"Pretty much."

I dig my fork into my pasta and come up with a piece of pepperoni. I tried to dig out as much as I could from my serving and put it on Brian's plate . . . just in case the meat is bad. I mean, he's got a cast-iron stomach. I've seen him eat potato salad that sat out in the hot sun all day and never break a sweat. If I'd done that, I'd have been camped in a bathroom for the next 48 hours.

I nonchalantly park the slice on the side of my plate and cram the rest of the bite into my mouth. As I chew, I tell him what I've found out.

"After he graduated from UGA, Pressley came back to Atlanta. I guess he grew up in Morningside. He ran for Atlanta City Council and got re-elected once before he moved on to the Georgia Senate."

"And now he's running for the US Senate." Brian saw me flick off the piece of pepperoni and he's well aware of the unwritten rule. Once a piece of food has been rejected, it's fair game. He reaches his fork across and nabs it.

There are some hilarious videos on YouTube about being either a dog person or a cat person. The dog person is always underfoot with his tongue hanging out, eager to please. The cat person is aloof, moody, and tries to cause trouble. As soon as I saw the video, I realized Brian is the dog person and I'm the cat person. And here's more proof: him snatching the pepperoni off my plate. It's finders-keepers, just like a chunk of food that falls on the floor.

"I've got a lead on a guy who was on the city council the same time as Pressley," Brian says. "He's got a design shop in Midtown. Maybe he can give us some insight on Pressley. You should call him."

"No, we need to pay him a visit."

CHAPTER ELEVEN

I've got this theory about interviewing people: if you send an email, or call them, it gives them the opportunity to put you off, say they're busy, or give you the ever popular 'no comment'. Besides, people are always ruder on the phone or in a letter. In person, most people will behave. And you can get great non-verbal cues in person that you miss otherwise.

That's why we're driving all the way to midtown to meet some guy who was on the Atlanta City Council with Darrell Pressley. I'm not sure what we're going to find out but it beats scrubbing the bathtub, and that was next on my to-do list.

We spend close to thirty minutes trying to find a place to park that doesn't have a warn sign: *Parking for residents only*, and end up walking four blocks to Parker Designs.

A drop-dead gorgeous woman is sitting at an antique table, her legs crossed to show off amazing calves and taut thighs. She's wearing heels higher than I'd ever dare. She stands to greet us.

"Welcome to Parker Designs," she says. "How can I help you?"

"We're looking for Alan Parker," I tell her.

Too late, it occurs to me that I should have called first because Alan no doubt is meeting with a client somewhere and his assistant will not be of any help—although she's giving Brian an eyeful.

"I'm Alan Parker," she says. "Well, now I'm Alana. So what can I do for you today?"

Well, first of all, Alana, you can help my poor choking husband who sounds like he just swallowed his tongue.

I don't know how I missed the clues, like the fact that Alana is as tall as Brian and speaks with a husky voice, but I regroup faster than Brian.

"I understand you were on the Atlanta City Council with Darrell Pressley."

"Ugh," she says, rolling her eyes. "Will that dark time in my life ever go away?"

"Bad, huh?"

"I've met some tawdry men over the years, but none as sexist as Darrell." She waves us to the table and sits, crossing those impossibly long legs again. Brian takes a moment to get a peek at her breasts. Then he gives me this wistful stare before he takes a seat across from her. I interpret the look as: 'If a man can look this good, why can't you?'

That hardly seems fair to me. My breasts look just as good, and they're real. And although my thighs may be a bit wider—okay quite a bit wider—my legs look pretty good in a skirt. Plus, I've got a magic button between my legs that really works.

"What did he do?" Brian asks.

"What didn't he do," Alana says. "He never had a problem remembering a man's name, but when it came to women, it was always 'sugar' or 'sweetheart', or 'doll.' Even when I was living as a man, I found him disgusting."

"I'm surprised he got re-elected," I say.

"Most of his bullshit was behind closed doors. When he was out in public, he was this 'rah, rah, Atlanta first' kind of guy. And I guess the conservative voters that were his base acted the same way, either dismissing young women or flattering rich old blue-hairs."

"What was his wife like?" I ask.

"She was a bit of a ball buster. Ran his campaigns, probably wrote his speeches. She'd be in the background usually."

"Do you think he ever cheated on her?"

"Oh, hell yes." Alana puckers her face in disgust and for the first time, I see a wrinkle. How can she have such flawless skin? She must be in her mid-forties. "After the council meetings, Pressley and his cronies from the northern districts would meet at some bar in Sandy Springs. I went once and that was enough for me. It was just a bunch of privileged white men exaggerating their success."

Alana swivels in her chair, crosses her legs the other way and leans on the table.

"The night I was there, Pressley was flirting with a waitress, trying to get her to sit on his lap, or give him her phone number. She said she was in a relationship but Pressley said he wasn't looking for a relationship. Then she told him it wasn't a boyfriend, it was a girlfriend. He used that tired line about what she needed was a real man to turn her around."

"Yuck," I say.

"If came on to me like that, I'd lobotomize his balls with my shoe." She swivels her pointy toe to make sure we get her drift.

AS WE WALK back to my car, I go phishing. "I can't believe how beautiful Alana is."

"No kidding," Brian answers.

"I suppose I could do something like that with my hair if I took the time. And maybe wear makeup."

Brian slings his arm across my shoulders. "Women like that are fun to look at but I wouldn't want to kiss one. I'm sure she'd complain that I was messing up her hair or smearing her lipstick." He pulls me closer. "I love you because you don't hide behind all that."

My insides turn all warm and gooey. Is it any wonder I fell in love with this guy?

As we round the corner onto Sixth Street, I see a woman up ahead hovering around my car. A few steps later, I realize she's sitting on the hood of my car. Once I'm close enough, I give her my best squinty-eyed stare but she just stares right back.

"Parking on this street is for residents only," she says, her long wavy hair wafting as she bobbles her head.

"Sorry," I say. "We just had to run a short errand. I don't think we were even here thirty minutes."

"I see," she says. "So if twenty people needed to run a thirty-minute errand, this spot would be taken for ten hours."

Oh, brother. I shouldn't have engaged with this woman. I should have just gotten into my car and started it up. I'm sure she would have gotten off before I drove away. That's when I notice that the car in front of mine has been backed right up to my bumper. There's no way I can get out.

She sees where I'm looking. "That's right. I've parked you in. And now I'm waiting for a tow truck."

"Tow truck!"

I can't afford to pay to get my car out of impound. Plus, Brian and I will have to find some way home, get his Jeep, and drive out to some godforsaken area of town to get the car back.

"Listen," Brian says. His voice is all calm and reasonable. "How much will the tow cost. Fifty bucks? Why don't we just give you the money and you move your car so we can leave."

Is that what this is? A shakedown?

"I'm not giving you fifty dollars," I say, taking a step towards her in what I hope feels menacing. "You should be ashamed of yourself for extorting visitors to Atlanta."

She comes right back at me. "And you should learn to read. There are signs posted all over this neighborhood that warn about being towed."

Damn! I've come up against another neighborhood busybody just like me. I wonder if she really does sit in her living room waiting for some unsuspecting boobs like us to park, then she hits them up for money. It's a brilliant idea.

ON CLOSER inspection, though, I note her baggy linen pants and Birkenstocks. She looks like she's in her sixties. Is she a throwback from the days of the militant hippie? Ever since they stopped the Vietnam War, this woman has been looking for a new cause and she's finally found it: illegal parkers.

There's no point trying to reason with her; a tow truck could be on the way. We've got to get out of here.

I turn to Brian and whisper, "Circle around the car and chase her my way."

Brian crunches up his nose in disgust.

"You don't have to touch her," I say. (We definitely don't want this on the six o'clock news. Man Attacks Helpless Woman in Midtown.) "Just look intimidating."

Against his better judgement, he goes for it. He squeezes past the car behind us and inches his way towards the front of my car.

Crazy Lady swivels around to keep an eye on him. She suspects an ambush. While she's distracted, I grab her foot and pull. I'm not going to dump her onto the ground. I just want to get her off my car.

She starts sliding forward so I latch onto her arm as well. I don't want her falling between the bumpers and cutting a gash in her shin. Unfortunately, she doesn't come along quietly. She yells 'Help!' and jerks the foot I'm holding so that I lurch forward. While I'm off-balance, she kicks at me with her free leg.

82

Her strength surprises me. She must be one of those yoga fanatics. I stumble backwards but manage to keep a hand on her foot. It doesn't stop me from falling. As I go down, I pull her off the car. I land with an oof in the grassy area between the street and the sidewalk. She lands right on top of me, driving her arm into my gut and knocking the wind out of me. She's pretty spry for her age.

I wrap my arms around her shoulders to keep her from taking a swing at me, and that's when I hear the jangle.

"Her keys!" I yell at Brian. "Get her keys."

He does a piss-poor action hero slide over the hood of my car and lands next to us.

"She's got her keys in her pocket," I say.

"I'm not reaching into her pockets!"

Yeah, I guess that could be construed as assault. I wrench her to one side, hoping to roll over on top of her. She braces herself, but now I have the advantage. I roll the other way and come up victorious. I brace my knees on her shoulders as I sit up. I'm panting like a bulldog but at least my tongue isn't hanging out.

While I'm sucking in all this air, I get a whiff of something stinky. And my elbow feels all wet. I take a quick glance. I've rolled through mud. No, not mud. I lean my head and take a sniff. I've got dog poo on my arm.

Gah! How am I going to get this cleaned off? I'm sure even if we give this woman money, she's not going to invite me into her house. I'll have to ride all the way home with this foul smell on me.

"Look at this!" I yell at her.

"It serves you right," she yells back.

That's when I lose it completely. I grab the front of her blousy shirt and wipe my elbow off. She screams and tries to buck me off, but I've got her by at least 30 pounds.

"If you want to be a neighborhood sentry," I say as I dig into her pocket, "you need to go after people who don't clean up after their dogs."

The fight has gone out of her. I'm sure all she wants to do now is get inside and find her Tide stick.

I struggle to my feet and toss her keys to Brian. "Move her car!"

He dashes away while I hop into mine and crawl over to the driver's side. As soon as he's got her car moved, I pull into the street. That's when I notice the small huddle of bystanders on the opposite sidewalk. At least two of them have phones held up. Great. There will be video of this fiasco.

Being the decent human being he is, Brian re-parks the woman's car, taking up both spaces. In the rearview, I see a tow truck turn onto Sixth. I toot my horn because it looks like Brian might try to apologize to Crazy Lady for my behavior. Instead, he tosses her the keys before he jumps into the passenger side and we zoom away.

Guess these in-town folks have learned not to mess with suburbanites like us.

Once the nervous giggling dies down and my fingers stop tingling, I loosen my grip on the steering wheel.

"That was . . . unexpected," I say, breaking the silence.

Brian doesn't answer right away, which makes me wonder if he's mad at me for duking it out with an older woman. Or if he found the scuffle disturbingly arousing.

"How did you know about the keys?" he finally asks.

"I heard them jingling in her pocket. And it all kind of made sense. Once the tow truck showed up, she wanted to get her car out of the way ASAP so he could haul the offender off. She wouldn't want to take the time to run inside to get them."

"I wonder if her brother-in-law owns the towing business."

"I wonder if we're going to be on the six o'clock news."

Brian's mouth drops open. Evidently he hasn't thought that far ahead, or he didn't see the cell phone brigade. This is probably a good time to change the subject so I start in on Pressley again.

"I wonder if Pressley has been a lifetime member of the Sexist Pig Fraternity."

"He was a member of Sigma Epsilon Nu, not Sexist Pig."

I offer a chuckle even though it isn't that funny. The last thing I need right now is Brian dwelling on my bad behavior. "Sigma Nu, huh? Does that mean something?"

"It's the premier sports house on campus. If a guy is in any kind of sports, he's probably a member."

"I wonder when Pressley's philandering started. In high school? College?" I drum my fingers on my lips. "I need to find out when he was at UGA and see if I can find a yearbook. Maybe some of his fraternity brothers can tell me more."

UNFORTUNATELY, the UGA website doesn't have a convenient tab for *Old Yearbooks*. But I seem to recall that Stan Richardson, a neighbor down the block, went to UGA. He's in his early fifties, maybe he bought a yearbook. But here's a bit of misfortune: the last time I talked to Stan was at the New Year's Eve party when I accused him of having sex with young girls in the back of his car.

As I stroll towards his house, I convince myself that he surely was as drunk as I was and doesn't remember the comment. Or if he does remember, that he was flattered that I thought a pudgy balding dweeb could entice young girls into his back seat.

I know it would be easier, and potentially less embarrassing to call first. That way if I got a chilly reception, I'd let it go. But let's say I call and he's all friendly; then we ascertain that he was indeed at UGA the same time as Pressley, and he did in fact buy a yearbook. He'll still put me off with some BS like 'I know it's around here somewhere' but then he won't look for it.

"Oh, sure," he says when he answers the door. "I bought one every year. Haven't seen any of them since we unpacked them in the last move."

Now, with me standing on his front porch, looking eager, he has no choice. He invites me in and waddles into their family room. They chose the house design with the built-in book shelves that flank the TV, and the cabinet doors at the bottom to hide all the junk.

He browses the upper shelves but I have a feeling they're in the back of one of the lower cabinets.

"Do you think they could be in here?" I ask, pointing to one of the doors.

"Maybe." He doesn't sound thrilled at the idea of digging around on hands and knees.

"Shall I look?"

"Knock yourself out," he says.

I drop to my knees and stick my tushy in the air as I root around. I know men love that kind of thing. Clear in the back, under a pile of photo albums, is a massive bound book. It has to be from UGA. Those things are huge.

I wriggle and pull at the thing while making little grunting noises, giving Stan quite a show. When I roll back onto my butt with my prize clutched in my arms, I glance up to see a nubbin poking his sweat pants. I graciously ignore it and stagger to my feet.

"This is it! Can I borrow it for a couple days?"

"Sure thing," he says. "Take as long as you need."

As he walks me to the door, he decides to get a little brazen. "Of course, you'll probably have to put it back when you're done."

Oh, you naughty boy.

* * *

IT'S A LONG tedious process of scrutinizing the caption under the group picture of Sigma Epsilon Nu fraternity, selecting the next name, then googling the guy to see if he lives anywhere in the vicinity. Most of Pressley's old frat buddies are scattered across the country.

I've wasted three hours this morning and still haven't started the laundry. Just the thought of that inspires me to keep searching. The next name in the yearbook is Jason Hadley. He's got a Facebook page and it says he lives in Atlanta. I read further and find out he's now a sports writer with the Atlanta Journal-Constitution. Paydirt!

I text the editor I know at the newspaper, Bryce Shackleford, and ask for an intro to Jason. Bryce and I are on pretty good terms because I gave the AJC an exclusive when Farouk Al Asad broke into our house and tried to kill me last month. We even included pictures Brian took of my bloodied face.

Shackleford texts me back immediately, asks how I'm doing, says he'll be glad to put me in touch with Jason Hadley. This is subterfuge for 'if you're digging up dirt on anyone, let me know first.'

A few minutes later, he texts me Hadley's phone number. I figure he gave Shackleford the okay to pass along his number so I call him. Hadley is very cordial, says he'd be glad to meet me at their offices in Dunwoody or for lunch someplace.

As we chat, I mention that I live in Mansell County and he says, "I'll be in your stomping grounds tomorrow. I coach baseball up in North Park."

If I meet Hadley at the park, I can wear jeans and tennis shoes; and the park is just a few miles away. If I meet him at the AJC offices, I'll have to wash my hair, wear nice slacks and at the very least, a pair of low-heeled pumps.

I make arrangements to meet him at Field #3 Friday. The younger boys Hadley coaches play their game at five, the next game starts at seven. I figure Brian and I will show up around six-thirty as the game is ending, talk to Hadley for a while, and hit Zaxby's on our way home.

Marsha Cornelius

Brian reminds me that he's got plans to go to a Braves exhibition game Friday night with Randy. He asked me first but I declined. Have I mentioned how boring baseball is? And when you're at a ballgame, there's no chance of polishing your toenails, or folding clean towels.

CHAPTER TWELVE

I get to the ballfield at six-thirty as planned. The bleachers are loaded with family; there are no actual fans of baseball at this age. Two little kids sit in the dirt just behind the seats driving toy cars along the roads they've excavated out of the red clay.

Half of the bleacher crowd roars as they stand and clap. The other half moans. I check the scoreboard: 13 to 5. Yikes. I hope the 5s just scored. One of the coaches claps his hands as he urges his team to 'shake it off', and 'we'll get the next one.' He looks enough like the photo in the yearbook to know he's Hadley. And his team is getting whupped.

I scan the bleachers for an empty spot and climb up to sit next to a woman who is watching alone.

"This doesn't look good," I say as I sit.

"Did you see the boy who got that last hit?" she asks. "He looks like he's fourteen. He's probably already shaving."

I click my tongue. "I'm glad I missed it."

We start with the mom introductions. I'm quite familiar with it since my sister Gwen has three kids and they've all been in some kind of sport. You don't say your name, like 'hi, I'm Sharon.' You say, 'I'm Nathan's mom.'"

The woman points out her son Trevor, who is scuffing dirt into a pile in the outfield. When she asks which boy is mine, I tell her I'm just here to see the coach after the game.

The next kid up to bat has biceps, like he works out. The poor guy on the pitcher's mound throws an easy curve and Biceps Boy whacks it into the next ball field. The score rolls up to 14-5.

Trevor's Mom groans. "I hope they score again and put us out of our misery."

My eyebrows knit in confusion.

"There's a 10-run rule," she says. "If the other team is that far ahead, they call the game. I've got to take my daughter to her soccer match and it's at Providence Park."

"Bummer."

"Yeah, my husband's out of town so I'm doing double duty tonight."

She scans the area and stops at three girls who are kicking a soccer ball to each other.

"Avery," the woman yells. "We're leaving in five minutes. Get your stuff."

Another boy steps up to the plate. The pitcher looks like he's about to cry.

"Do they always get beat this bad?" I ask Trevor's Mom.

"I'm afraid so." She checks the time on her phone. "This day is getting worse by the minute."

"How so?"

See, that's another big difference between men and women. A guy would never offer such a leading statement, and if he did, another guy would *never* ask him to clarify.

"My husband called me at four o'clock to say he was staying an extra day. Like I couldn't figure out he was going golfing. Then on the way to the ballfield, my son announces that today is our turn for snacks. I don't know anything about snacks."

"Oh, brother."

"Yeah," she says and lowers her voice. "And my son tells me it can't just be Twinkies or Snickers bars. It has to be healthy."

"God forbid you bring sodas."

"Right?" she says. "I got oranges and Gatorade."

"Good choices," I say.

"Listen." She turns to me. "I've got to go. Would you mind handing out the snack? It's right down there." She points to two plastic grocery bags setting just outside the dugout.

"Sure," I say. I feel like I've officially joined the ranks of motherhood.

Brian and I never had kids. It's not like we really tried all that hard to get pregnant, and we weren't too bummed out when it never happened. Neither of us considered tests or the basting bulb solution. My mother was more disappointed than me when I turned forty and she realized it was officially no longer a possibility.

As soon as I agree, Trevor's Mom hops up, yells at her daughter to meet her at the car, and stomps down the bleachers, making a hasty retreat.

The game ends as predicted with a final score of 15 to 5. I feel really bad for the losing team. And they don't even get a yummy consolation snack like a Rice Krispy treat or a chocolatey Yoo Hoo.

The parents stand to give their boys an encouraging round of applause while the kids shake hands with the other team. I make my way to the bags of treats.

I pick up the first, expecting to see a zip-lock bag of orange wedges. What I find is a mesh bag of whole oranges. What the hell? I won't even peel an orange. Trevor's Mom thought these boys would? The next bag is equally disappointing. She got two giant bottles of Gatorade. And I don't see any cups in the bag. How am I supposed to serve it?

I get the stink eye from each and every mother as I hand her son a stupid orange. A few of the boys have water bottles so I try to fill them with some Gatorade but end up getting most of it on my hands. Now they're sticky, and every woman has committed my face to memory so the next time she sees me, hopefully she'll have a rotten tomato in her purse. Has anyone snapped a picture of me to spread the word on Facebook?

Trevor accepts his orange and dashes away with a friend. I guess the friend's parents are taking him home. I wonder if he'll confess that it was his mother who brought this horrendous snack. That hope is dashed when I see Trevor and his pal drop their oranges in the parking lot and stomp on them. Juice flies everywhere.

Once the lynching mob has disbursed, I introduce myself to Jason Hadley. He's naturally confused since he thought I was a parent.

"Yeah, I got suckered into this," I say as I wad up the empty grocery bags. "Now I understand why the mom took off in such a hurry."

He laughs easily as I mimic one woman's particularly snarled expression. Then he asks why I'm interested in Darrell Pressley. I told him the 'who' but not the 'why' over the phone.

"I'm just looking into his background," I say. "How he went from football star to US Senator."

Hadley's smile fades. "Bryce thought you might be digging for dirt on Pressley. I'm not sure I'll be your best source for praise over that guy."

Hot diggity.

"Why don't you let me buy you supper and you can tell me all about why Darrell Pressley is such a turd."

HADLEY IS happy with Zaxby's. I figured if Brian and I had come, I'd have to pay for two so what's the difference? I'm pleasantly surprised when Hadley picks up the tab.

We sit down with our trays of food; he got the chicken finger sandwich, I got the wings and things. I have my list of questions, and I start in with the college scene.

"So Darrell was first-string quarterback at UGA for three years."

Hadley takes a huge bite of his sandwich that leaves mayo on his cheek. The food doesn't stop him from talking to me. He chews enough to get the wad manageable then shifts it to one side.

"He wasn't bad. I mean we went to two bowl games while he was quarterback." He gets a couple more chews in. "But he was such a whiner. He'd blame his receivers for a bad throw, or rant about the offensive linemen not doing their job."

"It's everyone's fault by mine."

"Exactly. He got into a big argument with Reggie Riggs his senior year." He washes down the bite with soda. "The press picked it up and ran with it. In a couple pictures, it looked like Riggs wanted to ream Pressley a new asshole."

"What was the fight about?"

"Oh, just some bullshit about Riggs not protecting his quarterback."

"I'm sure after that, Riggs was even more conscientious about defending Pressley."

We both chuckle. If I was depending on 300 pounds of beef to protect me, I don't think my first reaction would be to criticize the guy.

Hadley sets his sandwich down and wipes his fingers on a napkin. "So what did Darrell do?"

"I don't really know. Probably nothing."

Being a reporter, Hadley doesn't let it go. "I find that hard to believe."

"Okay, let's just say I'm not in a position to say anything yet. But the AJC will be the first to hear if I find anything."

"Good enough," he says, picking up his sandwich again. He takes another big bite and chews for a minute while he thinks. "After he graduated, Darrell got a job at a car dealership in Athens. You know, alumni got to meet their Orange Bowl hero and buy a car at the same time. One of the first things he did was push to get Reggie hired, too. Like he was trying to mend fences. They even had a little 'throw-down' rehearsed for the showroom."

"You mean like punching each other?"

"Nah, it was just bullshit banter. Customers loved it, though. Sold a lot of cars. They even took their 'show' on the road. Did a couple celebrity golf tournaments, charity events. Some of the material wasn't bad. They poked fun at each other and at themselves. Riggs is still in the car business. Has his own dealership in Stone Mountain."

"What about Darrell and women?"

Hadley leans forward. "Is that what this is about? Because he's a sexist pig."

"How so?"

"I don't know what he was like in high school, but for a while at UGA he was sniffing after every woman that crossed his path. A lot of the other guys at the house thought he was a player but I found his behavior disgusting. Especially with Dawn Shipley."

I'm scribbling like mad. Without looking up, I ask, "Who was she?"

"She was a cheerleader, a Theta, real popular on campus. But not a bitch or a bimbo. She was a genuine sweetheart. When Darrell hooked up with her, I was afraid it was the real thing." He pauses to reflect on what he just said, then gives me an embarrassed smile. "At the time I had quite a crush on her. Later, of course, I realized that she wanted a man who was into the physical aspects of sports, not just a guy who wrote about it."

Hadley shrugs it off. "Then the next thing I know, he dropped her for Charlotte Wilkins of all people. Really broke Dawn's heart."

"What was wrong with Charlotte?"

"Oh, nothing. Don't get me wrong. She's intelligent, she's motivated, she's compassionate. You know, she's Darrell's campaign manager. She's involved with fundraising for several charities. I think she's even connected to that run for breast cancer. She just never seemed like the type that would get mixed up with Pressley."

"You mean like the physical stuff."

"Yeah. And Darrell didn't seem to be interested in anything else. Back when he was on the city council, there was a group of businessmen who wanted to bring hockey to Atlanta. I guess some of the folks on city council helped pave the way. But Darrell couldn't care less. Then you know what he did? He heard about women's football—the Lingerie Women's League—out in LA. They basically wore sports bras and thongs with some shoulder and knee pads. And he did everything he could to get a team here. I think all he was really doing was 'interviewing' team candidates on his office couch."

"What a creep." I dredge my last bite of chicken finger into my Zax sauce. There's more than I really need but I can't let it go to waste so I drive that bite all around the bottom of the little cup, scooping all that spicy creaminess onto my bite. But just as I'm raising it to my mouth, a big blob drips onto my left boob. Lovely.

"It's interesting," Hadley says, trying to ignore the faux pas. "If he'd married one of the bimbos he fooled around with . . ." His eyes stray to my breast when he says 'bimbo', since by men's definition a bimbo must have big breasts.

I lose track of the conversation, frozen in the dilemma of what to do. If I was eating with Brian, I'd just scoop it up with a finger and lick it off. With Hadley, that may not be appropriate.

He's still talking but I can see he's also losing his train of thought. Probably because the blob isn't just sitting there, it's now inching its way over the peak and down the lee side.

I can't ignore it. I go for the napkin, but I also make a diversionary attempt to get the discussion back on track.

"Maybe Charlotte saw that his days as a sports hero were over . . ." I pull the front of my tee shirt away from my body, and give it one quick brush. Now the blob has been smeared to twice its original size. "Maybe she always wanted to be married to a politician."

"You may be right." He's finished his sandwich so he balls up the wrapper, tosses it onto his tray, and in an act of chivalry, he picks up the tray to return it to the stack over at the trash bin.

The instant he's gone, I yank the lid off my drink, wet a corner of a new napkin, and scrub. Naturally, the flimsy paper crumbles immediately. I brush away the white residue while keeping an eye on Hadley. He's taking his time. *Good boy*. He must be married.

I dip again with a dry napkin. Most of the sauce is gone, but now I have this big wet spot. I look like a lactating mother whose baby started crying. In a moment of clarity, I reach behind me and get the flannel shirt I draped over my chair and slip it on.

By the time Hadley gets back, I'm buttoned up. Now I just continue on like nothing happened. "Tell me about Dawn Shipley."

He seems relieved that the crisis is over and sits into a relaxed slump. "She's married. Her name's Dawn Ralston now. Her husband works for some athletic wear company. They're both fitness nuts."

Oh, boy. This won't be pretty. I feel compelled to talk to Dawn but I'm sure I'll be shamed to the core.

CHAPTER THIRTEEN

As soon as I got home from the ballfield last night, I searched for Dawn Shipley Ralston on Facebook. I couldn't find out anything without friending her. (You know how you can add art to your Facebook pic? Like a flower wreath for your hair, or a rainbow across the bottom? I added the UGA logo to mine. Clever, huh?) So now I'm waiting for her to accept my request.

It doesn't matter. I've got a full day today. I pull on a pair of sweats, zip up my jacket, and jog to Sarah's for our Saturday walk.

Ellie's already there and the two of them are talking about the Kramer's getting a load of horse manure for their garden.

"Once Mark gets it turned in with the dirt, it'll be fine," Ellie says.

"Well he's got it piled on a tarp in his driveway for now and it stinks," Sarah complains. "Someone needs to talk to Regina."

"Oh, don't rattle her cage," I say. "If she starts snooping around, she may find Brian's fish pond in the back yard."

"A fish pond?" Ellie says.

All I can do is shake my head. "It was either let him dig up the back yard or put in a new toilet in the guest bath."

They both recoil in horror. "Oh lordy, don't let him near the plumbing," Sarah says. "Ron tried four times to replace the flapper in the toilet tank. It never did stop running after we flushed. By the time he gave up, he'd spent more at Home Depot than the plumber cost."

"I let Joanie put a new pedestal sink in our bathroom and the faucet has dripped ever since," Ellie says.

We power walk to the corner of Hamilton Farms Avenue and Wisteria Drive and take a left. Roger Nelson is in his front yard spraying weeds.

"Hey, Rachel," he calls out. "Did you hear about the drowning?"

"Sure did," I say as I nod. At least most of my neighbors haven't gotten into the habit of calling me Gladys like Brian does. Although, Sarah and Ellie have adopted the moniker, now that I've made the news with my meddling.

"But thanks for letting me know," I call back as we continue swinging our arms and waddling our butts. I need to practice good public relations if I want neighbors to keep me in the loop.

"What *is* happening in the world of espionage?" Sarah asks.

I catch them up on Deborah Wiley's funeral, my visit to the fitness center, Six Flags Over Jesus services, and end with the zinger, that esteemed Georgia Senator Darrell Pressley was dicky-dunkin' Deborah Wiley.

There's an odd combination of guffaws and groans from both of them. Ellie hates him because he's homophobic. Brian and I loathe the man for not supporting the environment.

I'm not sure how Sarah feels about him but I think she's forming an opinion when she asks: "Do you think his wife knows he's cheating on her?"

Sarah caught her husband cheating on her a couple years ago with a twenty-something. Now he lives with the dental assistant who, according to Sarah, sounds like a parakeet when she talks, and he's barely making ends meet. Child support for his two kids sinks lower on his list of priorities each month.

"Maybe she got jealous and had her competition eliminated," Ellie says.

"Already considered that," I say. "According to the police, there's no evidence of foul play. And her daughter insists her mom was deathly afraid of the water so she thinks she panicked."

"But you're not buying it?" Sarah asks.

"I don't know," I say. "Truth is, even I think I'm barking at a dead horse. The only reason I'm still asking around is because I can't believe it's a coincidence that she drowned at Pressley's subdivision."

Dan Bellamy is standing in his front yard watering pansies as we stride by. I swear, the way he's holding his garden hose, it looks like he's peeing. Is he doing that on purpose?

We get back to Sarah's at eight-thirty. Ellie jogs the rest of the way home while Sarah and I stand out front making arrangements to go shopping at ten. There's a publishing convention this weekend at the Georgia Congress Center. Magazines from all over the country have gathered to exchange ideas on cutting costs, increasing advertising, and staying afloat in a digital world.

The Good Life, the magazine Brian and I work for, has a booth at the event. We're manning the table from 4 to 5 this afternoon to promote our column 'Off the Beaten Path.' But really, I'm more interested in showing my portfolio of work to other magazines.

Currently, I'm submitting to romance and crime magazines, but I'm always open to new genres. Well, anything but crafts like scrapbooking or gluing sea shells on bird houses. I'm curious if there are any magazines that cater to the BDSM crowd so I can get some pointers.

Being out in the public means I need to look good without spending a fortune on a new outfit. I've set aside my own mad money for a new pair of shoes. Sarah is my designated personal shopper for things like this. We'll go to Von Maur and Dillards to get ideas, then to the Goodwill to see what we can scrape together.

* * *

AS WE BROWSE racks of clothes, Sarah insists I look into Darrell Pressley's wife. "You know, in the TV shows, they always look at the spouse first."

"Yeah, I've got my eye on her but she's a prominent figure in Atlanta. I can't believe she'd let jealousy ruin everything. I mean, she's Darrell's campaign manager, plus she's on the boards of Scottish Rite Children's Hospital, the Jane Fonda Center, the Red Cross. She even has something to do with the Susan G. Komen Race for the Cure."

Sarah pulls out a gray skirt with black pinstripes and holds it up to me. "Do you think she participates or is she just a talking head?"

I drape the skirt over my arm to try on. "I think she might actually walk. There's a picture on her Wikipedia page that shows her walking with a group of women."

"You should register. If she walks, that would give you three days to get some dirt. I'm pretty sure they do it sometime in the spring so it could be coming up soon."

I make a frowny face. Three days of walking? I'm not sure I'm that committed to solving this crime.

"Ellie and Joanie did the walk a couple years ago," she says. "You should talk to them."

IN THE DRESSING room, I can see there's a major flaw in our plan. The styles are all short skirts, and frankly, my thighs are a tad bit saggy.

"I can't wear something like this. Look at me!" To emphasize my point, I grab some skin at my butt and pull the excess up then let it sink back into place.

"Do that again," she says.

I pull up the loose skin and we stand in front of the mirror, analyzing my legs. If there was only some way of keeping it all up permanently without spending thousands of dollars on plastic surgery, or dieting.

"Too bad they don't make those tape thingies like they do for women's faces." I say.

"It'd have to be some heavy duty tape," she mumbles.

After an hour of pawing through exorbitantly priced skirts and blouses, we take off for Goodwill. Now I'm in my element. I put my shoulder into heaving the packed hangers to the left so I can squeeze a hand in and browse through hundreds of skirts. Sarah won't touch the clothes ever since the time we were looking at blazers. I tried one on and then struck a model's pose with my hands pulling up the lapels. A cockroach skittered out.

I insisted it was an isolated incident but she's not taking any chances. So now she stands behind me and points at the items I need to try on.

I pause when I come to a blue and grey plaid skirt. It looks like part of a school uniform. My mind immediately jumps to me in knee socks, the skirt, and a tight, white blouse unbuttoned halfway down. Brian is watching TV. I walk in front of him and bend over, placing my hands on the arms of his chair. 'Professor Sanders,' I say, 'I'm having trouble with my biology project. Is copulation and fornication the same thing?' Then I suck in my bottom lip like a porn star.

"You've got to be kidding," Sarah says when I pull the skirt out. "I don't think school girl is the image we're going for here."

"This could be for something else," I say.

She shakes her head. "You bad, bad girl."

* * *

BRIAN PULLS into the driveway just as Sarah drops me off. He's got a clear plastic bag bulging with water and little fish. He's got one hand under the bag and the other with a firm grip on the knot at the top. He's heading for the door when I stop him.

"Hang on, Jacque Cousteau. Why don't you take those *around* the house to dump them in the pond?"

"Good idea."

Why don't men ever envision catastrophes? I can see that bag busting open the moment he steps inside, water gushing everywhere, helpless little fishies gasping for air, me having to scoop the slimy devils into drinking glasses.

I start for the door with my purchases, but Brian stops me.

"Aren't you going to watch me christen the new pond?"

Will champagne be involved?

"Yeah, sure," I say as I trudge along behind him. But if he has a speech prepared, I'm leaving.

The ceremony is short and sweet. He holds the bag over the pond, cuts a small slit in the bag which immediately spreads to a gaping hole. The water and fish splat into the pond like a bomb that causes a mini tidal wave. As the water sloshes back toward us, it slops out of the side and gets Brian's shoes.

It's a touching service that I'll always remember.

AFTER MY SHOWER, I stand naked in front of the full length mirror. I pull up my butt cheeks and see the remarkable difference in my thighs. If only I could figure out . . . that's when a brilliant idea comes to me: duct tape.

I throw on my robe and scurry out to the garage. Brian's work space out here looks about the same as his work space in his office: a total disaster. There's junk piled everywhere, and the handy plastic organizing trays and drawers I have bought over the years are crammed with junk in no discernable order. I peer in one of the larger drawers. A small can of 3-in-1 oil lays on its side, the contents a black sludgy puddle on the bottom. In another drawer, I find a box with two screws left in it. Finally, I locate the duct tape on a shelf between a box of nails and a stack of rusty circular saw blades he accepted from Jerry Bloomberg when he was moving. Does Brian have a saw that takes those blades? Of course not. But he insists that someday he's going to create some kind of yard art with them. When he first brought them home, I had this Gahan Wilson vision of a saw-blade mobile being blown by the wind and the lethal discs whirling away in all directions.

Back in the bathroom, I pull off a long strip of tape, rub one end securely to the bottom of my sagging butt, and hike everything up. I fasten the other end of the tape to my lower back. Not bad. I shimmy into the gray dress I bought at Goodwill and check the results. No visible sign, like a panty line or furrow on my butt cheeks. And I have to admit, I look pretty damn good. But the real test is, can I walk like this? I stroll around the bathroom, into the bedroom, down the hall. So far so good.

Unfortunately, the ultimate test fails. There's no way I can sit down or even climb stairs. Undeterred, I decide to take the tape with me. I'll slip into the women's bathroom as soon as we get to the expo, tape up my butt, and I'm set. I mean, no one ever sits at these events; they just shuffle from booth to booth like cattle, grabbing giveaways and stuffing them in the handy carrying bag supplied at the door. And even while we're manning our *Good Life* booth, I'll be standing.

* * *

BRIAN AND I spend the first hour or so flowing along with other attendees. He stops at booths to hand out business cards and schmooze with editors about freelance photography. I chat with publishers about writing articles.

I stop at a booth for a magazine called Persist. Several back issues are spread across the table. One has a picture of a woman politician on the cover with the headline 'Making Progress in Congress.' Another cover shows a group of young girls with labels on each: doctor, scientist, coder, diplomat.

Am I really the type who could write for a consciousness-raising women's magazine? I mean, Brian and I both consider ourselves feminists, but do I have the mindset to think up pressing women's issues and argue intelligently about them? If the woman on

103

the other side of the table knew I had my butt taped up, would she be appalled?

I take a couple magazines anyway, just to show my support.

At four o-clock, we take our places at *The Good Life* booth and watch attendees stream by. Now and then someone stops to take a pen or flash drive. Madeline sent me a terse email yesterday warning me not to put out more than three flash drives at a time. When folks see a big pile, they'll grab a whole handful. (I know I did when we first got here.) Madeline is the office manager at the magazine, and she's a penny-pincher in the same league as J. Paul Getty, who it was rumored put pay phones in his mansion in England for his guests.

Our main goal is to let people know about the magazine and encourage them to subscribe. But let's face it: 90% of the people milling about are here only for the freebies.

Along with the giveaway items is a small table poster of Brian and me standing outside the Tippecanoe Place Restaurant in South Bend. It's a gorgeous Romanesque mansion built in 1889 by the guy who manufactured the Studebaker cars. We're known for finding out-of-the-way places, and this is a perfect example. The picture is supposed to entice people to read more about our travels. But neither the poster nor my slim thighs are bringing in potential customers.

Now and then a hotel chain representative stops to chat, hoping we'll stay with them next time. A guy from Trailways hands me a brochure. What? Do we look like bus-riding journalists? While we're hanging around being ignored by people, I tell Brian about the Komen Race for the Cure.

"Sarah thinks I should do it. Maybe after three days of walking, Charlotte Pressley will crack and tell me something incriminating about Darrell."

"Hey, don't the women camp out at night? I could sneak into your tent and . . ." He wags his eyebrows at me. That's man talk for 'have sex'.

"I think men walk, too. We could turn this into a column."

He sneers. "Three days walking with women who are hot and tired and sweaty? I'd end up slitting my throat."

An announcement comes on thanking everyone for attending and requesting that they make their way to the gallery banquet room where the keynote speaker is someone from Oprah's O Magazine. I wasn't about to pay $50 each for overcooked chicken breast and chocolate pudding. It isn't even Oprah, it's one of her PR people, although they've been pushing the fact that there will be a videoed personal welcome from the big O. For that kind of money, they better be raffling off a Cadillac.

Brian throws all the giveaway junk into a box while I fold up the table cloth. We decide to keep the poster of us.

"I still think it would be cool to sneak into your tent."

I grab him by the shirt front. "Come on, Lover Boy. I'll let you buy me a cheeseburger."

OUT IN THE parking lot, Brian tosses the box of junk into the back. I open the passenger door of the Jeep and try to step up to get in. The duct tape on my butt pulls the skin on my legs and back. Ow, ow, ow. I'd pull it off right now but a lot of folks are getting into their cars. I'm not sure how they'll react to a woman raising her dress to expose her tape-covered ass.

My solution is to recline the seat back, twist so I can grab the overhead roll-bar with both hands, and try to pull myself in. Unfortunately, my arms are too weak.

Brian stands at the driver's side door watching my acrobatics. "What are you doing?"

I close my eyes and sigh. Then I tell him about the tape.

"No way," he says, a big grin on his face. "Let me see."

"I can't pull my dress up right out here."

He scurries around the Jeep. "Get in."

105

"I can't. That's the whole point."

"How about if you're face down?"

Oh, brother, now I know where this is going.

He folds the seat completely down and while I grip the back, he picks up my legs and drives me in. I wrap my arms around the headrest with my head hanging over the end. Oh, yeah. This is totally comfortable.

"I should probably get inside, too," he says.

How this man thinks he's going to mount me from behind in the middle of a parking lot is beyond me. But hey, no one's going to see *my* face.

Once he has the seat pushed back as far as it will go, he wedges himself between my legs in the foot-well.

"Okay, let's have a look," he says and pulls up my dress. "Holy shit!"

Did he think I was lying?

Here's what I think happened. Have you ever patched a car seat with duct tape? Once it's been on there a while, and the sun has heated up the adhesive, it's on there to stay. My body heat must have gotten the tape nice and gooey and now it's not budging.

"Just rip it off like a Band Aid," I tell him.

"I don't think so," he says. "That sucker's really on there."

"Try a quick pull and see what happens."

He jerks and half of my ass ignites in pain. I want to scream or cry but this is all my doing. I can't carry on like a big baby and make Brian feel guilty.

"Oh, shit," he says. And it isn't so much what he says as how he says it. I imagine a layer of my skin now clinging to the tape and my butt gushing blood.

"How bad is it?" I ask.

"I'd rather not say."

CHAPTER FOURTEEN

It took three glasses of wine and a hot soaking bath to get that darn tape off last night. Brian started my bathwater and brought the first glass while I was struggling out of my clothes.

That's the thing about men. Sometimes they're so aggravating, women take up signs and threaten to kill them all. But then they do something totally sweet.

He even brought in his iDock to play me some music but I suspect my whimpering and hissing as I pulled at the tape was disrupting his baseball game on our bedroom TV. Every now and then he'd call into the bathroom, 'Are you okay?' At least he didn't go downstairs and ignore my plight.

Once I got the tape all off, he rubbed Aloe on my poor stinging butt. I suspect there might have been an ulterior motive to that as well but then I'm always suspicious. I didn't have the heart to look at the damage. I also couldn't bring myself to tell Brian about the teeth marks in the headrest of his Jeep. He'll find them soon enough. This little episode will be repeated at parties, mark my words.

You know what the best part of this whole debacle is? While he was rubbing Aloe on my ass, he said, "I don't know why you can't just take my word that you look fantastic. There's nothing wrong with your legs or your butt." He even kissed my fanny when he was finished.

I'M FEELING brave this morning, so I slip out of bed while Brian is still sleeping and hobble into the bathroom. My flannel pants cling to my butt; not a good sign. I gently pull the fabric away from my burning skin and have a look.

I suck in a gasp as I glance over my shoulder. Flaming red stripes run from my lower back to the top of my thighs. And there's a massive petechial rash over the entire area. (That's those little red spots where the skin almost bleeds but not quite. I learned that term the first time I tried bikini waxing.)

And along the entire edge of redness is a border of grey goo from the tape. How many days will I have to suffer through my underpants sticking to me before that all wears off? My only other solution is to smear Goo Gone all over the sticky gunk and rub. I decide to test a little dab first, thank goodness. (Here's a tip for do-it-yourselfers. Goo Gone was never meant to come in contact with raw, painful skin.)

I call Sarah and have to endure her chortles before she suggests peanut butter. Now I'm positive my blunder will be the hit of the next party. After I've slathered creamy Jif all over my butt and wiped it off, I get into a cool shower and put out the fire.

The schoolgirl skirt hanging in the closet mocks me. My fantasy of crawling onto the bed and wiggling my fanny at Brian will have to wait. I really don't think he wants to pull down my panties and view this disaster.

I ease into my softest pair of sweats and head for the kitchen. This calls for pancakes.

WE SPEND the morning drinking coffee and reading the newspaper. It looks like we've dodged a bullet on my tussle with the hippie woman in midtown. There's nothing in the Sunday edition, and I haven't seen any video on the news. (To be more precise: no one has stopped me to say, 'Hey! I saw you on the news last night beating up an old lady.')

I catch up on Facebook and see that Dawn Shipley Ralston has friended me. Now I can get onto her page and see if she has revealed where she lives or how I can accidently bump into her.

Lucky for me, she has gotten sucked into a pyramid scheme selling healthy drinks that insure positive vibes and weight loss. And she's having a 'party' at a small craft shop nearby on Monday night. Oh, yummy.

All the coffee activates my morning call and I head for the bathroom. While I sit, I flip through one of the magazines I picked up yesterday. It's the one for activist women. They have a section of who's who, just like People Magazine, but instead of movie stars at gala events, it's prominent women doing good things.

One of the pictures is of Charlotte Wilkins Pressley at the Komen race. She's standing next to a woman in a pink tutu, and wearing a pink knit hat. The caption identifies the other woman as Audrey Wilkins McMurray, Charlotte's sister. Interesting. Looks like I've got another lead.

I NEED TO walk off the caffeine jitters so I power-walk over to Ellie and Joanie's. They've done the 3-day event and I want to get the details before I sign up.

"It's a blast," Ellie says. "You meet so many fabulous women."

"How far do you walk?" I ask.

"It's twenty miles a day, but you get so wrapped up in the experience, you hardly notice," Joanie insists.

"What if I get a blister? Or I have to go to the bathroom?"

"Oh, don't worry about that. There are pit stops and first aid stations all along the way," Ellie reassures me. "And if you really get so tired you can't go on, they'll give you a ride."

"Every day?" I ask.

Joanie gives me the stink eye. "The whole point is to make sacrifices."

"Yeah, I get that. Taking a dump in a port-o-let and sleeping in a tent rank right up there with me."

Joanie and I don't get along nearly as well as Ellie and I do. She's never been interested in our girl-talk walks. And she's definitely not a high-heels and lipstick kind of woman. (It's tough to find a couple where you like them both, isn't it?)

"The bathrooms are very clean," Ellie insists. "It's all handled by professionals."

"And what about meals?"

"They serve breakfast before we start each morning. Then there's a lunch stop along the route, and dinner wherever we stop for the night."

"Do I have to carry a backpack with all my stuff?"

"No, no," Ellie says. "They have a gear truck for that. All you do is walk and enjoy the camaraderie."

"Do you walk with the same people every day?"

"Oh, hell no," Ellie says. "It changes all the time. I mean, every time you stop for a break, you get back in line with new people."

So I could scope out Charlotte Pressley, sidle up next to her one hot afternoon when her pups are barking and she's craving a glass of wine. How easy will it be to spot her? Does she have an entourage?

"How many women are in this walk?"

"The first year we walked it was around thirty-five hundred. But I read that last year they had over six thousand," Joanie says. "And I never saw anyone give up and accept a ride." Harsh, Joanie.

How am I supposed to find Charlotte in a crowd like that? I press on.

"I saw that the tents are pink but where exactly do they pitch these tents? What if it rains?"

"The tents are waterproof," Joanie says.

110

Ellie jabs her with an elbow. "They set up in school gymnasiums. That way they can secure the area. Keep troublemakers out."

Hm. Doesn't sound like Brian's going to be sneaking into my tent at night. And I don't think he'd appreciate being known as a troublemaker.

"You should find a partner," Ellie says. "It's two to a tent, you know."

Oh, great. I'll end up sleeping with a woman who snores, or who suffers from irritable bowel syndrome.

Will it really be worth it to spend three days walking just to chat with Charlotte Pressley? Am I going to get any useful information from her? The compassionate side of my brain tries to shame me by pointing out how worthwhile my efforts will be. Speaking of which—

"So how do they raise all the money? How much is the registration?"

"The registration isn't that much," Ellie says. "It's the pledges of twenty-three hundred dollars per person."

"Twenty-three hundred dollars!?"

Joanie gets a big grin on her face. "Yeah. And if you don't get enough pledges, you pay the difference yourself."

"Geez! Why didn't you tell me this first?!"

I FUME ABOUT the high cost of caring on my walk home, but once I've decided that the Komen walk is off the table, I wonder how else I'm going to get dirt on Darrell.

I google the sister Audrey on my phone but don't find much.

Tomorrow Brian and I are going out to Riggs BMW to see if Reggie can shed any light on Pressley. The question is: will we be able to talk to him? He's the owner of the dealership so I doubt if he sits on the team bench waiting for his turn to make a sale. We'll have to be special customers to warrant his attention. And what would make us

111

special? Either we need to be famous and buying a top-of-the-line model, or we have a business that needs a fleet of cars. Looks like I'll be wearing a business suit and heels tomorrow. Good thing I still have that navy blazer from the Goodwill.

I see Marge Chronister at her mailbox, hanging one of those cute Easter flags with a bunny and colorful eggs. She's got a flag for every occasion from the New Year all the way to Christmas.

"When is Easter this year?" I ask. I don't really care but sometimes I get a little tidbit of news when I stop to talk.

"Third Sunday in April," she says. "Although we won't be here. We're going to my daughter's. Charlie Fisher is thinking about selling his camper and if the price is right, we'll take it to St. Louis."

"That'll be fun." Not!

"I'm a little leery of pulling a camper but Laura only has a one bedroom apartment."

"And she can't get away to come here?"

Marge shakes her head. "She's got a boyfriend." Her eyes roll up. "And she can't bear to be apart from him for three days."

"I remember when I felt like that."

She chuckles. "Yeah, me too, but it was my new German Shephard puppy."

We both laugh and I stroll on.

Easter is coming, which naturally makes me think of candy. I love the chocolate covered marshmallows, the crème eggs, the jelly beans, the Peeps, the malted milk balls. Let's face it, the only Easter candy I don't really like is the plain hollow chocolate bunnies. They're kind of boring. Although one year, I got out a knife and the peanut butter, and after I'd bit off the head, I filled the rest of the cavity. The ratio wasn't quite the same, but it was tasty.

That gets me thinking about an article for the magazine. How soon do candy manufacturers start production for the next year? The displays show up in the stores right after Valentine's Day so they must make the candy in the fall. Brian and I could tour some factories and get pictures of how different items are made. Who hasn't wondered how Cadbury gets that yolk in the middle of the egg?

* * *

I SEND AN email to Ray at *The Good Life* while Brian drives us to Stone Mountain and Riggs BMW. My idea for the Easter candy research is developing. We'd visit Mars (makers of M & Ms) in Hackettstown, New Jersey, then drive to Hershey, Pennsylvania (for an up close and personal viewing of chocolate rabbits and Reese's peanut butter delights) and a hop, skip and a jump to Bethlehem, PA for a tour of Just Born. (They make Peeps. Isn't that cute?) I threw in Fairfield, California for Jelly Bellys even though that's a long shot.

I've also been rehearsing my story about our small company that needs four of BMW's X1 series for our sales staff. I'm thinking Brian and I have a swimming pool company and the sales personnel sometimes have to transport supplies.

The skirt I chose is a little tight and my tender buns are protesting but they don't come close to Brian's constant grumbling and tugging at the tie I made him wear.

Ray emails me back that the candy idea sounds good although he nixes the California stop. I assume that's because Madeline wants us to drive instead of fly. I'll have to come up with a compelling reason to keep Jelly Bellys on the itinerary.

I text Ray about a possible second article on wineries *outside* of Napa Valley. (After all, we're known for taking the road less traveled.)

Brian pulls into the BMW parking lot and as we get out, I drill him on the scenario.

"Remember, we have a swimming pool company and we're looking for a fleet for our sales staff."

"Come on, Rach, I can't keep up with all of your stories. Why don't we just tell Reggie we're doing an article on famous people and their favorite out-of-the-way places?"

113

Damn, that's good! I wish I'd thought of it. Naturally, I don't want him to get too full of himself.

"Fine," I say with a resigned sigh. "We'll go with that."

Inside, I whip out one of my business cards and announce our desire to interview Mr. Riggs.

"I'm doing a story on celebrities and their favorite destinations," I tell her.

The woman at the reception desk seems impressed, although the way she's staring at Brian makes me think she'll let me do the interview with Riggs while she takes my husband for a little test drive.

I clear my throat to get her attention and she dashes away, embarrassed I hope, and returns shortly with Reggie Riggs. I introduce Brian and myself. He gives us a polite smile.

Then Brian pumps Reggie's hand. "My dad took me to a Georgia-Georgia Tech game when I was in high school. I'm sure he was hoping it would inspire me to greatness. But when I saw you steamroll Sammy Brown, I knew I wouldn't make it." He chuckles. "I didn't have the cohones."

What BS! Brian went to high school in Florida. If his dad took him to any games, it was between Florida and Florida State. But evidently his research worked because Reggie gets a toothy grin on his face and ushers us into his office. He asks his receptionist to get us drinks. For the next several minutes the guys talk about Vince Dooley and Bill Curry and winning seasons.

When the receptionist comes back with bottled waters, I take advantage of the lull in the conversation to dig into my purse and pull out my trusty notebook.

"Wasn't Darrell Pressley the quarterback while you were at UGA?" I say as I flip open to a clean page and cross my legs. I don't dab the end of a pencil on my tongue though; I'm using a pen.

"Yeah. Good guy," Reggie says. "Good guy."

"Didn't he have a romance going with Dawn Shipley?" I ask.

114

"If I recall, Darrell had romances with several of the beauties at UGA."

Nice. Reggie's good at the positive, generalized comment that politicians and savvy businessmen are famous for.

"How well did you know Darrell off the field?"

"When I was recruited by UGA, I was strongly encouraged to join Sigma Epsilon Nu since it was a sports fraternity, but I didn't hang out with the brothers much." He snorts at the 'brothers' reference.

"So who did Darrell hang out with?"

"His two best buddies were Lonnie Taggart and Adam Winston."

"Any idea where Lonnie and Adam are now?"

"Once I graduated, I lost touch with most of the guys."

"Do you think they're still in the area?"

"I'm sure Lonnie is still in Georgia. He got some girl pregnant and dropped out of school. He's got a farm somewhere." Reggie leans back and squints his eyes. "Are all of the celebrities for this article UGA football players?"

Yikes! I sputter for a second to get my head back on the right track. "No, no. I'm going to interview Dominique Wilkins and Chipper Jones, too." I straighten in my chair and poise my pen over my pad. "When you take a vacation, what are you looking for? A mountain cabin, a sandy beach, a bustling city?"

"There's plenty of city here. If I get away, I want peace and quiet."

I scribble his quote while I nod. "What's one of your most memorable destinations?"

"One year my wife and I went to Costa Rica. They have a lot of volcanos there and I'd never seen one. An active one, I mean. We went in the spring of '94 and stayed at the lodge in Arenal National Park. That place is fantastic. Have you ever been?"

Brian and I shake our heads no.

"Oh, you've got to go. Every room has these floor to ceiling windows looking out on the volcano. You can lie in bed and watch the lava flow."

"Weren't you afraid it would flow right over the lodge?"

"Nah," he laughs. "It's not that close."

Brian jumps in. "Do you have any pictures of you and your wife at the volcano?"

"Oh, sure. Tons of them."

"Maybe we could borrow one for the story?" Brian says.

We don't even have a story but Brian's talking about pictures? He's good.

AS SOON AS I'm back in the Jeep, I pull up Facebook, find Adam Winston and friend him. His profile picture was taken at a gym. He's got on an extra-large tee shirt with the sleeves cut off. My guess is there's a big belly hiding beneath. He has one knee on a weight bench and a hefty barbell in his opposite hand. His arm is cocked back to show off his biceps. Something about his dark hair looks weird so I click on the picture to see the larger version. He's wearing a black do-rag; a dead giveaway that he's balding. I'm sure he wants the other guys at the gym to think he's a badass who rides a Harley.

He lives in Ohio. His bio says he works for the Blanton Corporation. Unless I can get into a Facebook conversation with him, he's a dead end. There's absolutely nothing on Google for Lonnie Taggart except for sports articles that go back to his college football days. He really has fallen off the grid.

Maybe I'll have better luck with Dawn Shipley Ralston tonight.

CHAPTER FIFTEEN

Dawn's Juice de Vie party is at a small craft store in an out-of-the-way shopping center. I get there a little late so the party has already started. Conventional wisdom would suggest I get there way early so Dawn and I could chat about her school days. But if she's anything like me that would never work. Pre-party, I'd be running around making sure there were plenty of napkins and cups. And I'd probably find out something was missing which would call for a quick dash to the grocery store on the other side of the shopping center.

Then there's the other friends who come early to chat. And the pyramid builder (that's the woman who strong-armed Dawn into having the party) who needs to keep Dawn all pumped up about how much money she's going to make when she talks three of her friends into selling the products, too.

But after the party, everyone will scatter like roaches when Dawn comes around to take orders. Plus no one wants to stay for clean-up so that will be my moment to bond.

When I walk into the craft store, Dawn is laughing and joking with ten or so women who are sitting around a long table covered with a cheap plastic cloth. On weekday mornings, I imagine little old ladies are gathered around the table chatting as they make a quilt or glop decoupage glue on a plaque of cut-out pictures rose buds.

Dawn catches my eye and for a second there's a little hiccup in her introduction as she tries to figure out if she knows me. The head

Juice Lady, wearing a white lab coat, dashes over to whisper a welcome and escorts me to an empty seat at the table.

Each place has a little goodie bag with two sample packets of powdered drink mixes: vanilla and Dutch chocolate. I'm sure it will taste just like Godiva even after I've mixed it with kale, and banana, and flax seeds.

After Dawn wraps up her remarks, she turns the program over to Juice Lady who has a handy flip chart to show us just how beneficial her juice drinks are. On each page of the presentation, professional models dressed like medical staff add credibility to the research that has been done.

Dawn walks around the table with a tray of tiny plastic cups like they serve pills in at the hospital. Each cup is filled with either a pinkish concoction or a brown one. I won't even say what the brown goop looks like. I'm sure they've learned not to give attendees too large a taste. No need to discourage anyone before they've bought all the crap and made their own drink at home.

I take one of each like everyone else. Then we all sit holding the pink drink, waiting to see who will be the first to slug it down. Dawn's smile falters. She's telling herself she's made a big mistake, and now her friends will hate her for dragging them out into this chilly night to drink something with beets and brown rice bran in it. I tip mine back and swallow it down, even making a rude sucking noise to show I'm trying to get every drop.

Dawn's smile comes back to life, the other women give me a few seconds to either claw at my throat or run to the nearest wastebasket to barf.

"Mmmmm," I say, stretching my lips into a smile and raising my eyebrows in confirmation. "It's really good."

The rest join in.

A bitter aftertaste creeps up on me. I look around but there's no soda or tea to wash out my mouth; only the dreaded brown cup. Juice

Lady is carrying on about all the nutrients and antioxidants in every serving. The woman on my right is toying with her brown cup. I think she's moving it slowly to the edge of the table with the intention of knocking it off. The woman on my left is holding her cup. She takes a sniff. Well of course it's going to *smell* like chocolate. I wonder if anyone will notice if I plug my nose to drink mine.

This reminds me of the time Brian and I sampled kopi luwak, also known as civet coffee. A civet is a furry little animal that looks kind of like a weasel. These critters eat coffee cherries, then shit them out, and some enterprising individuals scoop up the poop, pick out the undigested seeds, and make coffee.

Evidently, the Dutch coffee plantations in the East Indies used to prohibit the workers from picking the cherries and making their own coffee. I'm sure if someone told me I couldn't have any of the cherries, the first thing I'd do is check out animal poop.

I refused to enjoy the sample. First of all, the only thing I'll eat that comes out of an animal's butt is an egg. And secondly, that stuff is *way* too expensive. If I've got that kind of money to burn, I'll buy shoes.

Two women sitting across the table are waiting for me to take another one for the team so I toss it back. The only way this can be construed as chocolate is the brown color and the faint smell. It tastes like mud which is actually better than what I thought it would taste like.

Juice Lady stands at a blender, pouring carrot juice into the pitcher and then shoving a whole banana into the opening on the lid. She wants us to see how easy it is to make one of these delicious and nutritious drinks every day.

I avoid making eye contact in case she asks who would like a taste. While I'm burrowing into my goody bag, I find a small packet of capsules near the bottom. I pull it out and feign interest by turning the pack over in my hand a couple times. What I'm thinking is: 'Why the hell didn't they tell me I could get the same thing in a capsule instead of that nasty drink?'

Dawn comes around again with cut up bars made from the drink powder. Ugh. I'm going to have to stop on the way home for an order of French fries to combat all this stuff.

As predicted, once Juice Lady finishes her presentation, the excuses from the attendees fly: 'Told my babysitter' . . . 'have to pick up' . . . 'early day tomorrow'. Within minutes, the place is deserted. I notice several of the samples are still sitting on the table. Poor Dawn.

And poor me. Because now she'll pour all of her selling skills on me. I consider writing a check, knowing it will bounce, but that's low even for me. I do have a semi-legitimate excuse.

"I just started the Plexus plan a couple weeks ago," I say. "I think I should give it a fair trial before I switch."

Juice Lady jumps in to tell me how awful Plexus is compared to Juice de Vie. (What a surprise.) I walk around the table one step ahead of the sales team, picking up empty cups and napkins. There's not much for cleanup; it's time to get off the pot.

As I turn to head for the wastebasket, I say, "I understand you used to date Darrell Pressley back at UGA."

Dawn skids to a halt. "Who told you that?"

"Jason Hadley. I freelance at the Atlanta Journal-Constitution. He's a sports reporter there."

"I know him. But why would he tell you—"

"I'm digging up dirt on Darrell," I say. Might as well.

Her mouth makes the same grimace we all did when we tasted the brown stuff. "You won't have to dig too deep."

She still sounds bitter. Of course, if I was in my mid-50s and had to join a pyramid scheme to make ends meet, I'd probably be angry, too.

"You're lucky you dumped him when you did," I say, hoping to sooth her anger while letting her save face by assuming she walked away from the relationship. "Or he'd be cheating on you."

"So he's cheating on Charlotte, huh?"

"I'd say for quite some time."

She sits as though the weight of the memory is too much. "I guess I'm not surprised."

"What happened between you two?" I ask.

Her head shakes slowly as she thinks back. "I don't even know. One day he's this voracious animal and the next day he can't even get it up. He couldn't sleep, he had nightmares."

"Sounds like something bad happened."

"I know, right? But he wouldn't talk about it. He just drifted around in a haze for about a week. I heard there was a big party at the fraternity house right before spring break. I left that morning for vacation so I didn't go. But one of my friends said Darrell went home that night with Charlotte and didn't come back until the next morning." She shrugs her shoulders. "That didn't bother me. I mean Charlotte was no competition, or so I thought. But then the next thing I know, he's running for student body president and Charlotte is handling the campaign."

"That's quite a leap from football jock to politician."

"He was very charismatic. Still is from what I've seen in the news and in the commercials. And she's what we used to call a ball buster. Nowadays, she's not domineering, she's motivated."

Juice Lady has packed up her blender and supplies. She's ready to give Dawn one more pep talk before she bugs out. But I've got my own agenda.

"Maybe that's what Darrell needed."

"I guess," Dawn says. "But it seemed to be more than that. Like he did something awful to her that night and he felt like he had to make it up to her. I don't know. I *do* know that he finally did snap out of his

121

funk. I'd catch him staring at me with that same lusty gleam in his eyes but he was afraid to act on it."

"That's weird."

"I don't know what Charlotte did to get her claws into that man, but once she did, there was no letting go."

"And she's still his campaign manager after all these years."

"Isn't that something?" She chuckles. "I'm sure there isn't a decision made that she doesn't know about."

"So she must know he's cheating."

"I'd bet my last dollar on it."

"Do you know anything about Charlotte's sister, Audrey?"

Now Juice Lady clears her throat and rustles the plastic bag in her hand. Dawn doesn't seem to notice. Or this is payback for roping her into this scheme.

"Oh, now she's a sweetheart," she says. "A gentle spirit inside, but a brave warrior on the outside. She's devoted her life to helping women."

"I saw her in the Komen Race for the Cure."

She puffs out a breath of contempt. "She does that for Charlotte. But her real cause is a women's center. It isn't just for battered women. It's for women who need a new start, a helping hand, a little shove in the right direction."

"I didn't see anything about that on Google."

"I think they keep it quiet since some of the women are trying to end a bad relationship."

"Do you know what it's called?"

Dawn doesn't know but we exchange phone numbers and she promises to text me. I think she'd love to see Darrell squirm. The Juice Lady takes advantage of the break in the conversation and snags Dawn.

As I'm walking through the parking lot, my phone dings with a text. Audrey works at Fuller House.

* * *

THIS MORNING has been quite productive. I've already got a bead on the Fuller House in downtown Atlanta. It's named after Margaret Fuller, an American journalist, critic, and women's advocate. Their website is as vague as you might expect. But they have a page for volunteers to sign up, so I do. This could be my best lead yet. If I can work some day when Audrey's there, I might be able to get some dirt on big sis and her good-for-nothing husband.

Plus, I got a Facebook acceptance from Adam Winston. I send him a brief note telling him my older sister went to UGA and had a huge crush on him. That should get a quick response.

While I'm killing time, I browse through the pictures on his Facebook page: hanging on a waitress in a bar; his arm slung over some woman's shoulders, his hand dangling right in front of her breast; pretending to pour a beer on some girl's head who looks mortified. The expression on his face is usually leering. Have the women in his office ever filed a discrimination suit against him?

A google search shows Blanton Corporation is a bunch of auto parts stores in Indiana, Ohio, and Kentucky. Their headquarters are in Columbus.

My iPad chimes. Adam Facebooks me back wanting to know my older sister's name. Thank goodness I still have Stan Richardson's yearbook. I flip through to the sororities and find a cute girl. If I'm lucky, Adam won't have a clue who she was but he'll be flattered and want to chat more. He sends a message back: *Can't believe I didn't know her. She's hot.*

Brian comes rushing into the kitchen. "I need a bucket quick!"

I hand him the bucket from under the sink and he runs out to the back yard. I stand at the kitchen sink and watch as he steps into his fish pond. There doesn't seem to be any water in there but I know it was full yesterday.

He lays the bucket on its side at the bottom of the black plastic liner and seems to be scooping water. I've got to get a closer look.

At the edge of the pond, I see a small puddle just a few inches deep. Brian's newly-acquired fish swim frantically, dodging his hand as he tries to herd them into his bucket. Each time he manages to get a fish to swim in, another swims back out.

"Come on, Comet," he says in exasperation.

I snort. "You named your fish after Santa's reindeer?"

He jumps at my voice and drops the bucket. All the fish swim back out.

"Damn it, Rachel!"

I hold my hands out. "Sorry, sorry." Then I slip off my shoes and step into the cold pond bed. While he holds the bucket, I push fish and water in. "Get along Dancer," I say, trying to add some levity.

He gives me a droll stare. "They aren't named after reindeer. That one is a Comet goldfish. And this one is a Pearl-scale."

"Ah," I say, nodding. "And I guess its name is Pearly?"

It's too bad Brian doesn't wear glasses because this would be the perfect opportunity to glare at me over the top of the frames. But at least all the fish are now in the bucket.

He climbs out of the pond and I scramble out the other side. Then he squats and grips the rounded edge like he's going to pull it out. Evidently, he's waiting for me to grab the other end and help lift. This is what I get for coming out here; and for taunting him about fish names.

I wrap my fingers under the curved lip and give a little tug. Nothing. What did I expect? All the water drained into the pit in the ground and has created a muddy tomb.

Okay, let's do this right. I squat in a sumo wrestler pose and heave. The black plastic quivers but doesn't really move. I take a deep breath, flex my muscles, brace my elbows on my thighs, and try to stand.

The liner inches up.

"That's it," Brian encourages. "Keep lifting. Don't stop."

I can't stop. My legs are screaming from the deep squat I'm in. And one of my fingernails is bending precariously from the weight. I've got to get this stupid thing out before I break something, either my nail or my back.

I clench my teeth and grunt like all the good weight lifters do. That does the trick. The liner comes out. Brian takes control and tips it to drain the rest of the water out. I hobble around the yard to work out a leg cramp while I examine the fingernail. Great. It's got one of those splits at the side. Now I'm going to have to clip it off or it will snag on everything I touch. That means I'll have to clip all the nails so they're the same length. Then there will be filing. I tsk as loud as I can.

Brian is oblivious to the disaster. "We need to clean all this mud off so I can look for the leak."

Oh, no. 'We' aren't going to do any such thing.

Now here is where I have irrefutable evidence that miracles do happen because my cell phone dings and I see that I have a message from Fuller House.

"I've got to take this," I say and sprint toward the house.

The message is from Audrey Wilkins McMurray no less. At first I'm flattered, but then I realize it's a form letter they send out to all volunteers. There's the cursory welcoming paragraph that thanks me for my interest in Fuller House followed by an interview date and time: tomorrow at eleven.

CHAPTER SIXTEEN

The Fuller House is a converted two-story Craftsman near Inman Park east of downtown Atlanta. There is no sign outside, just the street number on the building. I assume that's because some women who use the services don't want a boyfriend or ex-husband tracking them down.

The woman at the reception desk in what was previously the living room confirms my suspicions. Her desk is parked about three steps in from the front door. If I was some slug looking to cause trouble, I'd turn around immediately because this woman is built like a young Rhonda Rousey and has a red Mohawk like that scary guy in The Road Warrior. Her arms are covered with tattoos, and she's got piercings in multiple places on her face. I'd wager she's got a gun in one of those desk drawers.

I wish I'd printed out the email instructing me to come for an interview so I could wave it in front of me like a white flag.

But as soon as she sees me, she says, "Welcome to Fuller House. How can I help?"

I glance at the name plate on the desk: *Tanya.* I ask for Audrey McMurray but Tanya says she's not available. When I tell her my name, she glances at a sheet of paper on the desk. "Ah, you have an interview at eleven."

Then she leans back in her seat and calls out 'Samantha!' A woman scurries out of the kitchen wearing a gauzy skirt and Mary Jane flats. Her long gray hair is pulled back into a loose ponytail. The staff is an interesting blend so far: the intimidating amazon for security, and the compassionate Earth Mother for support. I wonder what Audrey is like in person.

After a gracious welcome and warm handshake, Samantha takes me on a tour of the facility. The first stop is the former dining room, now a small daycare. Two doorways are blocked with those plastic baby fences, and there are toys scattered around on the floor.

"We only take children from eight am to noon. It's strictly a service so a mother can go on an interview. The kids are great because it's the morning and they've just gotten up so they're fresh. You know, they aren't cranky and need a nap. And the mothers are very considerate. We hardly ever . . ."

My brain tunes out the rest of her hard-sell. Evidently, she's hoping I'll volunteer for child care. That probably wouldn't be a good match. I'm not a very responsible person. I'm missing that mom gene that allows a woman to look four steps ahead to potential danger. If two kids want to use lighted sparklers like saber swords, I don't see them maiming each other with that molten-lava piece of metal until someone has a third degree burn.

Samantha gets the drift that I'm not interested in that position. I'm pretty sure it's my glazed eyes and slightly snarled upper lip. She unhooks the first baby gate and we move on to the kitchen.

"We use this for a breakroom," she says, but I notice the cupboards are full of food. Does Tanya live here? I can't think of anything more life-threatening than waking her in the middle of the night.

Samantha gives me the lowdown. "If a woman is struggling, we give her a few days' worth of canned goods to see her through to payday."

127

Then it's up the narrow wood stairs to the bedrooms. The first room has three small computer desks for women to work on resumes and do job searches. The second room has 'business' attire hanging in the closet and stacked on metal shelving. Some of the fancy stuff, like suits can be borrowed but have to be returned within a week, cleaned and in good condition. The same goes for shoes.

The last room has six desks for training on interviewing, child care, nutrition, even substance abuse. It looks like they've got all the bases covered.

I need to put my bid in for computer assistance before they stick me with kiddie patrol or dressing for success. (Although my duct tape trick might get a few laughs.)

"I'm a writer," I tell Samantha. "I think I could be an asset to women who need to polish their resume."

We go back to computer room and sit at two of the desks. Samantha shows me some websites they use for job searches. They even have a box of used USB drives that women can put their resume on and take with them.

I sit back in my chair. "This is all so organized. Audrey sounds a lot like her sister Charlotte."

"They're both motivated, that's for sure."

"Are there any more Wilkins out there doing good things for Atlanta?"

"There's a brother, Nate. He has a degree in some kind of forensic science. You know, analyzing blood and tissue."

"Oh, sure," I say. "I love CSI."

"For a while, he worked as an expert witness at trials, explaining DNA and all that stuff. But the defense attorneys were ruthless. They'd do whatever they could to discredit his testimony, even attacked him personally. He couldn't take it."

"So he wasn't as thick-skinned as his sisters."

"It wasn't that," she says, then glances at the doorway to be sure we're alone. "He's bipolar. Started thinking people in the lab were talking about him. Worried they were going to send him back as a witness even though they swore they wouldn't. Finally, he just stopped showing up at work. Lost his apartment."

"Holy crap!"

"Yeah, it was real sad. Audrey didn't even know until she found him shuffling along Ponce de Leon, tattered clothes, smelled like hell. She barely recognized him."

"Damn."

Does Audrey know how Samantha readily gossips about her brother? Or is this some kind of psychological technique to show how lots of people have problems? Is there even a Nate?

"She and Charlotte got him into a facility, got him on meds. Then I guess Charlotte and Darrell paid for an apartment for him. He's okay for a while but then he thinks he doesn't need the pills so he stops taking them and the cycle starts over again."

"I think that's a pretty common dilemma."

"That's what they say. I see him now and then cruising the streets with other homeless guys. I heard he's a regular at some pancake house on North Avenue."

If this is all a ruse, she's doing a great job.

We hear footsteps clomping on the wooden stairs and Samantha whips around to the computer. "We allow our ladies to check their emails here so you may need to help them set up an account if they don't have one."

A woman pokes her head in the door. She looks scared to death.

"Hey!" Samantha says all cheery. "How can I help you?"

The woman clings to the doorjamb as though she may bolt at any second. "I need a job," she says quietly. Then she looks down the stairway like she's afraid someone may come storming up after her.

"Well you've come to the right place," Samantha says, motioning for the woman to have a seat. "Let's get started."

My first inclination is to ask the woman all about her troubles and how she ended up here. But suddenly Samantha is all business. She gets her name, Amber, then takes her through a mini-interview: Does she have a car? Are there children in daycare? Where does she live? In less than two minutes, I know this poor woman is in deep doo-doo. She doesn't have a car so she needs a job on the bus line. She has three kids, all in elementary school, so she'll have to be home by three at the latest. Her husband walked out on her so she's the primary caregiver. Her last year of school was eleventh grade. She won't say where she lives. I suspect she's trying to move; probably afraid her husband will come home drunk and smack her around again.

"What about a job at a school," I say. "The hours are right."

Amber shakes her head. "I tried working in the cafeteria but you have to lift heavy pans and cases of food. My back couldn't take it."

"Any other limitations?" Samantha asks.

Amber flexes her left hand. "I don't have much feeling in my fingers." She glances down. "Not since they got smashed in a door."

Whoa! I can guess how that happened. I'm not letting Amber out of this room until we've found her a job. It's going to be tough because of her limitations, though.

"Here's a custodial job," Samantha says as she scrolls through her computer. "Oh, wait, it's for nights."

"Most custodial jobs are at night," Amber says. "When businesses are closed."

That gets my mind in gear. What kind of places are open at night but closed during school hours? Bars. Maybe restaurants if they don't serve lunch. Concert halls.

"Hey!" I blurt. My enthusiasm frightens Amber and she jumps. I raise my hands in apology and lower my voice. "What about movie theaters? They don't open 'til noon. They must have someone who sweeps up popcorn and mops all the sticky spills."

Samantha likes where I'm going. "There are movie theaters everywhere. And I'm sure they're on a bus line. No heavy lifting."

Tears well up in Amber's eyes. This could be the first time someone has shown a genuine interest in her in years.

I'M SO PISSED at Amber's husband that while I'm driving home, I compose a short story for the crime magazine where I freelance. It's about a man who pushes his wife too far and she finally seeks revenge. I'm just sorry that Lorena Bobbitt has already beat me to the best retaliation, but I'll come up with something.

CHAPTER SEVENTEEN

My rage against crappy husbands has toned down by the time I wander out to the backyard. Brian evidently found the leak in his pond liner because he's holding a caulk gun and I can see he's blobbed about a pound of silicone on the bottom.

With a sigh, I slump into one of our sturdier chairs on the patio. I'm exhausted from an hour's work this morning. How am I going to make it from nine in the morning until three?

Brian takes the other chair. "How was volunteering?"

"Some of it's good, some of it's bad." I tell him about poor Amber and my suspicion that her husband slammed her hand in a door.

"Damn!" he says. "And you thought you had it bad with my chronic flatulence."

I smile. "Yeah." Then I lean over and he meets me halfway with a kiss.

"And guess what?" I say. "There's a Nate Wilkins, too."

"Brother?"

"Uh-huh. But I'm going to have to take it easy on him. According to Samantha, he's severely bipolar. I'm talking homeless here."

"Oh, boy. I'm afraid to think about how you're going to track him down."

* * *

THE ONLY pancake house on North Avenue is called The Pancake House. Clever. It's ten o'clock so folks have had their breakfast and gone to work; and it's too early for the lunch crowd so the place is deserted. At the back of the restaurant, off in the corner, is a shabby-looking man. His hair is long and stringy; his clothes look tattered. He's leaning back against the wall, his feet sticking into the aisle slightly. Taking a nap?

This has to be Nate Wilkins. I'm surprised he got past the No Shirt, No Shoes, No Service sign. But then technically, I guess moccasins are shoes.

Brian and I take a booth next to the windows. When the waitress comes, I order coffee and offer to buy the gentleman in the back a meal.

"He's already eaten," she says.

I give a kind-hearted humpf. "I'm surprised he has money."

"He doesn't. He runs a tab and somebody pays it every month."

"No kidding. I wonder who?"

She doesn't bite. But when she comes back with our coffee, I hit her with another question. "Does he come back for dinner?"

"The manager won't allow that. Too crowded at night. Only reason he can come now is 'cause we aren't busy."

I nod, mulling over what else I can ask her when Nate stands to leave. Did he overhear our conversation and got offended?

"Crap," I whisper and Brian turns around to get a look at Nate.

As Nate shuffles by, Brian mumbles 'Zombie'. Nate stops and turns. I'm flabbergasted. I mean, the guy looks rough, but we're trying to get into a conversation with him, not drive him away.

Nate looks at Brian with a confused expression, like 'are you talking to me?' He rakes his teeth rapidly over his bottom lip causing the mustache of his unkempt facial hair to jump. Then he glances down at his feet and my eyes follow. The lacing that holds the leather top to the sides of his raggedy moccasins is fraying. He doesn't look confrontational, just uncomfortable, like he's trying to decide if he made a mistake, and wondering how to walk away now that he has stopped.

Brian sees him struggling and says, "Dolores O'Riordan has an amazing voice."

Nate's head jerks up. I wouldn't really call it a smile, but his face relaxes. He bobs his head. *"No Need to Argue."*

"Yeah," Brian agrees, relaxing his shoulders. "Did you go to the concert?"

"Nah." Nate looks back down and even takes a step back like he's leaving.

"So which album did you like better?" Brian asks. *"Argue* or *Everybody Else is Doing It?"*

"Hmm." Nate gives the question some serious thought as he strokes his fingers down his beard. I'm half afraid something might come crawling out. The other half is fear that Brian is going to ask him to join us. I can smell him just fine from here.

"I kinda liked *Bury the Hatchet,"* Nate decides. "But then maybe it's just where my head was at the time."

Brian smiles. "Did you ever see any of their videos?"

Nate blurts out a laugh. "The yellow brick road?"

Brian joins him. "Or the cowboy one?" He shakes his head. "How did we go from November Rain to that crap?"

"You ever hang out in the Fourth Ward Park?" Nate asks. "There's a woman who sings sometimes in the amphitheatre. I love to sit and listen to her."

"Does she do covers or original stuff?"

"Oh, it's mostly original," Nate says. "I can't understand why she's not more popular."

"It's got to be hard to get a break in the business, especially with new bands always coming out."

Nate's hands shake; he darts his tongue in and out of his mouth like a snake. Is he agitated at the very thought of trying to get into the music scene? Or is he getting uneasy about having a conversation? I suppose his homeless pals aren't as coherent.

Brian notices his discomfort, too. "Have you heard of the Suicide Spiders?"

The tongue relaxes and Nate's eyes refocus on Brian. "No. What's their style?"

"It's hard to really pin down, but I like the heavy bass. Kind of Bush, or Les Claypool stuff. And they've got a female singer. Maybe not as raw as Florence but she's got a lot of energy."

"I'll have to check 'em out."

And suddenly Nate turns to leave. Is he planning to go check out the band right now? Or has the clock run out on how long he can talk to a stranger? Brian pushes his coffee cup away and rises. I point at the cash register to let him know I'll pay. He follows Nate.

They're both standing in front of the restaurant, still talking about music, when I come out.

"They never were as good after Serg Walken left," Brian is saying.

Nate has a big smile on his face. I imagine it's been a while since he's gotten into a conversation like this. I'd imagine most homeless guys spend their time searching for a meal or a dry place to sleep.

"You know," I say. "You look so familiar. Do you have a sister named Audrey?"

The smile vanishes. His eyes roll around as he looks for anyplace to focus besides me. Then he gives his head a vigorous shake of denial. Do we have the wrong guy?

I tilt my head to the side. "Aren't you Nate Wilkins?"

He growls through clenched teeth like a cornered dog. Then he pushes me out of his way. It's so unexpected that I reel back and fall flat on my ass. I try to catch myself and both palms skid along the pavement.

"Hey!" Brian yells, but Nate is literally running away.

Brian squats down. "You okay?"

I brush the grit from my palms and examine the scrapes. They sting but they're not bleeding. He takes an elbow and helps me to my feet.

"What was that all about?" he says.

"I shouldn't have been so blunt," I say as I take a swipe at my butt.

"But he didn't need to push you down. Jesus. Just walk away, Dude."

ON THE RIDE home, I lean my head back and close my eyes. My butt hurts but I can't make a big deal out of it since I brought it on myself. Brian was doing a great job. Why did I have to interfere? What am I even doing? Snooping around for what? I still don't have any evidence that Deborah Wiley's death was anything more than a tragic accident. So Darrell Pressley is a prick; aren't most politicians? Nobody has been able to give me any kind of solid lead. All I have is a bunch of loose threads that I can't connect.

I'm done with this. Like Brian said, I should just make up some bizarre story of how a newspaper carrier is killed and the murder covered up. That way I can actually make some money instead of winding up with road rash on my hands.

"Are you okay?" he asks.

I nod my head because I'm afraid if I speak, he'll know I'm getting choked up. Which is nuts. Why am I so depressed? I talked to a few people about Darrell Pressley and came up empty. All it cost me was a little time and gas. I thought I was on to something but I wasn't.

And what's with the lump in the throat?

Well, for one thing, solving the mystery of Farouk al Asad a couple months ago was the most exhilarating time I've had in years. It snapped both Brian and me out of our middle-aged doldrums, like beating the dust out of an old rug. (And let's face it. We've been having the best sex since we were young and horny.)

Somehow, I had convinced myself that because I could figure out one crime, I was an expert. Now I realize it was just beginner's luck.

I glance over at him. He doesn't look as depressed as me. In fact, he's tapping his fingers on the steering wheel to David Bowie. So do I drag him down into my funk or rise up to his positive mental state? I stare out the windshield at speeding cars and billboards.

"How did you know he was into music?" I finally ask.

"Huh?"

"Nate. How did you know?"

"He was wearing an old Cranberries tee shirt from their *No Need to Argue* tour."

"And you thought of the Zombie song."

"Yeah." Brian glances over at me. "But you know what's really weird? Where did he get the shirt? It's a collector's item. He says he didn't go to the concert. I bet that sucker's worth a hundred bucks."

"You're kidding."

He shakes his head. "No. So how does he have something like that?"

"From the Goodwill?" I say.

"If he did, I need to find out where he shops. There could be lots of good stuff."

BACK HOME, Brian dashes out to poke at the blob of caulk on the fish pond. I guess it's dry because he gently eases the liner back into the hole. Now the true test. Fill it with water and see if he has fixed the leak. I hope Comet and Pearly and the others can survive another day in the bucket.

At least he's doing something constructive instead of standing over the kitchen sink eating Girl Scout Thin Mints like me. The best way to stop obsessing over Darrell Pressley and Deborah Wiley, is to concentrate on stories that will make money so we can pay our bills. I have a book to write, too.

I head upstairs to my office and work on the rough draft of my battered wife short story. Since I can't have the woman lop off her husband's dick, I settle for her whacking it first thing in the morning while he's got wood. I researched whether a man's penis can be broken. It cannot. But it can get 'bent'. According to Wikipedia, if an erect penis is subjected to blunt force trauma it can rupture the vessels that carry blood into the organ. There's even a cracking or popping sound, lots of pain, and bruising.

The abused woman raises a hefty book overhead, and while her abusive husband snores away she drives the book down—

"Damn, Rachel, that's cold," Brian says and I jump. I didn't hear him come into my office. He's standing behind me, reading. "The guy could have permanent damage."

"Yeah, well his wife could have permanent damage when he slams her hand in a door."

"I get that," he says. "But aren't most of your crime fiction readers men? I don't think they want to read this."

He's right. And I don't think this will qualify as a romance. Now I'm going to have to start all over again.

"Did you come in here just to finish off my crappy morning?" I ask.

"No," he says all snippy. "You left your phone in the kitchen and someone is trying to call you." He hands me my phone and stomps away.

I look at the screen. Shannon Wiley has called twice. She sounds out of breath when I call back.

"Hey," she whispers when she answers. Then I hear a bell ring, like the ones that hang over doors to let a sales clerk know when someone comes into a store. She must be at work and she's trying to avoid being caught on her phone. "Can you meet me at two o'clock?"

I hear traffic. She's gone outside to talk.

"Sure. Sorry I called you at work."

"I need to show you something. How about Hardee's."

Is she hoping to get another free meal out of me? At least it isn't Outback steak.

"I'll be there at two," I say but before I can ask what this is all about, she hangs up.

Hard as I try, I can't stop the pitter patter of my heart. What is Shannon going to show me? I'm sure it's about Darrell Pressley. Is it going to be a stain on a dress a la Monica Lewinsky? I hope not. Proving Darrell and Deborah were having an affair is so 20th century. I'm pretty sure all politicians have mistresses now.

Maybe it's a suicide note; although I'm not sure that's going to get me anywhere, except an acknowledgment from Detective Baker that he was wrong.

Should I tell Brian I'm meeting Shannon? At least I should apologize for biting his head off. He's in the kitchen, finishing off the sleeve of Thin Mints.

"Sorry about that," I say.

I step in close, brush black crumbs from around his mouth, and give him a kiss.

"That's okay," he says in that little boy pout that tells me it really isn't. "What did Shannon want?"

"I don't know. She said she wanted to show me something so I'm meeting her at two."

Brian's eyes go from a dull listless haze to a gleam. "What do you think it is?"

I run my two scenarios by him, then ask if he wants to go with me.

"Hell, yeah!"

I'M SO ANXIOUS, I drive like I'm late for a buy-one/get-one free steak sale at Aldi's. We get to Hardee's at 1:45. And of course, when Shannon said two o'clock, she must have meant she got off work at two because she doesn't show up until 2:15. We've been killing time by sharing an order of fries.

I managed to get seven bites out of a single fry. Brian beat me with nine, but his was longer.

I wave when Shannon finally arrives and she hurries over to our table. I give a quick intro to Brian while she slides into the booth. She definitely looks excited.

"After my mom died, the police gave me a bag of her stuff that they got from her car. One of 'em was her iPhone. I said something about it being worthless since they hauled the car out of a pond but the woman at the desk said if I put it in a bag of rice it might dry out and be okay."

"I've heard that works," I say.

"So I did what she said. But I don't know why 'cause I sure didn't want to transfer all my pictures and stuff from my android to her iPhone. Then my friend Misty said I should try and sell it. But then I thought about people gettin' robbed when they meet somebody at a gas station and I didn't think it would be worth bein' stabbed for a phone."

I watch Brian's hands clench tightly as he clasps them together on the table. He's not good at 'ramble talk'. He's wishing she'd just get to the bottom of this tale. I slip a hand under the table and rub his thigh. That makes him jump and he yelps. And that startles Shannon.

"Sorry," he says, patting his stomach. "Just a little gas."

"Go on," I say as I roll my eyes.

"Well, then I went online and saw folks were asking over $300 for the same phone so I thought 'what the hell?' But first, I figured I'd get rid of pictures and texts and stuff she had."

"Smart thinking." Now I'm wringing my hands.

"Lord, you can't believe all the texts she had from Darrell. And some of them were pretty dirty. And pictures? I was embarrassed at some of the stuff she had on her phone."

I'm wondering if all of that has been deleted. Would there ever come a time when I'd want to threaten Darrell with sordid selfies?

"So then I get to the videos," she says, leaning across the table at me.

I get a little tingle. "Videos?"

"Wait a minute," Shannon says, waving a hand. "Let me back up. A while ago, Mama made plans to spend the whole weekend at Darrell's place. His wife was headin' up to Minnesota 'cause their daughter just had a baby. But after a couple days she got sick."

"The baby?"

"No, Darrell's wife."

"Charlotte," I offer.

"Yeah. Whatever. But she was afraid the baby might get sick so she came home early. So Darrell is bangin' away—that's what my mama said—when they hear Charlotte luggin' her suitcase down the hall to the bedroom. Mama pushes Darrell off, grabs her clothes and shit and runs for his closet. Darrell hasn't even got his pants pulled up when Charlotte walks into the bedroom."

"Holy shit!" Brian whispers.

"Yeah! It takes the bitch about two seconds to figure out what's happenin'. 'God Dammit, Darrell', she says. 'I told you not to bring them whores here'."

"Ouch!" I say.

"Mama thought it was pretty funny. When she came home she told me about it. She didn't think it was any big deal, and I didn't either 'cause Darrell kept coming to our apartment. Then I found this."

She presses the iPhone and then turns it so Brian and I can watch.

The video starts when Charlotte yells, 'God Dammit, Darrell.' It's obvious that Deborah is in a closet but the door is open enough to video some of what is going on. 'I told you not to bring those whores here'.

Darrell acts all innocent, like he doesn't know what's going on. So Charlotte stomps over to the bed and yanks the top sheet back. 'It smells like a cat house in here.' Then she looks down at the bed. 'For Christ sakes,' she yells. 'These are eight hundred count sheets. Look at these stains!'

'Chill out,' Darrell says. 'I'm going to send them to the cleaners.'

'The cleaners!' she screeches. 'So all those damn Koreans will think it was me?'

'What would you like them to think?' he says, getting in her face. 'That it's another woman?'

Now they're practically nose to nose. She says, 'We had an agreement. You can have your whores at the apartment. Not here. If you can't stick to the plan—'

'Don't threaten me, Charlotte,' he snarls back. 'If you're not happy, I'll be glad to give you a divorce.'

But ole' Charlotte doesn't back down. 'And don't you threaten me with that bullshit again. You seem to forget I'm the one holding the Aces.' She jabs him in the chest. 'Or do you need to be reminded about Tommy Martin?'

Brian and I turn to each other, and at the same time we say, "Who's Tommy Martin?"

CHAPTER EIGHTEEN

The video ends with Charlotte hauling her suitcase back out of the bedroom, screaming that she'll be at the Ritz Carlton until she can get the stink professionally cleaned out of the house. She turns to the closet door as she passes by, like she knows someone is in the closet but she doesn't want to be bothered with a confrontation.

We watch the drama a couple more times before I ask Shannon if she'll send me a copy. She insists Deborah didn't tell her about videotaping the confrontation. Or maybe she did but Shannon forgot. The point being, Shannon never saw it or she would have told me sooner.

"I'll bet that was awkward when your mom came back out of the closet," I say.

"I guess," Shannon says with a shrug. "But like I said, she thought it was funny by the time she got home."

"Do you have any idea who Tommy Martin is?" Brian asks.

"Not a clue."

"DO YOU REALLY think Deborah took all that 'whore' talk lightly?" I ask Brian as soon as we get into my car. "I'd probably be in tears."

"She was messing around with a married man," he says. "Doesn't that kind of come with the territory?"

He's got a point. But still . . . "I wonder what the conversation was like after Charlotte left. Did Deborah feel guilty enough to consider breaking it off? Did Pressley grovel to keep her around? If she was hiding her real feelings, maybe that was enough to make her decide to kill herself."

"I'm not buying suicide," Brian says as I pull out into traffic. "Not with Darrell paying her rent and buying her stuff. It still goes back to 'part of the package.' You want the goodies, you take the shit."

Then another idea occurs to me. "Do you think Charlotte was so pissed, *she* did something?"

"Like what? Push Deb's car into the pond? Hold the door closed so she couldn't get out? Don't forget Deborah called nine one one. If someone was harassing her, she would have told the operator."

Damn! It always comes back to the 911 call. Deborah Wiley didn't feel threatened. She was just too afraid to get out of the car and swim to safety. And I'm right back where I started: with no case.

"I'm still going to look into Tommy Martin," I say.

"Oh, definitely."

WE'RE PULLING into the driveway when my sister Gwen calls.

"I'm desperate," she says when I answer. "Allison has a soccer tournament in Orlando starting tomorrow. We should be on our way to the airport right now. Jackson was supposed to stay with his friend Kyle but he fell at school and he's at the hospital—"

"Jackson?"

"No, Kyle." Gwen is freaking out. I can picture her careening around her kitchen flailing her arms, her eyes bugged out, her face red with stress.

144

And I assume she's hoping Jackson can stay with us. She must really be desperate.

"I got this," I say. "Get going. I'll pick him up in the next half hour."

"I called the airline to get him a ticket but the flight is sold out."

"I got it. Go!"

She clicks off. I'm barely through telling Brian about our house guest when Gwen calls back. They must have piled into the car and are on their way. It's like she never disconnected. "I called mom," she whines, "but they're out in Taos with the RV."

"It's no problem," I assure her. "I've got that daybed in my office. We have a refrigerator and a stove so he won't starve. He's potty trained, right?"

That should get a chuckle out of her since Jackson is twelve, but it doesn't. She has trust issues with Brian and me as responsible adults. For example, when Jackson was seven we babysat while Gwen and Jake took Allison to see The Nutcracker at the Fox Theatre.

I was in the shower when they came to pick up Jackson after the show. Evidently he and Brian had been playing cowboys and Indians, and Brian was literally tied up in our living room. Jackson answered the door with chocolate syrup dribbled down the front of his shirt and although he denied it, I'm pretty sure he was sucking it right out of the bottle.

It was years before Gwen stopped talking about all the horrible things that could have happened to Jackson: he might have wandered outside and gotten hit by a car; he could have started a fire and burned our house down. I was tempted to point out that a seven-year old who played with matches or stepped in front of a speeding car might need to be tested but Brian nixed that.

One good thing came out of it all. That's the last time either Gwen or my mother harangued us to start our own family.

145

"I got a text from Kyle's mom, like half an hour ago," Gwen rambles on. "He fell down the bleachers during gym class. He's still unconscious. They're freaking out that there may be swelling on the brain. Everyone's rallying around his mother, I can't very well start calling moms and ask someone to take Jackson."

"Gwen!" I have to yell since I can't slap her. "What about Jackson?"

She finally settles down and takes a deep breath. "He has a bag packed. It's right inside the front door. He and Kyle were supposed to work on a project for their science class but I guess I'll email his teacher and see if they can put it off for another week."

"Don't sweat it," I tell her. "I'm sure Brian and Jackson will have a ball working on it this weekend."

I'm tempted to get Jake on the line and tell him he's going to owe me big-time for this favor, but it's probably better to wait until they get back and Jackson is still alive.

* * *

NOT ONLY does Jackson have a small duffle, he's got three of those cloth shopping bags loaded with stuff. It must be the materials he needs for his science project.

I fix a healthy meal for us all so when we order our usual Friday Night pizza tomorrow I won't feel guilty. Then after dinner, I make Jackson sit at the dining room table to do his homework. I've got some investigating to do in my office.

After my shower, I google Tommy Martin, narrowing it down to UGA and 1985, but there's nothing noteworthy in any of the results. Brian has been pursuing the sports angle but he's not having any luck either. He called Alana Parker this afternoon at her design business but she'd never heard of Martin. I tried calling Jason Hadley at the newspaper but got his voicemail.

While I wait for Jason to call me back I do a google search on BDSM toys. I didn't really feel comfortable picking up packages and reading all about hand and ankle cuffs at Ricco's adult store. Now I can shop at my leisure.

It blows my mind to see all these sex toys on Amazon of all places. There's everything from low temperature candles—for dripping wax on flesh—to lifelike dildos with a suction cup to keep it from sliding off a kitchen counter, I guess. Every time I think I've seen it all, something else comes along: like the soft pliable tube with a mouth at the end for male masturbating. Guaranteed lifelike lips, tongue and teeth to give a man the full treatment.

I justify all the time I've spent looking at this stuff by telling myself I'm really going to write an article about the expense.

My eyes are buggy after visiting just seven of the 400 pages of items. I decide to go downstairs for some ice cream. Jackson is right where he should be—at the dining room table—but he's hunched over his cell phone and giggling. I'm not saying I was actually creeping up on him, but I do manage to get a glimpse of a teenage girl baring her breasts and trying to lick one. She's got her hair pulled back with one hand and she's turned to the side so everyone can see her face.

Holy crap! What would her mother think if she saw that?

I must have gasped because Jackson jerks his head up and hides his phone between his legs. Great. Now I'll have to give him a lecture about inappropriate behavior which is funny since I was just upstairs googling sex toys.

"She's got big breasts," I say as I pull out a chair and perch on the edge. "How old do you think she is?"

Jackson is too embarrassed to answer. He just shakes his head and hunches it between his shoulders.

"Does she go to your school?"

Another head shake.

"So one of your buddies sends you the video, you watch it a few times and send it on. I'm not very good at math but I've got to figure that in a couple days, that video's going to be viral."

"Lots of girls do this."

"Because they want to be popular? Are they looking for a boyfriend?"

I think about poor Amber at Fuller House. What was her life like in high school that her only solution was to get pregnant, drop out, and marry a prick who hits her.

Jackson shakes his head. "I don't know."

"If you were looking for a girlfriend, would you chose one who did something like this and sent it out?"

He won't answer which means he wouldn't. I figure I've gotten my point across.

"I'm getting some ice cream. Do you want a bowl?" I don't wait for an answer; I just get up and go to the kitchen.

For a moment, I stand at the refrigerator, thinking about our conversation. Normally, I would have ignored the situation, figuring it was Gwen's problem. But after spending time at Fuller House, I couldn't let it go.

"Turtle Tracks or chocolate chip cookie dough?" I call out.

Jackson wants Turtle Tracks. Brian raises his hand from the sofa in the family room. "Cookie dough."

Once I've served the king and the royal prince, I take my bowl and head back upstairs. I hear my phone ringing on my desk so I start running. My toe catches on the last step, the spoon in my ice cream goes flying and hits the wall, leaving a long streak of chocolate syrup.

I'll get it later.

I manage to get to the phone while it's still ringing and see that it's Jason.

"Hey!" I pant. "Thanks for calling me back."

"No problem," he says. "What's up?"

I take a deep breath to slow my racing heart and sit to collect myself. "I'm trying to track down someone named Tommy Martin. Does that name ring a bell?"

"Wow. Tommy Martin." I hear a chair squeak and figure Jason has lounged back. "I haven't heard him mentioned since school."

"What can you tell me about him?"

"He was a gay guy on campus. I'm mean flamboyantly gay. Of course, this was back in the 80s when gays were really coming out big time. Especially in Atlanta. But it was a different story in Athens. UGA was such a rah-rah jock school. Even so, Tommy refused to tone it down."

"Do you think he still lives in the area?"

"Oh, no. He was killed. Murdered, actually. The 'official' ruling was that he was turning tricks and some john killed him. But there was speculation that maybe a straight guy decided to take a walk on the wild side but then he had post-coital remorse and killed Tommy to shut him up. Personally, I thought it was some kind of hate crime.

"Whoever it was, they gave him a good beating. It was big news for a while on campus. But the school worked hard at making it go away. They never want to cast an unpleasant light on the university."

"I know that mindset." I say as I doodle on a legal pad. "None of the schools do, whether it's a robbery or a rape, but especially if it's a death. They want parents to feel safe about sending their kiddies there."

"Regardless of the speculation, no one was ever caught. I guess technically it's still an open case."

"Did you see the police report?" I ask.

"Nah. I was already hooked on writing sports. I wasn't . . ." The rest of his sentence is dropped, like he's getting beeped with another call.

"I gotta take this," he says.

"One more quick question," I say. "Was there ever any link between Martin and Darrell Pressley?"

"You mean like friends? Are you kidding? They were opposite as night and day."

I RUSH PAST the ice cream dribbling down the wall. I've got to tell Brian the latest. I find the guys flaked out in front of the TV watching Dave Chappelle. I'll be the first to admit he's a funny guy but every third word out of his mouth is the F-bomb. Probably not appropriate for a twelve year-old.

"What's going on here?" I ask. I'm momentarily stunned at how much I sound like my mother.

Brian looks over like he has no idea Jackson is sitting beside him.

"Isn't it your bedtime?" he says.

Jackson slithers past me and rushes upstairs. I try to give Brian the stink eye but he's back watching the TV.

"I've got some primo news," I say, "if you can tear yourself away from that."

He turns his head to the side a fraction and tilts up an ear, but he's still looking at the TV. I lean over and whisper in his ear. "Tommy Martin was murdered."

"What!?" Brian fumbles to put the show on pause. "How do you know?"

I straighten and raise one eyebrow. "I have my sources."

He smiles and pats his lap. "Why don't you have a seat right here and tell me all about it."

He reaches up, grabs my wrist and pulls me down. Hard as I try, I can't keep the girly giggle away. I settle onto his lap, and wrap my arms around his neck. Then I walk him through the short but sordid story of Tommy Martin.

"Do you think Darrell Pressley had anything to do with it?" He asks when I'm finished.

"I don't see how. According to Jason Hadley, they didn't know each other."

I feel some twitching under my butt like Little Brian may be awake. I wiggle on his crotch to get a better reading. Yep, he's awake.

Brian does his own wiggling to get the maximum benefit of my butt. "Darrell had big plans for his future. I can't believe he'd do anything to damage his career."

"So why did Charlotte bring it up? There's got to be something there."

Brian's hand roams under my pajama top and up to my breast. "And the even bigger question. What does any of this have to do with Deborah Wiley?"

"I don't know but first thing tomorrow, I'm going to start digging again."

"How about if I do a little digging tonight?" Brian says as he brings his hand down and between my thighs. "I've got just the right tool."

"Is that so?"

"Well, I must be honest. It's more for drilling than digging."

If Jackson wasn't an overnight guest, we'd both be tempted to commence excavation right there on the sofa. Instead, we head upstairs. I lock the door to our bedroom and turn on some music to drown out any moaning or squeals of delight. Brian strips down to take a quick shower.

While he's busy, I kick off my pajama pants and wriggle into my school-girl outfit. The skirt hits me about mid-thigh; I decide panties are a waste of time. Then I get out my nice, lacy push-up bra and slip into the white blouse that's two sizes too small. I couldn't button the top three buttons if I wanted. The finishing touch is the black thigh-high stockings and the Giuseppe Zanotti knock-offs I found at T J Maxx. I rarely wear a three-inch heel, and it's startling how much I paid, but it was some of my mad money, and they're black so I'll have them forever.

This will be our first dress rehearsal in role-playing. If Brian gets into it, I can come up with a lot of costumes: the naughty maid, the naughty school teacher, the naughty nurse. (See? There's three more times I can wear the shoes.)

I hike up the back of the skirt to take a quick look at my butt cheeks in the bedroom mirror. The tape wounds have faded nicely. I smooth the skirt back down and wait just inside our closet.

Brian walks into the bedroom and looks around but doesn't see me.

"Mr. Sanders?" I say in my best little girl voice as I step into the room.

When he turns, I cock my butt back in a classic Betty Grable pose, pull my knees in tight, and place a finger on my pouty lips. "I have a question about our last biology assignment." I bat my eyelashes. "It's about the mating habits of mammals."

The towel he has wrapped around his waist takes a little jump. He blinks a couple times but I can see he's not quite sure what's going on.

I stroll across to the bed with my left arm crooked. "I have my textbook here," I say. Then I bend over the bed like I'm flipping through the pages, and expose my nether-region. "But I have several probing questions."

My elbows rest on the bed as I glance over my shoulder. His erection knocks his towel to the floor.

"Well, Ms. Sanders," he says, clearing his throat. "I believe I can be of assistance."

He walks over and flips my skirt up. His hands massage my ass. "You see, mammals, unlike reptiles and birds, do not lay their eggs outside the body. So if the male wants to fertilize an egg . . ."

Brian slips his tool between my legs and rubs.

" . . . he must first insert his organ into the female."

"Oh, Professor," I groan.

CHAPTER NINETEEN

I'm in a euphoric haze this morning, sipping my coffee and mooning over our little tryst last night; especially that part where Brian reached around at the last second and gave my magic button a little pinch. Holy cow! What an orgasm. I get all tingly just thinking about it.

"Rachel!"

My eyes fly open as Jackson clomps into the kitchen. "We need to get going."

I'm in such a sexual stupor that all I can manage is a stammering 'Uh-h-h-h-h-h.'

"School," he reminds me. "Now."

At least I wasn't drooling. I glance at the clock on the microwave. "It's not even eight o'clock. Your mom said school starts at eight-thirty."

It's like he doesn't even hear me. He hikes his backpack higher on his shoulders and moves towards the door to the garage.

"Can I at least put on some shoes?" I ask.

"No!"

I shuffle out to the garage in my house slippers. He's already in my car, glaring at me. The school is only a few miles away. What's his problem? Is he meeting some kids out behind the gym to get high? Is there some cute girl who always gets to school super early? He probably didn't get his homework done because he was so busy gawping at tittie girl last night and he's got to finish it this morning.

I'm tempted to say something about responsibility but what's the point? He knows.

I plop into the driver's seat and get a faint hint of our love juices from last night. Can Jackson smell it, too?

I doubt it because as soon as I close my door, my eyes start to burn. He's wearing so much cologne I'm surprised there isn't a cloud over his head. I roll down my window and lean that way to get some fresh air.

Once we're on the road, he digs into his backpack and pulls out a granola bar. It's one of those healthy ones with added protein and fiber. He didn't get it at my house. Which means Gwen must have packed it in his bag when she realized he'd be staying with us—the childless slugs from hell.

Traffic is slow but it's moving; until we get closer to Cogburn Road. The light at the intersection turns green but the cars ahead of me just sit there.

"Great," Jackson mutters. He bites into his bar and rips off half of it with his teeth like a cowboy out on the range gnawing on a piece of jerky.

"Take it easy," I say. "It's just now eight o'clock. We've got half an hour."

He turns his head slowly to stare at me. I know he wants to call me an idiot or something.

Ten minutes later, we've just turned onto Cogburn. There's a solid line of cars all the way to the school entrance.

"What the hell is this?"

"It's carpool line," he says.

I'm in deep shit. The school sits back off the road so the long drive can accommodate all the parents who think their little angels are too good to ride the bus. If Cogburn Road is backed up, that means the carpool lane is too.

At 8:15 we still haven't reached the turn to the school. Jackson is definitely going to be late. He fidgets with the zipper on his backpack: opening and closing it as fast as he can.

"Look, why don't you hop out and walk the rest of the way."

"I can't!" he says, his voice cracking. "The crossing guard watches for kids who get let out. She'll make me come right back to the car. Sometimes they make the driver go to the end of the line."

"What? Are we living in Russia now?"

It occurs to me that if my brother-in-law Jake is an ass to me, he might be just as ass-ish with others, including poor Jackson.

"Is your dad going to be pissed if you get a tardy slip?"

"Yeah! Especially since this will be my third one."

Crap! I scan the area. To the right is a church and then a few houses. I turn in at the church.

"What are you doing!?" Jackson screams.

"Surely the crossing guard doesn't know you. And she won't see you get out of my car. Just sneak up along the side of that house and pretend you're coming out the front door."

He wants to rub in the guilt a little more but there's no time. He hops out, slamming the door as hard as he can, then trots across the parking lot and into the yard. I watch as he ducks along some bushes before reaching the front walk. I've got to admit the kid's good. He even takes off his backpack, then pretends he's just slipping it on as he hits the sidewalk out front.

I wait to see if parents blast their horns and wave their arms to get the crossing guard's attention. 'Look what she did!'

There are no repercussions, so I circle back around to Cogburn Road. Here's where the foolishness of my decision sinks in. I've got to turn left. And all the drivers who weren't on their phones watched me drop Jackson off. They're not about to let a lawbreaker like me get out.

(But I'll bet a couple of them are thinking of doing the same thing tomorrow.)

Jackson is still meandering along the sidewalk like a typical kid. "Get going", I whisper. But then I realize a running kid is a dead giveaway.

My car sits idling for so long, the engine cooling system kicks in. I may as well turn it off and check emails on my phone.

There's a message from Madeline. Our story about wineries outside Napa is approved. She will schedule us to fly into San Francisco and spend two days on the road. That's Madeline-speak for taking a cheap late night flight out, bust our butts for two days visiting four or five wineries, and returning at four in the morning.

If we want to stay longer, we'll have to spring for the extra overnight accommodations. That's fine with me. San Francisco is one of our favorites; it will be totally worth the extra money to feast on apple fritters at Bob's Bakery, and sip Anchor Steam beer at some corner bar.

I also have a private Facebook message from Adam Winston in Ohio. *Your even hotter than your sister. Are you married?* Ugh. He's hitting on me? From what I've read on his posts, he's married and has grown kids. And obviously, his stint at the University of Georgia did nothing to improve his spelling and grammar.

I don't want to discourage him by saying I'm happily married so I type back: *At the moment.*

His message back is: *Sure wish you lived closer to Cincinnati. We could get together.*

I answer: *Yeah, you look like you could show a girl a good time.*

Wait a minute—Cincinnati? I thought the Blanton Corporation was headquartered in Columbus. So what does Adam do for a living? Manage one of their auto parts stores?

It's after nine by the time I get home. At least while I was stuck in traffic, I made a list of things to do today. Number one is more research into Tommy Martin's murder.

I WALK INTO my office and it's in complete disarray. The quilt is on the floor, the sheets are a tangled mess, there's an open bag of chips propped up between the day bed and the wall. Hmm. Barbeque kettle chips. Something else Jackson brought with him. Now I'll have to fight the urge to eat some. Some? Ha! By the time Jackson gets home, the bag will be empty. I've got to get those out of here.

Every stitch of clothing Jackson wore yesterday is on the floor. The air is thick with that horrible cologne. How long has it been since he's taken a shower? I probably should have insisted on that last night. I open a window and turn on the ceiling fan before I get down to business.

My google search doesn't come up with anything. I've tried *Tommy Martin murder UGA*. Then Thomas Martin. I guess at what year it might have been along with *student murder* and *UGA*. Nothing.

I swivel my chair away from the monitor while I think. What else can I use for a search? I'm roaming my eyes around the room when I spot something under the day bed. It looks like one of the special hand towels I put out at Christmas. How did that get there?

I drag it out. It's kind of balled up and when I try to straighten it, I find a crusty snarl in the middle. "Damn it, Jackson!"

As I stomp past Brian's office, he asks me what's up. I hold up the assaulted towel. "Look at this!"

Brian grins. "So he's been buffin' the banana."

"On my good hand towel."

"Just put it in the wash like I do."

"It wasn't meant to be washed. It's just for decoration. Everyone knows that."

"They do?"

Didn't his mother teach him anything?

"These are special towels. See the satin Christmas balls and the little pearls? They can't go through the wash."

"So what are people supposed to dry their hands on?"

"The regular towel hanging on the rack. Or a paper towel from a basket. If there's absolutely nothing else to dry your hands on, use the bath mat or your clothes."

I toss the offending implement of masturbation on top of the mountain of laundry in our closet. The fact that our bed looks just as mangled as Jackson's gives me a moment's pause. Did he know what we were doing last night? Is that why he jerked off in bed? Dear Lord.

Maybe it's time I washed our sheets since I can't remember the last time I changed them. I grab a corner of the fitted sheet and pull it up. As I'm moving to the other side of the bed, a new search string comes to mind. Maybe 'murder' is what's causing the glitch.

Leaving the bed half undone, I scurry back to my office. I get a hit when I google *Martin* with *death* and *UGA*.

A very small story appeared in the *Athens Banner-Herald*.

The body of a UGA student was discovered early Saturday morning on the bank of the North Oconee River in Oconee Hill Cemetery. The victim, Alvin Thomas Martin, was pronounced dead at the scene at 10:32 am.

Police officer Greg Olsen responded to a call at 8:16 am. APD later told reporters that there were signs of a struggle but it was unclear if Martin wandered off after an altercation and fell into the river. Next of kin was notified but no funeral arrangements have been made at this time.

ALVIN THOMAS Martin. No wonder I couldn't find anything. I google the full name and find a brief obituary in the *Atlanta Journal-Constitution*. The article says Tommy grew up in Morningside and went to high school at Paideia, a private school on Ponce de Leon. The parents are listed. No siblings. Still no cause of death listed.

At least I've got the police officer who filed the initial report: Greg Olsen.

When I tell Brian, he's just as excited. I know this because he lays down his game controller and looks up.

"We should drive over to Athens Monday. See if we can find Olsen," I say.

Brian takes advantage of the break in his game to stick a finger in his ear and pick. "He's probably retired by now."

"I kinda figured that. But we can go to the police station, ask around."

He smirks. "You really think they're going to give you his contact info?"

"I'll stop at a donut shop on the way. Take a dozen for everyone."

"That's so clichéd," he says. "Thinking cops love donuts."

But he agrees with my rule about confronting—I mean interviewing—people in person. The only question is how.

BRIAN DOES HIS own research and comes into my office a few minutes later. "Okay, like we thought, Olsen retired a few years ago. But now he's on the board of the Georgia River Alliance. He's a big proponent of keeping the North Oconee clean and healthy."

Nothing about those statements sound useful so I keep typing.

"Tomorrow, they're organizing a clean-up on part of the river."

"And—?"

"I think we should go. Show some support. Meet Olsen, get on his good side instead of pissing him off."

I'm sure the 'pissing him off' comment is for my benefit.

"We can't go. We've got Jackson," I say.

"He can go, too. What better way to teach the kid about community service?"

"What better way to get a kid washed down a river or bitten by a snake," I mumble.

I'm not too keen on slogging along a riverbank in boots picking up water bottles and used diapers.

* * *

WE'RE LEAVING SO early for Athens that I have to forfeit my Saturday morning walk with Sarah and Ellie. We'll have to have to get together for wine later this weekend so we can get caught up.

Jackson is not thrilled with the idea of getting up early. I told him last night what we were doing and when we had to leave, but this morning when I wake him, he acts like he doesn't remember any of it. I can see that he's well on his way to being the typical male.

Then he comes downstairs wearing shorts and a tee shirt.

"You can't wear that," I tell him. "It's going to be cold this morning, and we're slogging along a riverbank. You've got to have long pants and sleeves."

"I don't have any long pants with me."

"And you can't wear those shoes. You need something that can get wet and dirty."

"These shoes are old," he says. "They'll be fine."

I pooch out my bottom lip and pull it over the top one as I contemplate the situation. "Okay, here's what we'll do. You can wear a pair of my sweats and an old sweatshirt. What size shoe is that?"

"These are fine," he insists.

While he's changing his clothes, I pack a heavy-duty first aid kit, a change of clothes for each of us, a package of yellow rubber gloves, a bar of Fels Naptha soap, a bag of trail mix I found at the back of the pantry, and a sharp knife in case one of us has to cut an X in an ankle and suck out snake venom. We each have a travel size bottle of hand sanitizer for our pocket, too. I'm not coming home with e-coli under my fingernails.

I learn about unexpected repercussions when Jackson comes back downstairs in my sweats.

Geez," he says. "Look at these things." He pulls out the waist band. "They must be XXLs." He reaches around to pat all the extra fabric at his butt, too.

I try not to take it personally; he's just being cranky so I'll tell him to stay home. He grumbles when I point a finger towards the garage door.

"Go!" I say in a commanding voice. I'm not sure what I'll do if he doesn't.

He pouts in the back seat for at least fifteen minutes before he settles in with his phone. I'm not sure any of his friends are up this early but by noon they'll all know that the aunt and uncle he thought were so cool are total douche bags—or whatever kids call ogres like us these days.

WE ARRIVE AT the designated meeting place at nine. It's a gravel parking lot in the middle of nowhere. I'd bitch about slogging through mud and garbage, but I'm the one who wants to talk to Greg Olsen. Besides, if Jackson knew my true feelings, he'd never let up.

A few clusters of people stand around waiting for direction. I approach one of the groups and ask for Olsen. They tell me he's already at the river, so we head down a well-worn path.

I've got on my cute plaid rain boots that I found at Aldi's. The stripes are all different colors so I can wear them with anything. Although I'm not usually out in the rain. Today is a great opportunity to break them in.

The trail gets steep as we get close to the river and without warning, I step on a particularly muddy patch. Zing! Down I go, flat on my ass. Some man in waders and a bright yellow rain jacket scurries up the trail to help.

"Are you all right?" he asks. I hear Jackson snickering behind me.

Brian grabs one arm, the man grabs the other, and they stand me back up.

"Well, that was embarrassing," I say, hoping to sound upbeat as I wipe at the mud on my butt.

I introduce us all and add, "We drove over from Atlanta to help."

He is indeed Greg Olsen. His smile looks forced as he says how happy he is to have us. What he's really thinking is, 'Oh, hell. I got me some city folk hoping to add community service to their resume.'

"How did you find out about us?" he asks.

Brian tells him about the post on their website.

"Great," Olsen says even though it's obviously not great. "Have you ever helped with a river cleanup before?"

We all shake our heads. I tell him we think it's a wonderful opportunity for young people and his smile vanishes. I've got to make sure Jackson doesn't do anything to piss off Olsen.

The folks mingling around the parking lot are coming our way. "I was wondering if we could chat a little bit," I say in a rush. "After the work is done."

"Yeah, sure," He says. Then he waves an arm for everyone to gather around as he gives us instructions.

It's pretty simple. Some guy hands out sturdy trash bags and we're supposed to fill them up. Big items like tires can be piled along the bank and someone will take care of them.

The work is as disgusting as I thought: soggy plastic bags, half empty soda bottles with mold growing inside, shoes, shirts, hats, you name it. Thankfully, I have the yellow gloves. I keep an eye on Olsen but he's always busy hauling out a dumped sofa or a soaked mattress.

162

We haven't even been at it for fifteen minutes when I look around and see Jackson has taken off my sweats; he still has on his shorts. And he's not wearing the gloves. I'm sure he waited until we were surrounded by people so I won't ream him out. How do parents put up with all of this?

I clomp further along the shoreline towards something caught on a fallen tree. It's a sleeping bag. Most of it is submerged in the river. I wade in carefully so the water doesn't come up over the tops of my boots. I can't quite reach it, so I break a branch off the dead tree to snag it. I pull the soggy bag towards me but just when I almost have it, the current threatens to pull it off my stick. I grapple for the strap/handle at the top end and heave. The stupid thing must weigh 50 pounds. On second thought, I'll just drag it through the water until I get to the take-out point.

My foot catches on something along the bottom. Most likely, it's a root, but there's no way I'm going to reach my hand into this murky water. Instead, I pull up with the toe of my boot. The water is so muddy that I can't see what it is until it's nearly to the surface. But I don't see brown, I see something green.

"Snake!" I scream.

CHAPTER TWENTY

I kick at the writhing reptile, let go of the sleeping bag, and splash like a deranged woman for shore. My foot slips and I go down on my knees, sinking into a foot of muck. I'm losing my balance but I refuse to put my hands in the water. My arms pinwheel to keep me upright until Brian can get to me. All the while, I'm making this panting groan, 'Ah! Ah! Ah!'

He grabs me by the armpits and pulls but my knees are mired in this blasted silt. I'm pretty sure I hear muffled laughter and it's more than just Jackson this time; I can't get turned around to see who it is. Olsen sees the dilemma and comes over to help. All of his misgivings have been realized. We're nothing but trouble.

While Brian pulls my arms, Olsen reaches into the water and frees one of my knees. I get my foot under me and tug on the other knee. I'm free! But the sudden loosening throws both men off balance. Brian tumbles into the drink. Olsen manages to stay on his feet. I can't remember the last time I've been in such a humiliating situation. (Actually, I can, but that's neither here nor there.)

I step towards the shore with my right foot, but my left boot is now bogged down since I used it as leverage to stand. I'm so disgusted,

I pull my foot out of the boot, scramble up the steep bank and stand with hands on muddy knees, struggling to catch my breath.

"Hey, Rachel," Jackson calls. "Here's your snake."

I turn and look. He's holding a section of green garden hose. Everyone gets a good laugh, even Greg Olsen. There's no point in letting my vanity spoil the moment; I laugh, too. But inside, my heart is thumping like a drum and I think I might faint.

I sit down, still shaking my head at what a goof I am. Then I pull off the one boot I still have and dump the water out. That gets another laugh. They're still laughing when Brian pulls my missing boot out of the river with a noticeable farting sound. He drags himself up onto the bank next to me and dumps the water out of his boots, too.

"I told you this would be fun," he says.

I pull off my sopping sweatshirt and wring it out. The tank top underneath is brown with river silt. I'm guessing my bra is, too. Not ten seconds later, a horsefly takes a big bite out of my shoulder. Yeah, I'm having a ball.

ONCE WE'RE dismissed, I trudge up to the Jeep to get some dry clothes. Have you ever tried to take off wet pants in a stinking, fly-swarming Port-O-Let? That's a lot of fun, too.

I've held my breath as long as I can, so I don't bother with a dry bra. I just pull on a tee shirt and scramble to open the door. I puff out poo-tainted air and suck in freshness.

Olsen is at the other end of the parking lot, leaning into a car window, chatting with the driver. He stands and pats the roof and the guy drives away.

He sees me and comes my way. "You okay?" he asks.

"Nothing damaged but my pride," I tell him.

"You sure livened up the day," he says. "I don't suppose I can get you to come to every clean up."

I force a weak smile. "We'll see."

165

"You need some plastic for the car seats?"

"Thanks, I brought a change of clothes," I say. I pull my pant legs to the sides to show I'm wearing different clothes. I manage to keep from saying 'duh'.

"So you did," he says.

I smile and ask, "Can we talk for a minute before you go?"

"Sure. How about over at my truck."

I follow him to one of those big trucks with four doors and two tires on each side of the back. He folds down his tailgate, then unhooks the straps to his waders and lets them drop. Brian sprints over. Is he thinking he may need to defend my virtue or does he just want to ogle Olsen's monster truck? My money's on the truck.

Jackson is right behind. But here's the thing. Talking about a murder probably shouldn't be done in front of Jackson. I don't know what Jake's stance is on that, but I'm not going there.

I fish out the bar of Fels Naptha from my backpack and tell him to go sit on one of the rocks along the shore and wash his legs and arms. I don't trust him though, so I tell Brian to make sure he does.

"What?" Brian says. "He doesn't need me."

What he means is, he'd rather talk to Olsen.

"Imagine this," I say, leaning close. "We search until dark but never find Jackson's body."

The two plod off in the direction of the river.

Olsen appears confused; does he think I want to get on the river-cleaning board?

I decide to dive right in. "Back in the eighties, there was a murder on the UGA campus. Or rather, in the Oconee Hill Cemetery. A student named Alvin Thomas Martin was beaten and he drowned in the river. I believe you were one of the officers who investigated."

Olsen sits on his tailgate to rake the waders off his feet. "I sure was. That was my first murder so I remember it pretty well."

"Can you tell me about it?"

"What do you want to know?"

"Everything," I say.

Olsen snorts. I think he's going to blow me off so I reach down casually and massage a knee. Yes, it's a lame bid for his sympathy. I don't care.

"I could call you at a more convenient time," I say when he still hesitates to talk.

"No, that's okay." He scoots back on the tailgate to get comfortable. "I'm just trying to get it straight. I haven't heard his name in a long time. The way I remember it, we got a call early on a Saturday morning. My shift was ending, but dispatch sent me out to check on a report of a body in the Oconee. A fisherman called it in.

"I drove over to the cemetery. The fisherman met me at his car and showed me where the body was caught up on some logs along the shoreline. He was dead all right. And naked. Since there was no reason to attempt CPR, I left him there and called for back-up. Charlie Atwell was the detective who came out. The medical examiner showed up, lots of day shift cops combed the area for evidence. I helped for a little and then went home."

Olsen leaves it at that. End of story.

"But . . ." I say, coaxing him for more.

He scratches at the beard stubble under his chin a moment, trying to decide if he should go into more detail.

"Come on," I say. "You're retired. The chief is probably dead by now."

He tilts his head in a what-the-heck shrug. "The official report said Martin went to the cemetery to meet a john. The john handcuffed Martin, the encounter got too rough, Martin fell against the step of a mausoleum, and was knocked unconscious. The john thinks Martin is dead, he panics and rolls him down the hill. He splashes into the river and drowns."

That's a lot different from the newspaper account. "But you didn't agree with that."

"I was new on the force, only six months in, working the graveyard shift." He gives me a wry smile at his pun so I smile and nod in agreement. "When the chief says that's how it happened, that's how it happened."

"What did you think?"

"It wasn't just me. Charlie Atwell had problems with the official report, too. And we were pretty tight so he filled me in on details as they came up. I first met Charlie in Beirut; while we were in the service. He's the one who got me the job on the Athens PD."

"What did he tell you?"

"The basic story is the same. Martin went to Oconee Hill Cemetery on Friday night around ten. He walked to a mausoleum near the river. He took off his shirt and pants, folded them neatly, and laid them on the step to the tomb. There was some debate on whether he was alone or not, but Charlie and I figured he was.

"He had a small prayer rug which he unrolled on the grass and knelt on it. Charlie thought it was some kind of ritual or maybe he and his john were into role-playing. The john wanted Martin in a supplicant position. That included the handcuffs. But here's the thing. When they pulled him out of the river, the handcuff was only on one wrist."

"Hang on a sec," I interrupt so I can think about what that means. I even raise my own arm and look at my wrist. "Maybe the john was just getting to the handcuffs when Tommy says 'no way' or something like that. They get into a scuffle."

"Don't get ahead of me now," Olsen says, shaking a finger at me. He makes a big deal of regrouping his thoughts. "So . . . the mausoleum is off the drive a little ways. I didn't see all the blood on the steps until the crime scene team showed up. And believe me, there was a lot of blood. I figured Martin died right there. But then other inconsistencies popped up."

"Like what?"

"First let's take the blood. The medical examiner said the amount wasn't unusual for a head injury, especially during a fight. The guy's adrenaline is ramped up so his heart is really pumping. But after a while, the blood coagulates enough to stop the flow from the wound. So Martin is still alive but most likely unconscious. The ME tested the blood to determine how coagulated it was, how long it had been on the step. That's where we got the time of the beating. And that was pretty much a certainty."

"Around ten o'clock," I say just to show I'm paying attention.

"But the coroner placed the time of death at around two am. That was based on Martin rolling down the hill into the water, and drowning."

"Because there was water in his lungs," I blurt out like I'm a Jeopardy contestant.

"Well, not really. It was based on lividity and rigor mortis."

"There's quite a time gap between ten and two," I say. "How do you know the john didn't drag Martin down to the river immediately but the body got caught up on a branch for a while?"

"No way. Martin laid in that pool of blood long enough for it to congeal around his face. That had to take a few hours."

"Any chance the john stuck around to get his jollies off on the corpse?"

Olsen bugs his eyes at me like I'm a total creep. I pull my head back and hold up my hands in surrender. "Sorry."

He's still giving me the stink eye so I give him the indifferent shrug, like 'What the heck, Dude? You were a cop. You saw it all.'

Finally he continues. "That brings me to another inconsistency. No semen. Not oral or anal. And no residue from a lubricant. I don't think the john ever showed up. Or if he did, he saw Tommy getting pounded and took off."

"How bad was the beating?"

"Significant. None of the injuries was life threatening, but he had broken fingers, cracked ribs, and a lot of blunt force trauma from both fists and shoes."

I scrunch up my nose in disgust. "That sounds like somebody who didn't like gays, not someone who wanted to get his rocks off."

"Doesn't it?" Olsen says. "Course back then, we didn't have hate crimes and police in general weren't as sympathetic to gays as they are now."

"Okay, so let's suppose Tommy woke up, crawled down the hill, knowing there was water where he could clean up," I say.

Olsen shakes his head 'no'.

"Or," I say. "What if whoever beat him up was interrupted? Say they heard voices, or saw headlights and ran. But Tommy is sure they're going to come back and finish the job so he crawls into the woods to hide. He doesn't realized how steep the incline is so he tumbles down into the water."

"Where he lies for three to four hours," Olsen says, "not drowning but not getting revived enough to get back out of the water."

"Good point."

"Here's the problem," Olsen said. "If he'd crawled on his own, there would have been scrapes on his chest, his elbows, and the fronts of his legs. We found plenty of abrasions on his chest, and some on his thighs. So that covers some crawling. But it wasn't just his elbows that were scraped; it was the whole underside of his arm. That's more consistent with being dragged. And crawling doesn't explain the scratches on his back which would indicate rolling." Olsen circles his fingers to illustrate the tumble. Then he pauses. I get the feeling he's waiting to see if I can figure it out.

I brush my fingers back and forth across my lips as I think. "Someone sees him lying by the mausoleum. He's unconscious but he still has a pulse. They're afraid he's going to wake up and identify whoever beat him up."

Olsen nods to encourage me.

"So they drag him off into the woods . . . by his feet since his head's all bloody . . . they don't want to get it on their hands. Once they get close enough to the river bank, they roll him into the water."

"That's what I think."

A man in bib overalls waves for Olsen to come over to his truck. Olsen hops off the tailgate. "Sorry, I gotta go."

I shout out a thank you as he trots across the parking lot. Brian and Jackson wander up the path.

"Where's the soap?" I ask.

Jackson gives me the vapid stare of a pre-teen. "It was gooey."

"It was in a baggie. You put it back in there and then rinse your hands."

I get the same vacant stare that makes me wonder if he's ever been tested.

I'M DYING TO tell Brian all the details about Tommy Martin on the ride home but I can't because of Jackson. Even back at the house, he seems to be sticking as close to us as goo on a guest towel.

"We all need to take showers," I announce, "And I'm going first."

I've got the water set to scald so I can annihilate all the invisible vermin on my body. I'm right in the middle of the second round of shampooing when the water turns cold. I leap blindly away, then cup my hands, and splash shampoo from my eyes so I can open them.

There's no way I've used up all the hot water. The only logical answer is Jackson. How does he not know the proper protocol for showering? One at a time.

I turn the cold way down to get more of my share of hot and quickly rinse out the shampoo. Seconds later, the water turns cold again. He has cut off the cold water, too. We're battling over a puny stream of tepid water. I need to make a list of this child's bad habits.

171

By the time I've dried my hair and gotten dressed, both Brian and Jackson are cleaned up and parked in front of the TV. It's still March Madness. A moment of depression weighs heavy on me. I can either watch the game or do laundry. The lure of hot wings from Freddy's draws me to the sofa but after gnawing on five extra spicy, my lips are on fire and I'm sick of watching men run back and forth in baggy shorts. I go start a load of wash. And I finally change the sheets on our bed. I'm a domestic goddess.

I'm actually looking forward to snuggling my head into a pillow case that smells like fabric softener, not stagnant drool.

THE GAME finally ends around 10 o'clock and I tell Jackson to go to bed. When he complains that he's not tired, I tell him to read a book.

Alone at last, I give Brian all the details I got from Greg Olsen. He's just as stunned as I was.

"I wonder if two different people were involved," he says.

I can't come up with a scenario where that fits. "You mean, one guy beats him up and leaves him for dead. Then four hours later, at like two o'clock in the morning, another guy ambles into the cemetery, sees the body, and rolls it into the river."

My head has a little bobble going because the idea seems ludicrous. Brian doesn't appreciate my skepticism. "How do *you* explain it?"

"I can't. But I googled the cemetery. The walk back to the river is quite a distance. What if Tommy is unconscious for a while but then he wakes up. He's scared the attacker will come back. I mean, this whole story sounds like a Jeffrey Dahmer horror story. Tommy's got to get out of there. But he's disoriented, confused. He turns the wrong way and suddenly he's falling down the hill and into the water."

"But if he was conscious, why wouldn't that cold water wake him up more?"

"Yeah, that's kind of what Olsen said." I eye the three hot wings still in the box, but if I'm going to eat any more, I'm going to need some Chapstick to keep from burning my lips again.

"I've heard the bridge was a favorite spot for late night drinking," Brian says, "because the beer cans got tossed right into the river. Under-aged students didn't worry about getting caught."

"Okay, so some kids take their beer to the bridge, they see a dead guy, or almost dead guy, and their first reaction is to roll him into the river." I'm putting a tad too much sarcasm into it and Brian gets snippy.

"Maybe it wasn't their *first* reaction. They're walking along, they got a good buzz going, and all of a sudden they see this naked guy lying in a pool of blood. Somebody says 'We should call the police.' But somebody else says, 'No way. We're drunk'. Or 'They might accuse us.' They talk it over. Somebody says 'Let's get outta here.'"

I get into the scene. "Someone else says 'Just leave him alone.'"

"Yeah. But some numb nuts decides he can't drink with the stiff nearby so he drags the body by the feet into the trees, just to get him out of sight. But the body accidentally rolls down the hill, kersplash, into the river. Are they going to climb down there and haul him back out? Remember there were no cell phones. They'd have to walk back out and find a gas station with a phone. They think he's already dead so what difference does it make?"

"I like it," I say. Then I pick up one of the wings. Yes, I'm willing to sacrifice my lips because I don't want to go find my purse and dig around the bottom to find my lip balm.

"You do?"

"Yeah, it could definitely happen."

"If you like that idea," he says, "I've got another one, and you could definitely make it happen."

"And what's that?"

Brian cups his junk and gives me a big smile.

173

"No way! I just changed our sheets, and I don't need Jackson listening to you moan while he's wackin' the Kraken on another one of my good towels."

CHAPTER TWENTY-ONE

The guys went through a whole package of bacon this morning. They left me one piece, and none of the pancakes. It's like a couple of giant sucking leeches wormed their way through the kitchen consuming everything in sight before slithering out to the back yard.

As I wash the skillet from a second batch of pancakes for me, I watch them playing with Jackson's drone. It doesn't look nearly as fun as it does on YouTube. Brian has the controller but all he's doing is moving the drone up a foot into the air and bringing it back down.

In the laundry room, I rake a load of clothes out of the dryer and into my mangled laundry basket. When I pass the kitchen window again, I see the drone hovering a couple feet off the ground. It moves to the right and lands on a bare spot in our lawn. Jackson gives Brian a high five like he's done something extraordinary. And I thought baseball was boring.

The mountain of clean clothes are piled on our bed, and I'm digging around for socks when I hear a loud buzzing. My shoulders hunch, my knees buckle to a squat, and I glance overhead, expecting to see a giant hornet. The sound of guffaws outside the window draws my attention. And there's the drone, hovering, the camera eye aimed right at me. When I start towards the window, it flies away.

I open the window. "Very funny," I yell down at Brian.

"This thing is amazing. You should come try it."

"I'm folding clothes."

"Suit yourself," he says and turns to fly the drone over to the Bradford's house. If he flies that camera around Lisa's bedroom window, he's liable to get himself arrested. She may look like she's twenty-one but she's only seventeen.

Perhaps I need to supervise these hooligans. Sock-sorting and shirt-folding will have to wait.

Outside, I watch the drone fly over our neighborhood, and if I look at the phone Jackson is holding, I get an aerial view of our subdivision.

"Fly over Jerry Kemp's house," I say. "I want to see if he really got rid of his camper."

A couple months ago, Jerry bought a used pop-up camper. He had it in his driveway while he made repairs but the HOA insisted that no mobile units were allowed and demanded he tow it away.

Brian flies over the house. Just as I suspected, Jerry just moved the camper from his driveway to his backyard. He's lucky none of his neighbors are on the Homeowner's board.

The drone hovers down close to the camper before it rises up again and moves away. We can see it all on Jackson's phone.

"I'm impressed," I say.

"Wanna try it?" Brian asks.

Oh, yeah. Owning a drone could open whole new vistas in crime solving.

Jackson objects. "But she hasn't practiced flying it. No one gets to use it unless they pass the training session."

If that doesn't sound just like Jake. I can hear his bullhorn voice lecturing Jackson about being responsible.

"Don't worry," Brian says as he steps behind me. "I won't let her fly solo."

He wraps his arms around mine and holds the controller out front. "There's two toggles. One is the throttle and the other is directional."

I take hold of the controller and pinch the two levers. Brian rests his fingers on mine so I don't get carried away.

Against his better judgement, Jackson holds his phone out where we both can see where the drone is flying. We turn left and aim the drone out of our subdivision and over to the house I suspected was making porn videos. Another family has since moved in.

"Let's take it down," I say.

We cruise through the backyard for old time's sake. The owners have added a small metal shed for storing a lawn mower. It's clear in the back near a stand of trees. When we fly lower, we see two kids standing behind the shed, passing something back and forth.

Brian chuckles. "They're smoking weed."

Evidently, the kids hear the drone because they both look up. When they see us, they flip us the bird. Brian toggles the drone so that it wobbles back and forth—I guess that's drone-talk for same to you—then flies away.

I can see on the phone that we're heading up Braxton Lane when suddenly the drone turns around and heads back for Hamilton Farms.

"What are you doing?" Brian asks me.

"Nothing. It just turned around."

Jackson taps his phone. "It's running out of power. If that happens it automatically comes back."

After a moment, we hear the familiar whine. Sure enough, the drone is coming back on its own. It's still high above our backyard when it suddenly starts spinning.

"Hey!" Jackson yells. "Stop that."

"I'm not doing anything!" I yell back.

The drone is in a spinning freefall. Brian lets go of the controller and Jackson drops his phone in the grass. They have their hands out to catch the stupid thing, but it's careening wildly. With his head craned back, Brian staggers right, then back to the left. It reminds me of an outfielder who's trying to catch a high fly but the sun is in his eyes.

The drone is close enough that he gets a bead on it and jogs to the right several steps.

"Watch out!" I yell just as Brian steps into the fish pond.

A wave of water sloshes over the rim of the pond. Poor Comet and Pearly must be freaking out. Brian, too. I'm sure he's hoping he didn't just bust open the leak he patched. At least he managed to catch the drone so we won't have to explain that to Jake.

SINCE THE drone is charging, the guys are parked in front of the TV again. Guess what they're watching. Some vague thought has been needling me all afternoon, but it isn't until after four o'clock that it wends its way to the front where my brain is functioning at full power.

"Oh, crap!"

I stomp downstairs and stand right in front of Jackson so he can't see the game.

"You have a project due for school tomorrow," I say, leaning down to get in his face.

He has the decency to look guilty, and when Brian turns toward him, Jackson ducks like he expects a whap to the head.

"What class is it for?" Brian asks.

"Science class," Jackson says, his head bowed.

"Cool. What are you going to do?"

"I don't know. Kyle and I were going to decide in class Friday and then do it at his house this weekend."

Brian clicks his tongue. "Maybe your teacher will give you more time since Kyle got sick."

"No!" I say. "I told Gwen we'd make sure he got it done without Kyle."

After I get the bug-eye from Brian, he turns back to Jackson. "Well, buddy. Looks like we've got a science project to do."

They google science projects and come up with something fairly easy: The Water Cycle: Evaporation, Condensation, Collection, and Precipitation. The biggest stumbling block is the folding project board that all good students use for their exhibits.

"You'll have to go to Staples or Office Depot," I say. "And you should make a list of supplies you'll need so you don't have to make two trips."

They both stare at me with vapid expressions, like I'm speaking Chinese. "What?"

"Don't we have any cardboard around here we can use?" Brian asks.

"You mean like cut up an old box or something?"

"Yeah!" they both say.

Evidently, Jackson will be satisfied with a C for the project, which I'm sure all students will get just for turning in their work on time. Brian doesn't want to drive all the way to Milton Marketplace.

The best I can come up with is a poster board from the last time I had a yard sale. The back side is fairly clean and only one of the corners is bent.

I spread newspapers all over the dining room table while Brian and Jackson search drawers for magic markers, colored paper, and glue.

Once they have the tools needed, I sit at the head of the table and fold my hands. "Okay, what's the plan?"

"Uh," Brian stammers. "The plan is for you to take a bottle of wine over to Sarah's and tell her all about *our* project." He's referring to Tommy Martin.

Now other husbands might insist that his wife help since she was the one who insisted it would get done. But after fifteen years of marriage to me, Brian knows that it will take twice as long if I make them do a professional job. His goal is to slap something together as fast as possible. Fine with me.

With a bottle of pinot tucked under my arm, I text Ellie that I'm on my way to Sarah's. She shows up before I can even unscrew the cap. They both want to hear the latest about Darrell Pressley, hoping to see him go down in flames.

"Well, I'm sorry to say, I don't have any news on Pressley," I say as I flop down on Sarah's couch.

"Then why are you here?" Sarah says in mock disgust.

"I've got a juicy story about a college kid named Tommy Martin."

I slug down a big gulp of wine and tell them what I've learned so far. Since I'm sitting right next to Ellie, I don't realized how steamed she's getting until she explodes.

"That's such bullshit! Labelling him a prostitute. How do they know it wasn't a boyfriend?"

"I don't know," I say. "Maybe because they were meeting in the cemetery?"

"What do you think would have happened if they'd met in a dorm room?" she asks. "This was back in the 80s. I'm sure there were plenty of homophobes around."

She's got a point. If the other guys on the floor had seen Tommy and some dude locking themselves in a bedroom, there would have been hell to pay.

"And believe it or not," Ellie continues, "some heterosexuals fuck without even knowing the other person's name. They never get labeled as prostitutes."

"That's true," Sarah says. "I slept around in college a lot, but I wouldn't say any of them were boyfriends. I even got it on in the bathroom of a dive in Charlotte once." She wags her eyebrows at us.

Ellie makes a poo-poo face. "I assume no money was exchanged."

"Just fluids," Sarah says.

I howl. "Is that how you met Ron?"

He's her ex and a dead-beat dad who always seems to be late on child support for their two kids. I wonder if he knows Darrell Pressley. I'm willing to bet he voted for him. They're both pigs.

Instead of answering, she turns the tables on me. "How many guys did you sleep with at school?"

Oh, boy. This is going to be embarrassing. "Just Brian."

"You're kidding," Ellie says.

"Is he the only man you've ever had sex with?" Sarah asks. She's got this leering grin on her face.

I shrug. "What can I say? He's good."

When Sarah gives me the smirk of doubt, I tell them about the school girl costume.

"See?" Ellie says once my tale has reached its climax. "You guys get into kinky stuff but no one thinks that's disgusting. But if two men, or two women want to experiment, that's perverted."

Hmm. I wonder if Ellie and Joanie have one of those dildos with the suction cup.

"Anyway," Sarah says. "What does all this have to do with Darrell Pressley?"

I shake my head. "I don't have a clue. But there's got to be something because Charlotte Pressley seems to be holding it over Darrell's head."

CHAPTER TWENTY-TWO

Gwen and her family aren't flying back until this morning because there was a banquet for all the soccer teams last night. I'm determined to pull off this mothering stuff, so I get up early to make Jackson breakfast before I take him to school. He balks at scrambled eggs.

"I don't have time," he says.

I figure if I had to make them he has to eat them. "It's seven-thirty. You eat and I'll get your project."

When I try to pick up his poster, several pages of newspaper are stuck to the sides. And a couple are also stuck to my dining room table.

"How much glue did you guys use?" I ask. (I've seen Brian with a caulking gun so the question is really a moot point.)

It takes an X-Acto knife to trim away all the glue and newspaper from the poster. By the time we have the project secured in my trunk, we're running late again. How do parents cope with this day after day?

I pull the same stunt as Friday, turning in at the church and letting Jackson walk the rest of the way. While I'm waiting for traffic to die down, I check my emails. I've got a message from Jason Hadley to call but when I do, I get a busy signal. I leave a message and move on.

Brian texts me from a local farm that raises llamas and ostriches. He's shooting for another of the magazine's writers and doesn't think he'll be back for lunch.

After our 'school girl' escapade last week, I've got another idea; and this morning will be the perfect time to search for props while he's away.

Sensory deprivation is another biggie in the BDSM community. I'm sure we've got some old headphones somewhere. And I still have one of those eye masks for sleeping that an airline handed out. The only other thing I need is a gag for Brian's mouth. Sarah said she had some old ping pong balls but even if she can't find one, I can just use a scarf as a gag. I'm not sure why kinky folks like stuffing a ball in another person's mouth but it's worth a try; especially since it will be Brian, not me.

I have another Facebook message from Adam Winston. *Maybe we could meet halfway some weekend.* Yikes! This is escalating fast. I can't believe I'm flirting with him in the hopes I'll get some information about Darrell Pressley.

I shoot back a message: *I don't know. My husband is the jealous type.*

He doesn't respond so hopefully I have suppressed his desire. Either that or he has an oil spill on Aisle Seven of his auto parts store.

I'm pulling into the driveway when my phone rings. It's Hadley. He says he remembered something else about Tommy Martin.

"I don't know how I forgot about this," he says. "I remembered after you asked if there was a connection between Darrell and Tommy. Back in the 80s, Atlanta had a bunch of gay nightclubs. One of the biggest was the Limelight. It was like Atlanta's Studio 54. We heard rumors about it at school but none of us at the fraternity had ever been."

"I remember it vaguely. My older sister used to talk about it. But I didn't know it was a gay bar."

"Technically, it wasn't. It was an anything goes bar. A woman might hike up her skirt and have sex on a guy's lap. Or two guys might hook up in a bathroom stall. People smoked pot and snorted cocaine. It was out of control.

"Anyway, I'm pretty sure it was Darrell's twenty-first birthday. A bunch of the brothers decided to take him to Limelight. I wasn't part of the 'in' crowd so I was in a second car and we didn't leave at the same time. But when we got there, the place blew my mind. The glass dance floor had live sharks swimming underneath. And there were hot, sexy women in tight pants or short skirts everywhere. Men wore flashy silk shirts and platform shoes."

"And were you all decked out?"

Hadley laughs at the idea. "No way. I was just there to observe. But I guess Tommy would go to Atlanta every weekend and hang out at the clubs. He was at the Limelight when Darrell showed up with his entourage. Tommy sashayed up, his hands all over Darrell, and he went on and on about how he never knew Darrell was 'one of us'. He must have been really drunk or doing drugs to pull a stunt like that."

"That sounds pretty crazy."

"No kidding. Darrell freaked out. I mean, he's a football star and here's this gay guy not only coming on to him, but convinced Darrell is gay. Supposedly, Tommy grabbed Darrell's crotch. Darrell punched Tommy and sent him flying into the crowd of dancers. I'm sure if they'd been outside, Darrell would have killed him. We got there after it was all over, but evidently it took three guys to pull Darrell off."

"Jeez. Did Tommy press charges?"

"Oh, no. This was before gay rights. No one really blamed Darrell for 'defending' himself. And there was no social media or cell phones to create a ruckus about it either way. I'm not even sure the cops investigated. If they did, they probably thought Tommy had it coming, too."

"Do you remember who was with Darrell?"

"It had to be Adam Winston and Lonnie Taggart. They were like the three musketeers. Or the Three Stooges. Adam was a wide receiver on the team. A real tool. A Darrell wannabe only not nearly as good looking or charismatic. I had my suspicions about him with some of the girls on campus."

"Oh, yeah?"

"It's not like I could prove anything, but I got the impression he forced himself on women."

"I friended him on Facebook and all I can say is I'm glad he's all the way up in Ohio or I'd be looking over my shoulder. What about Lonnie?"

"Lonnie was a hunk of meat on the offensive line who protected Darrell like they were brothers. He got more penalties than any other player because he'd grab a face mask or head butt anyone who got close to Darrell."

Interesting that when Reggie Riggs was telling us about Adam and Lonnie he didn't mention any of this. I guess it's some kind of code that you don't rat out your teammates. But since Jason was all about finding the news angle, he zeroed in on bad behavior.

"So there was bad blood between Darrell and Tommy."

"Definitely."

I'M SO EXCITED about this latest tidbit that I zoom into the garage too fast and don't get stopped before I ding the old refrigerator we keep out there. I back up quickly and hop out, my fingers crossed that I didn't knock the door off its hinges. That would be my luck to destroy Brian's beer cooler. The door opens just fine; well there's a bit of a catch if I open it too wide so I'll have to remember to stock only the left side of the fridge with beer. Since Brian parks on that side too, he may never notice the dent.

I close the garage door and scurry inside to find Greg Olsen's phone number. I want to see if the Athens police knew about the Limelight incident and if they questioned the boys at the Sigma house.

"To tell you the truth," he says, "We didn't question hardly anyone. Whoever killed that boy timed it perfectly. The campus was deserted. Most of the students had taken off for spring break by the time the body was found. And both the school and the chief were trying to keep it hush-hush."

"I remember you mentioning that."

"Martin's family figured as much because they hired a private detective. Any time he came up with a lead, his mom insisted we pursue it. I seem to recall a story about a dust-up at a gay bar in Atlanta. Maybe the detective interviewed the guys at the fraternity. Nobody from our department did."

"I guess since Tommy was gay, the chief didn't think it mattered."

"That's about right."

"You don't happen to remember the private detective's name do you?"

"Nope. I don't think Charlie Atwell ever talked to him, just Martin's mother. But you're not going to get any info from Charlie. He died in a boating accident a few years back."

"I don't suppose you could find out who the PI was?"

"Sorry, Rachel. I'm retired. There's no reason for me to start digging into a cold case. But if you do find out anything, you should call the station."

Swell. More dead ends.

I go back to the obituary in the paper and find his parents' names. Tom and Dolores Martin. A Google search pulls up a brief sidebar in the *Atlanta Business Chronicle*. Tom's company transferred him to Arizona less than a year after Tommy's death. Coincidence? Or was it too painful to stay in Atlanta after losing their only child?

After a couple tries, I find a phone number and call. A man answers, and once I'm sure I've got the right Thomas Martin, I tell him I'm hoping to get the Athens police to reopen the case of his murdered son.

Do you know what he says? "Why?"

I sputter for a moment before I can answer. "Because I think there might be new evidence."

"I'm not interested."

What the heck? How could a father not want to know what happened to his son? Because he's a rotten dad, that's why. Before he can hang up, I blurt out, "Wait, wait. Is Mrs. Martin home?"

"Mrs. Martin," he says with unmistakable anger, "Is now Mrs. Packworth. And she lives in Denver."

He hangs up.

I find Dolores Packworth on Facebook. She doesn't know enough to have her settings on 'private' so I can see all kinds of posts about her and her new husband, Harry. When Dolores answers her phone, I give her the same spiel about her son's murder. She's delighted that I'm looking into the case.

"He was our only child," she says. "I knew early on that he wasn't like other boys. I'm sure Tom did too but he wouldn't face up to it. He was always trying to get Tommy to play sports and he just wasn't into it. Once he got to high school, I knew for sure, but Tom was still in denial. He pushed Tommy to date, go to dances. When Tommy said he had a date for senior prom, Tom was ecstatic. Then we found out he was going with another boy. It broke Tom's heart."

I'm surprised a school would have allowed that back in the 80s, but then he went to Paideia which is a pretty progressive private school.

I ask her what she remembers about Tommy's murder, but she doesn't tell me anything I don't already know.

"Can you give me the name of the private detective that looked into the case?"

"I sure can," she says. "It's Harry Packworth." Holy crap. She ran off with the PI. No wonder the husband was so pissed.

"Can I speak with him?"

"Sorry, honey, he's out golfing. I can have him call you when he gets back."

I'M TEMPTED to call Brian to tell him about the Limelight, and finding the private detective, but it's so much more fun to give him news in person. That way, I can wave my arms and add facial expressions. What can I say? I was born for drama. Maybe by the time he gets home, I'll have talked to Harry Packworth as well.

It's not like I don't have anything to do. First on my agenda is the daybed in my office. I strip the sperm-riddled sheets off and start a load of laundry. Then I get back to my short story about the battered wife who seeks revenge. Now I'm gearing the story for a romance magazine. The woman still whacks her hubby's pee-pee with a book but when she's arrested, she hires a handsome young attorney who is sympathetic to women who are abused. He's going to win her case, they'll fall in love, and live happily ever after.

I'm typing like a woman possessed when my phone beeps. It's another Facebook message from Adam Winston. *Tell your husband a cousin died and meet me at the Lyndon House in Lexington. I garantee to rock your world.*

Lexington? This guy wants me to drive five hours just so he can demonstrate his sexual prowess? I 'garantee' it involves Viagra and porn. Oh, Adam, if your wife only knew. I'm tempted to tell him to shove it, but I'd like to hear his version of the Limelight story so I message back: *My husband would never let me drive all the way to Lexington alone. Could I bring my friend Sarah?* That ought to give him a stiffy.

Just for giggles, I do a google search of the Lyndon House. It's a gorgeous mansion on what must have been millionaire's row in the heart of Lexington. I've got to hand it to him, Adam goes first-class when he cheats.

A message comes right back. *Hell, yeah! I can handle two gorgeous women. Just give me a date.*

It may take a few weeks I answer. *First I'll have to tell hubby my cousin is sick.*

Tell him today. I'm rock hard just thinking about you.

Dear Lord. Why do men think they're so irresistible?

I HEAR THE garage door going up and race downstairs. My eagerness is two-fold. Sure, I want to tell Brian all about Tommy Martin at the Limelight. But I also want to distract him so he doesn't see the refrigerator dent. Then when he sees it tomorrow or this weekend, I can say 'It's been like that for a while' or even better, 'I was going to ask you the same thing.'

He climbs out of his Jeep and I'm momentarily distracted by the Culver's sack in his hand. Did he buy me a Butterburger and some cheese curds? I'm embarrassed to say I get an ever-so-slight tingle.

Like a five year-old when grandma visits, I wait in the kitchen with clenched hands until he reveals what he's gotten me. It's not a Butterburger, but it's the next best thing. Ice cream sundaes: one Turtle Dove and one Bonfire S'Mores. I squirrel them away in the freezer for later.

Then I tell him to sit while I perform the 'Tommy Martin at Limelight' story. His eyes sparkle as he watches me fawn over invisible Darrell and punch Miss Thing for being so gay. I also fill him in on my call to Doug Olsen in Athens, and the fact that none of the guys at Sigma Epsilon Nu were questioned by the police. I also tell him about Tommy's family hiring the PI and that I've tracked him down in Denver.

"I can't talk to Detective Atwell because he died in a boating accident a few years ago."

Brian jumps up and claps his hands on his head. "Oh, no! You aren't going to add his death to the investigation are you?"

"Very funny."

"My head is swimming with questions," he says as he begins pacing. "Let's start with the Limelight. How soon after the brawl was Tommy murdered?"

"Good question. I did a search for Pressley's birthday. He turned twenty-one in March. Tommy was killed almost a year later."

"Do you think Darrell Pressley had anything to do with it?" he asks. "That's a long time to wait if you want revenge."

"I know. But he definitely didn't like getting propositioned."

"Sometimes the men who protest the loudest—"

I click my tongue. "I don't think so. I mean, what about Deborah? And you should have seen Dawn Shipley. She's gorgeous even in her mid-fifties."

"Maybe Pressley's door swings both ways?"

"More likely, he had to wait for the right opportunity," I say.

"Like the anniversary of the Limelight episode?"

"That's too obvious," I say, dismissing his suggestion.

Then I pace too. How does all this come together? Will it ever connect back to Deborah Wiley? Why did Charlotte Pressley throw Tommy's name in Darrell's face?

"What about this," I say. "Pressley pretends to be a john."

"And he waited until a year after Tommy's proposition—"

"Sure, whatever. He leaves a fake name in a phone message for Tommy to meet him in the cemetery. Then he skulks over there at night and kills him."

"Wait a minute. He beats up Tommy, then waits around for four hours before rolling him down the hill?"

I click my tongue. "You're right. That doesn't work either. And like Ellie said, everyone is jumping to the conclusion that Tommy was in it for the money. Why couldn't he just love having sex with men?'

"Well there's got to be a connection. Otherwise, why did Charlotte bring it up?"

"Maybe she killed Tommy."

Brian rolls his eyes. I shrug my shoulders. He scratches the back of his head. I open the refrigerator door. It's our non-verbal communication. We've got nothing.

"Anyway," he says, "I've got to get these pictures to Madeline today."

"You're kidding."

"No! Can you believe it? You always give me at least a week."

He's right, but usually that's because I haven't hammered out an article in a single day since I was in college. Speaking of which, if I don't get my short story submitted this week, we'll be eating peanut butter for dinner.

Besides, sometimes it helps to push a thought away. When it bounces back, it's from a different angle. I shove all thoughts of Darrell Pressley into a gloomy closet in the back of my mind.

I try not to look into the hall bathroom on the way to my office but I can't help noticing a pile of towels on the floor. Jeez, the kid was here three days and used a clean towel every time he took a shower? What does he think this is, a hotel?

While I'm bending to pick up towels, my eyes betray me by glancing at the toilet. Dear God, there's pee pooled up on that spot behind the seat. And there are dribble streaks of urine running down the bowl and onto the floor. What did he do? Close his eyes so he wouldn't see his penis and remember he hadn't jacked off for at least half an hour?

I pull on a pair of yellow rubber gloves and get a spray bottle of cleaner from under the sink. If I needed a distraction, this is certainly it.

WE DINE ON baked potatoes topped with canned chili. In my constant effort to fit into my jeans, I omit the mountain of grated cheddar on top since we've got sundaes for dessert. But Brian sabotages my plan by getting the cheese out anyway. What am I supposed to do? Make him feel guilty about the added calories? I compromise and sprinkle half a mountain on my potato.

I'm just about to dig in when my phone rings. It's Harry Packworth. I put it on speaker phone so Brian can hear. Once we get past the preliminaries, Harry give us the lowdown.

"Dolores hired me two weeks after the murder," he says. "She realized the cops had already made up their minds and had written Tommy off. I wandered around on campus for a few days, asking questions. He lived in an apartment complex and some of the other residents were gay."

"Did you find out if Tommy had a steady boyfriend?"

"No. His mother was anxious to find out the same thing." He hesitates, and I wonder if he's walking into another room. I take a bite while I wait. His voice is lower when he comes back on the line. "She hated that everyone thought Tommy was turning tricks."

"I'm sure she did," I say.

"It was small consolation that Tommy was just promiscuous. There was no money involved that I could tell."

"That shouldn't have made any difference. There is no justification for murder."

"That's how we felt," he says. His voice comes back up to normal level. "Anyway, one of the residents at the apartment complex told me about a ruckus at this nightclub in Atlanta."

"The Limelight," I say, managing to spit a bit of potato on my phone.

"That's the place," he says. "Finally, I had a lead on something. I snooped around Sigma Epsilon Nu. Caught guys on their way to class or coming back to the house. And here's something strange. I interviewed two different guys who both look like they'd been in a real donnybrook: black eyes, busted lips. They were healing up, but it was too much of a coincidence that they were in different fights. I poked until somebody told me they had tried to beat each other to a pulp the Sunday they came back from spring break. But nobody knew why."

"Holy crap!" Brian chimes in. "That was just a week after Tommy's body was found."

"Yep."

"Did you talk to Darrell Pressley?" I ask.

I can hear Packworth flipping through his paperwork. "Yeah, here it is. He said they were fighting over a girl."

"Did he say who she was?"

"If he did, I didn't write it down."

"Do you think he was telling the truth?"

"Nah. Those guys were all on the football team and brothers in the same fraternity. I don't care if a guy murdered his mother, none of them was going to rat him out."

IT'S NOT UNTIL we're propped up in bed waiting for our sundaes to thaw to just the right consistency that I have a revelation. We're watching a crime show and the cops are chasing a suspect through the woods. They're dodging trees, hopping over logs; there are small saplings that slap their arms. There's no way Tommy could have 'accidentally' tumbled all the way down the hill and into the river. The trees and debris would have stopped his body almost immediately. Olsen was right; he was dragged pretty close to the water's edge.

"How about this," I say. "Adam and Lonnie follow Tommy into the cemetery. They both idolize Darrell. What better way to please their lord than by giving Tommy a sound thrashing. After they beat him up, they scurry back to the Sigma House to brag to Darrell about what they did. But he gives one of them the Three Stooges forehead smack—I'm guessing it was Adam—for being so stupid. 'When Tommy wakes up, he's going to say you did it. You could get kicked off the team.'"

I wag my eyebrows at Brian to see if he likes it so far.

"Go on."

"So one of them sneaks back later to finish the job. Dumps him in the river."

"And Lonnie and Adam get into a fight because—"

That's a good question. While I'm thinking things through, I reach over for my ice cream on the nightstand and give it a little poke with my spoon. The top has melted enough to create a little puddle, but the ice cream is still firm enough that it isn't soup.

I think I've got it. "One of them—let's say Lonnie—is pissed that Adam has really put them in the hot seat. They come back from spring break and everyone's talking about it. Lonnie beats up Adam for being such an asshole."

I'm proud of my deductive reasoning. To reward my genius, I create the perfect bite: caramel ice cream, a chunk of chocolate and a piece of pecan. Once it's in my mouth, I swoon.

"Oh, that's good."

"Are you talking about your new theory or the ice cream?"

"Both."

Brian does the same thing with his S'Mores sundae: ice cream, a bit of the swirled marshmallow crème, a piece of graham cracker, and a chocolate chunk. "These people should get a Nobel Prize."

"Or slapped with a lawsuit."

"Hey," Brian says. Then with the back of his spoon, he wipes a little ice cream on my arm.

"Gross. Lick that off." I shove my arm in front of his face.

Brian licks off the smear. Then he turns my arm to the inside and licks that soft spot at the inside of my elbow. A shiver runs down my back.

I use my spoon to wipe ice cream on his neck right below his ear, then start low and lick all the way up. With the tip of my tongue, I tease his ear lobe.

He scoops out a big bite of ice cream and holds it in his mouth for a few seconds before swallowing. Then he pulls up my night shirt and sucks in one of my nipples. Holy cow! The cold sends a charge all the way to my toes.

I jerk off my shirt as he wriggles out of his boxers. I push him down on his back, then I drizzle a stream of melted ice cream from his chest to his belly button. I straddle him and start with the puddle on his belly. I even dart my tongue into his navel, and beneath me, Mr. Happy leaps with glee. As I run my tongue up his torso, Brian groans.

We don't stop until I've hollered three orgasmic screams.

CHAPTER TWENTY-THREE

I wake up to chocolate smears on my pillowcase and a piece of pecan wedged in the crook of my elbow. It feels like every surface of my body is sticky. I've got to get a shower.

The water sprays my back as I comb my fingers through my hair. There are several gummy tangles here, too.

Brian comes in as I'm drying off. He's walking kind of funny, like a cowboy who's been in the saddle too long.

"My balls are sticking to my legs."

We may need to rethink the combination of food and sex; at least right before we go to sleep.

Once I've got the coffee going, I reach for my iPad and send a Facebook message to Adam Winston. *Guess who I met yesterday. Jason Hadley. He said you guys were in the same fraternity. Small world, huh? He was telling me some bizarre story about a gay guy getting beat up at some nightclub in Atlanta. Do you remember Tommy Martin?*

That ought to cool his hard-on for sure.

I haven't heard back from Adam by the time I need to drive downtown for my volunteer job at Fuller House. My phone is in my lap though, in case he answers me.

* * *

THE MOMENT I walk in the door at the women's center, Tanya the receptionist tells me there's a woman upstairs who needs some assistance. I scurry up and find a woman sitting in front of a computer. I give her a cheery greeting and ask how I can help.

"I need a job . . . bad."

'Well, you've come to the right place," I assure her.

I introduce myself but when I hold out a hand to shake, her eyebrows furrow. The fact that she's unfamiliar with women shaking hands is just the beginning of Sheila Newton.

"My husband fell off one of those rolling step ladders at Home Depot. Now his back is all messed up."

I sit at the computer next to her and pull up the small questionnaire Samantha showed me. It's meant to save me a lot of time; like when Ellie and Joanie told me all about the Komen Race for the Cure? The first thing out of their mouths should have been the cost.

Question one: Do you have a high school diploma or a GED?

Sheila shakes her head no. "I got pregnant my junior year and never went back."

Her comment jogs my memory. Didn't Reggie Riggs say something about Lonnie Taggart getting a girl pregnant? I need to find out who she was.

I tuck that into the back of my mind and move on with more questions. Does she have a car? What about young children? Can she work weekends? How late at night can she work?

She has two kids, has never written a resume, has no real skills; in fact, she's never used a computer. At least her husband can watch their kids while she works. I help her fill out an application to work in the bakery of a supermarket.

We're just finishing up when a woman comes in with a baby in her arms and a toddler at her side. I tell her I'll be right with her. She

197

sinks down onto a chair with a sigh, exhausted. They must have walked from the bus stop.

After I finish up with Sheila and she leaves, I start in with this new client.

"I got a email that said I could earn up to three hundred and fifty dollars a week at home," she tells me. "But when I clicked on the button, it went to a bunch of ads for schools online. If I don't have any money, how can I pay for school?"

"Sounds like clickbait," I tell her. She has no idea what I'm talking about. "There are a lot of scammers out there trying to get you to click on their message. Like these schools. I'm sure they're willing to work out some kind of payment plan. Others are trying to hack into your system for information."

"So how do I make three hundred and fifty dollars a week?" she asks.

She still isn't getting it. "There is no job that will pay you to work at home. They're lying."

The look on her face is depressing. She's dragged her kids all this way for nothing. I take her through the rest of the questionnaire but her answers are short 'yes' and 'no's. Her confidence is shot. She grabs her son's hand and walks out. I follow her down the stairs, urging her to come back some other time and we'll try again but I doubt if she will.

Since I'm downstairs, I might as well get a cup of coffee. Guess who's in the kitchen? Charlotte Pressley's sister Audrey. She has a cup in her hand and she's stirring with one of those plastic sticks.

Now a novice might walk right up, shake her hand, and congratulate her on being the brains behind the center's operation, but that would be a big mistake.

I pretend my phone just vibrated and pull it out. As I read a non-existent message, I huff out a breath. "My brother-in-law is such a douche. I don't know why my sister ever married him."

She glances my way. "It happens a lot."

"But he's cheating on her," I say, all indignant.

She gives me this knowing shrug like 'what else is new?'

"You don't get it," I say, ramping up my anger. "She knows he's cheating but she won't do anything about it."

Audrey feels compelled to offer some advice, just like I hoped she would. "Sometimes it's better to overlook the behavior because women think that's easier than starting over."

"Ouch," I say. "Sounds like you've been there."

Her left eyebrow shoots up. "Not me. My sister."

She throws the swizzle stick away and turns to walk around me.

Have I mentioned how impatient I am?

My strategy was to meet Audrey, build up a rapport over several weeks to gain her trust. Then broach the subject. But all of these scenarios about Darrell and Tommy and Deborah are swirling around in my brain, and the woman who could provide an important clue is about to walk out of the room. Next week when I come back, she might not even be here.

I know I shouldn't, but I push harder. "It's not just the cheating." I say as she passes me. "I bet you never suspected your brother-in-law of killing someone."

Her hand jerks and she slops coffee onto the floor.

"Oh, crap," I say and grab a napkin off the table nearby. "Let me get that."

I dive to the floor, essentially blocking her path of retreat, and as I'm sopping up the spill, I hit her with the zinger. "I heard about this guy once, Tommy Martin . . ."

I glance up. The cordial Audrey is gone, replaced by suspicious Audrey.

"Who did you say you are?" she asks.

"Oh, sorry." I wobble to my feet. "I'm Rachel Sanders. I volunteer upstairs in the computer room."

"The writer," she says, giving me an excellent resting-bitch-face before she walks away.

My hands shake as I fix myself a cup of coffee. I've shocked myself with my boldness. Ever since I took snooping to this level, I've become a different person. I'm just not so sure that's a good thing.

I sit upstairs in the computer room waiting for Tanya to come up and throw me out. Or at the very least, tell me I'm fired. But I don't hear any more footsteps on the stairs. After my initial wariness fades, I ponder the situation.

Audrey is older than Charlotte, so even if she went to UGA, she would have graduated by the time Charlotte was a junior. Was she even aware of Tommy Martin on campus? Did Charlotte know about the Limelight incident and tell her? Did she also tell Audrey she suspected Darrell had something to do with his murder a year later?

When I get tired of playing out endless scenarios in my head, I go to my Facebook page to see if Adam has answered my last volley. He's unfriended me!

This is why it's always best to interview people in person. They can't hang up on you, or unfriend you. Plus, you don't get the visual cues like the darting eyes or the jaw drop. Or in Audrey's case, the spilled coffee.

I am hitting nerves all over the country this morning. I've got confirmation from two different sources that Darrell might have been involved with Tommy Martin's death. Or as Brian would put it: 'You have suspicions.' But he's such a negative Neddy, what does he know?

The rest of my shift drags by, no one else comes in, and I'm wondering how I can get out of volunteering again next Tuesday. I certainly won't be getting any more information from Audrey.

While I'm driving home, I call Reggie Riggs at the dealership and put my phone on speaker. He still sounds happy to hear from me. Of course, that's because he still considers me a possible customer.

"How you doin'?" he says when he picks up his phone. "You and Barry ready to come test drive an F series?"

I overlook his misstep. "I'm all for it, but I haven't convinced *Brian* yet. Give me some time, I'll wear him down."

"There you go," he says. "How's the article coming on celebrity vacations?"

"Great. Great," I sputter. Then I add something about waiting to hear from Chipper Jones. He gives me the non-believer's 'uh huh.'

"Listen, I'm working on another article. I was hoping you could tell me a little more about Lonnie Taggart. I can't find anything on him. He's not on Facebook or LinkedIn. I even tried Twitter. The only thing I got was a short mention in the campus newspaper about him not coming back to play his senior year. It's like he's fallen off the face of the earth."

"That was real strange," Reggie says. "He quit school after his junior year. Didn't say goodbye to any of us. Never came back to visit or catch a game."

"Do you know why?"

"I got it on pretty good authority that he got one of the cheerleaders pregnant."

"You said that before. But it seems extreme that he'd drop out for that. I can't believe the school didn't beg him to come back his senior year."

"Darrell told me Lonnie hoped he'd be drafted by the NFL. That's why he didn't come back."

"Did you believe him?"

"Nah. Lonnie wasn't on any team's radar to play pro."

"Maybe his grades were so bad, he thought he was getting the boot."

"Are you kidding? He was first string on a winning college team. They don't get dropped. Not for grades."

At a traffic light, I drum my fingers on the steering wheel. Nothing about this story makes sense.

I come at it from a different angle. "So this cheerleader, what was her name?"

"Cynthia Davis."

"And she left, too?"

"Sure did. We heard they got a farm somewhere and were living off the grid."

"Do you know where?"

"Not a clue."

Crap. I'm getting nowhere fast. The car behind me toots their horn and I see that the light has changed. I hit the gas and almost ram into the car ahead of me. If I wreck another car, Brian will have a conniption fit. I wrecked two trying to solve our last caper.

I think back on TV shows I've seen. What do they always ask?

"Did you notice any suspicious behavior before Lonnie left? Was he acting distracted?"

"Not really. It was my senior year, football season was over, I had my eyes on moving up to pro."

I hear papers shuffling and then Reggie's chair squeaks. Is he signaling for someone to come into his office so he can get off the phone? Seconds later, I hear a woman's voice in the background. Then Reggie says he's got to go.

"One last question," I say, "and I promise I'll let you go."

"I hope it's a quick one."

"Can you think of anyone who would know where Lonnie's farm is?"

"I'll ask around."

I apologize for taking up so much of his time and thank him. He insists it was no problem and clicks off. I'm pretty sure that's the last time I'll talk to Reggie Riggs. If I call again, the receptionist will tell me he's with a customer.

I WALK IN the door and Brian comes downstairs to meet me in the kitchen.

"Reggie Riggs just called," he says. "Wanted to know when I'd like to take a test drive in one of his new F series BMWs. Would you know anything about that?"

"Oops. I might have made a vague reference . . ." I'm not coming up with a good excuse so I give him a quick kiss. "Sorry. Did he say anything about Lonnie Taggart?"

"Yeah. He said he had an address and we could get it when we come in for that test drive."

CHAPTER TWENTY-FOUR

I scurry upstairs to call Reggie back and apologize for misleading him about my *Celebrities and their Favorite Destinations* story.

"I figured you were playin' me so I decided to play you back," he says.

"I really am going to write that article," I insist but I don't fess up that it won't appear in the magazine for many months. I've got a lot on my plate already.

"Whatever," he says. "All I could find out is that Lonnie's farm is north of Macon. A dirt lane off Flovilla Road. And before you call me back *again*, I'll just tell you that Cynthia Davis is married and is now Cynthia Stamps."

If there was any way in the world Brian and I could afford it, I'd drive to Stone Mountain right now and buy a BMW.

"FEEL LIKE A road trip?" I ask Brian when I get back to the kitchen.

"Where we going?"

"Somewhere in rural Georgia. I've got a lead on Lonnie Taggart."

"Is this going to be an all-day trip?" he asks.

Now this is where Brian and I differ. I'll google Flovilla Road, then click on the satellite link and zoom in to get the lay of the land. How many remote farms I find on dirt roads, stuff like that. I used to look up rest stops along a route but now with our new GPS, it tells me when one is coming up.

Brian, however, will google eateries along our route. His favorite is BBQ joints—the more the place looks like a shack the better. He doesn't believe in health inspections. He always says they don't have quality control in European countries or Asia but I don't know where he got that information. If I'm eating in China and something looks like an insect or a cat, I'm not eating it.

"You know what we should do?" he says. "Take Jackson's drone. If we can't find Lonnie's farm, maybe we can fly over potential properties."

"And what? Look for a big Georgia G on the roof of a barn?"

There's no good reason to take Jackson's drone. Brian just wants to play with it again. But I figure, what the heck? Gwen and Jake owe us a favor for taking care of Jackson. I'll call her and see if we can borrow it.

But when she answers her phone, the first words out of her mouth are, "I was just going to call you." And it doesn't sound like she wants to gush over the excellent care we provided for her son. "We just got home from the doctor's office. Jackson has poison ivy all over his right hand and arm."

"What?!" I glower at Brian.

"The doctor gave us cream AND pills. He even gave Jackson an injection of cortisone."

"How could that happen?"

"Well, I guess it happened when you dragged him to some ivy-infested river swamp and let him roam around unattended."

Crap! Why does this always happen to me?

"I swear I told him to scrub with Fels Naptha, just like mom used to do." (I'm hoping to bring back fond memories of our own bouts with the vicious weed.)

"Yeah? Well it didn't work. I can't wait for Jake to get home so I can tell him how much I had to spend."

I stutter in confusion. "I . . . I . . ."

"Know what else we had to do today?" Gwen says. "Buy new shoes. Because you told Jackson it was fine to wade through muck in the only decent pair of shoes he had."

I apologize several times before she lets me off the hook by hanging up. Then I turn my wrath on Brian.

"I sent you with Jackson to make sure he washed his arms and legs."

"He did!"

"Whatever," I say. "You can forget about the drone."

And I can forget about any special favors from Gwen or Jake for the next ten years. Once again, I'm reminded of why Brian and I would not make good parents.

Not five minutes later, I see Brian texting.

"Who are you talking to?"

"Jackson."

"Are you kidding me? What if Gwen finds out."

"It doesn't matter," he says, sounding dejected. "He won't let me borrow the drone without asking his dad."

"What did you expect?"

"I figured if I offered him twenty bucks, he'd let me use it."

"Twenty dollars?" I scoff. "Did you think you were talking to The Beaver?"

Brian's phone dings with a text. He reads it and chuckles. "Jackson says he'll lend me the drone if I take him to some rock concert. His dad already said no."

"Do you really think either of his parents will let him go with you after this?"

"No, but I'm sure he'll sneak out and tell them some BS like he's going to a friend's house to study."

"Well, I must say it's an excellent plan. If I never wanted to be responsible for Gwen's kids again, this is the way I'd do it."

For the life of me, I can't figure out how the kid could get poison ivy on just one arm. He walked through it all morning in his shorts, but his legs are fine. Even one of his arms is blister-free. Did he rub against a plant after he washed? How would that get ivy oil all over? It's almost like he rubbed his arm with an ivy leaf. Surely, he's not that stupid. Or if he wanted revenge for us dragging him along, he sure picked a dumb retaliation.

I pick up my phone to text Jackson myself. As I hold it, I imagine it's a bar of soap. He sits on a rock and scrubs his legs. Then he scrubs his left arm, sets the soap down, and rinses in the river.

Ding! The light comes on. Once he put the soap down, he never picked it up again; never washed his right arm. He didn't even want to pick up the soap to put it back in the baggie. What a knucklehead.

My text says: *Guess I should have said wash BOTH arms and legs.*

* * *

BRIAN ARRANGES to meet Jackson at a buddy's house at 8:30 tonight. There's no point in me arguing against it. He'll just tell me some BS like he's going to a buddy's house for a beer and then still meet Jackson.

While he's gone, I do a quick search for Cynthia Stamps and find a Facebook page. She doesn't look a day over forty even though she must be in her mid-fifties. As a bonus, she has posted a link to a hardware store in Powder Springs called Stamps DIY.

How did the police carry on an investigation in the olden days before Facebook and Google?

I do a search for the band Jackson wants to see; they're called Bat Shit Crazy and from the looks of the motley crew, they are. I've never heard of them but they want fifty bucks a ticket? And they're playing at some abandoned warehouse in an industrial area of downtown Atlanta. Brian is sure to get stabbed in a parking lot and his Jeep stolen. I hate to agree with Jake, but this is a dumb idea.

As soon as Brian comes back with the drone, I message Jackson that there's no way Brian is taking him to that concert. Sure, he'll feel betrayed, but he may as well get used to grown-ups lying and deceiving him. It'll only get worse. What's he going to do? Tell his dad?

I AM AWAKENED at the crack of dawn by an eager husband. According to his research, there's a Patty's Porch in McDonough that serves the best biscuits and sausage gravy in the South, but they usually run out of biscuits around nine so we have to get there early.

Then we can roam the hinterland of central Georgia until noon, when Brian has reserved us a table at Cooter's Bar B Que in Shady Dale. (Just kidding. I'm pretty sure you can't reserve a picnic table.)

Assuming we still haven't found Lonnie Taggart by mid-afternoon—or he invites us in for some homemade muscadine wine and we visit all afternoon—we can swing over to the quaint town of Abide Awhile on Highway 162 for banana pudding and peach cobbler at Keeley's.

NOT ONLY DO we each order a massive plate of biscuits and gravy at Patty's, we order a second biscuit to split so we can slather it with butter and drizzle it with pure cane syrup.

We head cross-country at Locust Grove and find Flovilla Road around ten o'clock but this isn't going to be nearly as easy as we hoped. Every road that turns off Flovilla is a dirt road. There's no way we can possibly find Lonnie's farm. I wonder if Reggie knew that when he told me.

My phone dings with an email. It's from Samantha at the Fuller House. I've been fired. How embarrassing is that? Terminated from a volunteer position. At least I don't have to come up with an excuse for why I won't be there next week.

After wandering aimlessly for an hour, we end up in the burg of Flovilla. I see an old general store at an intersection and tell Brian to stop. I'm really just interested in using their bathroom, but then I see a sign in the window for a post office and it gives me an idea.

The store is so old it still has the creaky wooden floors; the ceiling has the old-timey tin tiles. The place smells like it's been around for a hundred years. One aisle has food, the next has motor oil and diapers. At the end of an aisle, I find a twirly stand of greeting cards. They're covered in dust. I select the cheapest card, wipe the cobwebs off the envelope, and take it to the front counter to pay. Then I carry it to the back of the store where the post office is located.

I pour on the dumb city-girl routine. "I just bought this card for Lonnie Taggart but I must have left his address back home on the counter. You don't happen to know where he lives. It's right off Flovilla Road."

"I don't recognize the name," the postwoman says. Her ID badge reads Helen.

"He's a big guy, used to play football, kind of keeps to himself," I say.

A woman walks up behind me. "She's talkin' about Looney."

"Martha!" Helen says.

I turn around. The woman must be in her seventies. She's wearing a floppy canvas hat, a man's flannel shirt that's at least two sizes too large, a pair of dungarees (no one could possibly call them blue jeans), and rubber boots.

"Well, he is looney," Martha says. "Got signs hangin' everywheres tellin' folks to keep out. Even got barbed wire crossed the top of his fence."

209

"Do you have an address?" I ask, waving the greeting card at her.

"Might save yourself the stamp. It's only a couple miles from here."

Helen glares at Martha for revealing this information. I'm sure somewhere in the postal code is a rule about giving out addresses.

Ignoring Helen, Martha gives us directions to Old Bullpen Road. It's a dirt road off a dirt road. "Cain't miss it."

As I'm heading for the door, she calls after me, "Watch out for them dogs!" Great.

MARTHA WAS RIGHT. It would be hard to miss Lonnie's place. The fence that runs along the road is topped with barbed wire, and there's a hand-made sign on every post. Some say 'Keep Out', others say 'This Means YOU'. A couple have 'Beware of Dogs'. One simply has a picture of a gun.

Brian thinks this is a bad idea. He slows down to check out the dilapidated house turned gray from lack of paint. The roof of the front porch sags dangerously at the far end. And yet Lonnie has a ratty old sofa parked on it. Isn't he afraid he'll flop down onto a flea-infested cushion someday, choke on the dust created, and shake the porch until the roof collapses? He might not be found for years.

Any kind of trash that can't be burned or composted has been tossed into the dirt front yard. And it looks like the dogs Martha warned us about use the discards as toys because a couple of plastic jugs have been chewed to bits; an old bike tire is in shreds.

The minute Brian stops at the gate blocking the driveway, three dogs come tearing out from behind the old farm house, barking at us.

I figure, we've come this far, and I open my door. Surely Lonnie hears the commotion and will come out to investigate. The dogs get hysterical, jumping on the fence, and snarling at me. One of them actually clamps his teeth on a steel cross piece of the gate like he's going to chew it off.

"Holy shit!" I slam the door shut and Brian zooms away throwing dirt and stones behind us. My heart is doing one of those drumline routines in a marching band and my stomach is getting swiveled around like a bass drum.

The Jeep slides into the turn at Flovilla Road. Half a mile later, dust flies everywhere as Brian skids to a halt. Once the car is in park, he flops back against the seat and hoots out a laugh.

"What kind of maniac lives like that?" he says.

I blow out my own shaky breath. "He's like the Unabomber."

"I can't believe someone who went to UGA could be that unhinged." Brian turns in his seat to look out the back. I guess he's making sure we weren't followed.

"Hello. He played football. Maybe he got hit in the head one too many times."

"You could be right," he says as he straightens back in his seat. "So now what?"

"I'd at least like to get a look at the guy. What if the nutjob back there is an eighty-year-old white supremacist?"

Brian gazes up the deserted road, then behind us again.

"There's more than one way to skin a cat," he says as he reaches into the back for the bag with the drone.

"Or in this case, a possum."

We both get out and Brian practices a couple times with the drone before he flies it toward the mystery house. Randy, our techie friend, explained how to link the drone to an iPad; I hold mine up so we both can see where the drone is going.

He flies it high over the farm, giving us a nice aerial view. There's a barn in back of the house and several goats in a field. Further along we see a big section of plowed dirt, probably for a garden.

Another small shed must be a coop. Brian flies lower and sure enough, chickens run in all directions.

"Don't get so close," I say.

"He really is off the grid," Brian says. "He's got the goats for milk, chickens for eggs and meat. By the looks of that pile of wood, he doesn't have a furnace."

"I didn't see any power lines."

Brian turns the drone in the direction of the house. Standing in the dirt yard is Leonardo DiCaprio from that movie <u>The Revenant</u>. At least that's what the guy looks like with the bushy beard, long, stringy hair, and the classic bib overalls. At his side is a shotgun.

"Geez," I whisper, like he might hear me. "He looks more rabid than his dogs."

Brian snaps some pictures. "Could this be Lonnie?"

Schizoid Man raises his gun and aims right at us. I can practically see down the barrel. Before Brian can retreat, I see a flash and instantly the picture on the iPad goes black. A second later, we hear the crack of the shotgun. Lonnie just shot Jackson's drone.

CHAPTER TWENTY-FIVE

The drive home is a somber one. Not only will we have to replace Jackson's drone, there's a good chance Jake is going to find out about this. I'm already in hot water over the poison ivy and ruined shoes. Our next family gathering should be a doozy.

I do a quick search on my phone. Jackson's drone isn't one of the most expensive, but it sure isn't cheap. (There goes the last of the mad money.) I'm afraid to tell Brian just how much this is going to cost because he's going to insist we drop the investigation.

In my mind, it's too late to walk away. I've got to at least come up with a plausible ending so I can sell this story. And I have to get paid enough to break even. All of this worry reminds me that I've got a deadline on the book I've already promised and I'm way behind on my page count.

I can tell Brian is also freaked out because when we stop at Cooter's in Shady Dale for the barbecue, he doesn't order the deluxe combo platter with a bowl of Brunswick stew on the side. We each get a sandwich and split an order of fries.

Back home, he slumps into his chair and turns on the TV, a broken man. I head into the kitchen to drown my sorrows in a big bowl of cappuccino fudge swirl.

* * *

I WAKE UP with renewed determination to solve this case. Well, it's more like a half-hearted desire to find something to do today besides work on my book or mop the kitchen floor. My next candidate for badgering is Cynthia Stamps. Reggie Riggs was kind enough to give me her married name right before he told me never to call again.

I call Stamps Do It Yourself and ask for her. The man who answers says she won't be in until noon.

Just to be sure, I say, "Didn't Cynthia go to UGA?"

"She sure did," he says. "She was a cheerleader."

My enthusiasm level makes it past the halfway line at least. I poke my head into Brian's office to see if he wants to ride down to Stamps DIY with me.

"No can do," he says. "I'm going downtown to hang out at the Old Fourth Ward Park. Nate said he likes to hang out there. Maybe I'll get lucky and run into him."

Isn't it weird how much we're alike? Last night we were both in the dumps, but a good night's sleep and we're both right back at it. I give him a big kiss and tell him he'll be on his own for lunch.

I've got some time before I have to leave so I get on eBay. I find a used model the same as Jackson's drone. It's half the price of a new one but it's still going to set us back. Good-girl Rachel lectures me on the consequences of sticking my nose where it doesn't belong. I ignore her and order the drone.

I ARRIVE AT Stamps DIY early and there's no sign of Cynthia. I wander through aisles of insecticides and plumbing supplies until I come to a section of bolts and nails. There are a couple of metal buckets with heavy-duty rings and fasteners. An image pops into my head: Brian laying on the bed, his arms overhead, his wrists securely tied to two rings on the wall.

I look in the other bins and find these U-shaped nails that I could pound into the wall and hold the ring in place.

I'm holding a ring in one hand, the U-shaped nail in the other, wondering if this will work, when a vivacious woman whooshes into the aisle. As she gets closer, she smiles and asks if she can help. I immediately recognize her; and Cynthia is even more gorgeous in person than she is in her Facebook picture. Her mocha-colored skin is as flawless as a teen's. I wonder if Reggie had a thing for her back in school and that's why he knows so much about her now.

"Uhhhhh," I stammer. Between the thoughts in my head, and her beauty, I'm flummoxed momentarily.

She grins and nods at the ring in my hand. "What size ring are you looking for?"

"I . . . don't know."

"What are you going to use it for?"

Oh, boy. I'm tempted to toss it back into the bucket and run. Instead, I say, "I was thinking of hanging this on the wall and draping a scarf through it?"

"How many scarves do you want to hang?"

"Uh, two?"

She nods but I know she's confused. If I only have two scarves, why would I hang them on the wall? Then she gets a grin on her face.

"Would these rings be above your bed?"

My face flames with embarrassment. I drop the ring into the bucket likes it's hot.

"I think that size will work," she says, reaching in and pulling it back out. "What you'll need is a loop fastener." She takes the U-shaped nail out of my hand and tosses it into the bin. Then she reaches into another bin and comes up with a heavy-duty loop that can be bolted to the wall.

"Depending on where the studs are, you can screw these into the wood, or you can get a couple molly-bolts to make sure everything

215

is nice and secured to the drywall. Who's getting tied up—you or your partner?"

I'm guessing my gaping mouth gives me away. She eases my discomfort with a smile. "My husband and I are into soft BDSM. Nothing rough, just adding a little variety to sex."

"Wow, you're pretty straightforward."

"The only way to be," she says.

As we walk towards the checkout counter, we pass a cardboard box of kids' felt cowboy hats. I perch one on my head. It's small but it could work. She turns back and sees me.

"Oh, now that'll be perfect," she says. "I don't suppose either of you has chaps."

We discuss possible cowgirl costumes while she rings up my purchases. When she hands me my bag, I tell her I need to be honest with her.

"I'm trying to contact Lonnie Taggart but he's—" I don't know how to finish.

Her nose scrunches up as she gives me a good long stare. I don't think she's pissed about me sticking my nose in his business. It seems more like she's being protective. Can I be trusted? I guess she figures I'm okay because she invites me to a small office in the back of the store.

She sits behind the desk and nods at a folding chair in the corner. I unfold it and sit. Then pull up the only picture we got of Lonnie and show it to her.

"Yeah, that's him," she says as she leans back in her chair with a sigh. "Poor Lonnie. I tried so hard to help him get past whatever was ailing him, but I never could." She twists her lips into a smirk. "Have you seen his house?"

"Yeah. And the dogs."

"If you knew him from school, you'd never guess he'd turn into that lonely, angry man. He was so lovable."

"But something happened."

She nods, a melancholy curve to her mouth. "I used to know this story well. Every day for years, I'd think about where I went wrong. Then I met Travis and he helped me get over Lonnie."

"What do you remember?"

"It started when I found out I was pregnant. This was early February of our junior year. I was traumatized. I didn't want to have a baby in September, I wanted to enjoy my senior year, be a cheerleader one last season. But when I told Lonnie I was going to get an abortion, he begged me not to." Her smile turns wistful. "He was so excited about being a daddy. I let him talk me out of the abortion. Then that whole spring semester got messed up. My hormones had me stressing all the time. Lonnie was acting weird but whenever I'd ask if it was the baby, he swore it wasn't." She shakes her head. "I was sure it was."

"When did he start acting strange?"

"It was right before spring break. He was going home to spend the week helping his daddy on their farm. I was going home, too. We both debated on telling our parents about the baby while we were there. I chickened out but I think Lonnie told his parents and they weren't happy. You know, that whole mixed race thing."

I raise my eyebrows at that.

"You have to remember," she says, "this was back in the eighties. And Lonnie's daddy was a Southern good ole' boy."

"Yeah, I get it."

"Anyway," she says, "Lonnie and I talked on the phone that week and he was . . . different."

I let her wander with her thoughts for a moment before I get her back on track. "So you get back to school on Sunday."

She nods, her face drawn with sadness. "I heard Lonnie and Adam got into a horrible fight at the fraternity house. I mean punching with fists. Nobody seemed to know what it was all about. I was sure Lonnie had told Adam I was pregnant and Adam told him to dump me."

"Typical macho male reaction," I say.

"Isn't it? I begged and prodded Lonnie to tell me what was going on but he wouldn't. I thought maybe I'd go ahead with the abortion and then tell him later I lost the baby. But my being pregnant seemed to be the only thing that made him happy. He wasn't doing well in school. I think he flunked all his finals. It was only six weeks until the end of the semester but it felt like forever."

She picks up a paperclip and bends it back and forth.

"Once the semester was over and my apartment lease ran out, we found a cute little house out in the country. I thought being away from the campus would help, but he just got more restless."

"How so?"

"He was having terrible nightmares. He'd thrash around in the bed and wake up in a sweat." The paperclip breaks and she tosses it on the desk. "I was sure it was about the baby but he'd get so mad when I brought it up that I stopped."

"Do you remember when Tommy Martin was murdered?"

"Who's Tommy Martin?"

I'm looking right at her face. She isn't bluffing; she doesn't know who he was.

"He was a gay guy who got beat up at the Oconee Hill Cemetery and drowned in the River."

A glimmer of recognition flashes in her eyes. "Oh, yeah. I didn't know him, but I remember kids on campus were talking about it. I didn't really pay much attention."

"Did Lonnie know Tommy?"

She gives me a shrug. "I don't know. Seems pretty unlikely if the guy was gay. Although I'll tell you something weird. When Lonnie and Adam got into that huge fight, I wondered if they'd gotten drunk and some homosexual feelings came to the surface. I mean, when Lonnie and I first started dating, there were plenty of times when Adam would coax him into hanging out with the guys instead of me. Maybe

Adam had some issues he couldn't face? But then he made some kind of advance on Lonnie, they both totally freaked out over it, and ended up bashing each other to prove they weren't gay?" She throws her hands into the air.

"All I know is, after that fight, Lonnie hated Adam."

Cynthia seems totally in the dark about the incident with Tommy Martin. It looks like she was so absorbed in her own crisis that nothing else registered. When I tell her that Tommy was killed on the Friday night before spring break, she's surprised. I can see she's thinking back but it was so long ago, I'm not sure she'll have any other useful information. Not right away at least.

But I get the feeling she may be calling me some day.

CHAPTER TWENTY-SIX

I get home first and can hardly wait to tell Brian about Cynthia. But he's totally wired about running into Nate at the Old Fourth Ward Park so we have to draw straws for who gets to tell their story first.

Brian wins.

He grabs two beers, I get a bag of tortilla chips, and we head out to the patio. The sun is shining and somewhere it's five o'clock. We sit at the umbrella table and I drag my chair to the left until I'm not in the beam of light that shines through the tear in the canvas.

He sets both beers on the table and twists off my cap. "Have you seen that dent in the refrigerator?"

Yikes!

"In the kitchen??" I sound, all alarmed.

"No, in the garage."

"Oh, yeah," I say. "I noticed it a couple weeks ago. So tell me about Nate." (Smooth, Rachel.)

"He was glad to see me," Brian says. "We talked about bands for quite a while. I worked the conversation around to concerts I went to in college. He told me some of his. I asked where he went to school. University of Tennessee. He said he hitchhiked to Louisville to see the

Blizzard of Ozz Tour. He saw AC/DC's Highway to Hell tour in Greenville and again at the Fox in Atlanta."

I take a big slug of beer and munch on chips. This is going to take a while to get to relevant material.

"I told him about my cousin taking me to the Roxy to see Marilyn Manson and the Spooky Kids. Nate remembered all the members' stage names, too. How they were taken from serial killers. Berkowitz, Bundy, Speck. We talked about how Madonna Wayne Gacy had all this weird shit on her keyboard, like dismembered doll heads and kids' toys."

"Good thing we nixed taking Jackson to that concert," I say. "His brain would get even more damaged than it is now."

"Yeah," Brian says, ignoring my interruption. He's on an extended trip down memory lane. "So then I asked him 'what's the earliest concert he went to—"

He gets my eye roll now. For someone who's intolerant of 'ramble talk', Brian's pretty good at it sometimes.

"Okay, so anyway, I asked him what he studied in school and he said forensic science, but when I said 'like blood splatters and DNA', he got all jittery. I switched back to music and asked if he ever went to concerts with his sisters. And get this. He says his sisters are bad."

"Oooh," I say, rubbing my hands together.

"I said, I thought Audrey ran a center to help women. He said, that's what she wants people to think."

"Dang. He sounds kind of paranoid."

"Yeah. It gets better. He said Charlotte tried to get him to stay in a fancy apartment in Alpharetta but the place was bugged. He's sure she was spying on him."

"Wow! Deborah's apartment."

"That's what I think," Brian says. "He got up like he was leaving so I walked along with him. I said, 'why would she spy on you?' And he says 'because I know she killed a man. She thinks I'm going to tell'."

I crow like a rabid rooster. "That's unbelievable!" Then I clink his bottle with mine.

"I know," he says. "After he said that, he kind of lost it. He veered off into a rant about some kid who beat him up back in grade school. Then he complained about his mother. I mean, the guy was all over the place."

Brian takes a sip of beer before he leans across the table. "He says 'I ran her stupid lab tests but what was the point?' Then all of a sudden he freezes, like he said something he shouldn't have. He stares at the ground like he sees something horrifying. He's so freaked out, he's vibrating all over. He yells 'I don't know where it is!' and just runs away."

"Did you go after him?"

"Nah. He was out of control. People would have thought I'd done something to him. But after he was gone, I look at the ground where he was staring. And there's this old, dirty sock lying in the grass."

"A sock."

"That was it."

This is going to take some processing. I grab Brian's empty bottle, drain mine and head inside for the next round. And maybe some salsa for the chips.

Ole' Nate is one troubled puppy. He thinks his sisters are spying on him, and it sounds like he may have run some forensic tests for somebody. But why? And what was he testing? I'll have to pace and ponder this later.

Once I've settled back on the patio, I fill Brian in on Cynthia. (Not the part about lashing him to the wall, though.) As I run through the whole pregnancy business and the fact that the name Tommy Martin meant nothing, Brian dredges chips into the salsa.

"How could she not know about a murder on campus?"

"I'm pretty sure she was freaked out about being pregnant. Her hormones were raging, Lonnie was acting weird. It wasn't on her radar."

Brian's phone dings with a text. He pulls it out of his pocket and looks at the screen. "Shit."

"What?"

"Jackson wants to know where his drone is."

"Tell him we're still using it."

"I can't do that," he says.

"Then don't answer."

I scurry inside for my iPad and check on my order. The seller says my package has been shipped, and UPS says I'll get it Saturday.

You know that saying about *don't think of mistakes as failure, think of them as lessons*? Jackson is learning some valuable life lessons this week.

* * *

CYNTHIA STAMPS calls me first thing Saturday morning.

She says, "I've been thinking about Lonnie ever since you told me about Tommy Martin."

"And?"

"I'm looking at everything from a different angle now. You see, the last time Lonnie acted normal was on that Friday before spring break. We had lunch at the student center and he was talking about us renting a house out in the country over the summer.

"He was so excited about us being together, watching my belly grow, pretending to be married I guess. That's when I changed my attitude. Was being a cheerleader really that important? I could be starting a whole new life with a wonderful man."

Her voice cracks. After all these years, she still has feelings for him. Maybe it's one of those first-love things. If I lost Brian, I'm sure

I'd still get choked up thirty years later. And she had a kid with the man so I'm sure they've stayed in touch.

"Then the frat house had a big party that night," I say, nudging her back onto the trail.

"Yeah." There's a wistful sigh before she continues. "I never went to functions at the house. It was still a thin line for black and white couples back then. Neither of us wanted the hassle."

I remember one of Brian's theories and throw it out to her. "So the party is rockin', but more students keep showing up. The beer is running low. Would Lonnie make a beer run?"

"Oh, no. First of all, he didn't have a car. And he certainly didn't have extra cash to go buy beer for other people. He wasn't much of a drinker himself because he couldn't afford the habit."

"Did Darrell have a car?"

"No. But Adam did," she says. "I swear that's why Darrell hung around the asshole. And Lonnie hung around Darrell."

"Do you think all three of them would make a beer run?"

"Mmmm. That doesn't sound like something Darrell would do. He loved being the center of attention. So he'd delegate somebody else to do the steppin' and fetchin'."

I think out loud. "Darrell hands them some cash and sends them for beer. Adam is driving. He sees Tommy Martin near the cemetery, or maybe going into the cemetery. He says, 'Check out the faggot' or something like that. He pulls over and they follow Tommy back towards the river."

"Yeah. That sounds like something Adam would do. And I guess I can see Lonnie going along to get along," she says. "I mean, he was a beast on the football field, but the rest of the time he was like a loveable puppy. Maybe a mastiff puppy, but still."

"Here's a twist to the story that I didn't tell you before," I say. "When Tommy got back by the river, he took off his clothes and knelt on a rug."

224

"Day-um!" she says. "The guy was into kink before kink was cool."

"Looks that way. And maybe when Lonnie and Adam saw him, they just freaked out and beat him up a little?"

"I don't know. Lonnie wasn't a violent kind of guy. Especially if it was a defenseless naked guy on his knees. He believed in a fair fight. Like the guys he tackled. He used to say they signed up for the game so they paid the consequences."

"What about Adam?"

"He's as slimy as they come. And he learned from the master— Darrell Pressley. He'd be the kind of guy who'd sneak up behind you to get an advantage."

"So Adam beats up Tommy to show him a lesson. But he has misgivings later. 'What if Tommy identifies us?' So he goes back and rolls Tommy into the river."

"I could definitely see that happening."

"And that's why they got into that horrible fight. Lonnie didn't know Adam went back until he returned from spring break."

"It all makes sense now," Cynthia says. "Lonnie came to my apartment after the party. I expected him to be drunk and buzzed. But he was like a zombie. He crawled onto my bed and just curled up. Maybe it was because he saw Adam beat up Tommy."

"Maybe he was afraid Tommy was dead."

"Oh, God," she says. "I feel so stupid. All this time I thought it was because of me."

I'm getting an idea but I don't want to cross the line. "I've got a question for you, but please don't hesitate to say 'no' or tell me to go to hell."

"You want to talk to Lonnie," she says.

"The problem is, I don't know how since I'm sure he doesn't have a phone."

"You know what? I want to talk to him, too. You feel like driving back down to the farm?"

I sure do!

I'M FEELING lucky. (Not lucky enough to go buy a lotto ticket, but still.) I call Greg Olsen. He's probably out saving baby turtles or building a Habitat House. The fact that he answers tells me I haven't worn out my welcome yet. I know that day is coming.

"When you went through Tommy's clothing at the cemetery, was a sock missing?"

"A sock?"

"Yeah. You said he folded his clothes neatly and put them on the step. I wondered if a sock was missing."

He pauses and I'm pretty certain this is the last time he'll take my call. But then he says, "It's interesting you're asking that. At the time I thought it was odd that he would fold his socks together, like when you do the laundry. So no, both socks were there."

That ends my lucky streak pretty fast. Good thing I didn't waste money on the Power Ball.

I pull up a map of the UGA campus on my computer and zoom in on the cemetery. Then I google the address for the Sigma house. It's on River Road. So could someone at the fraternity see the cemetery from the roof? I really doubt it, not with all the trees in the way, and it was at night. So how did Lonnie and Adam know Tommy was there? They had to be near the entrance.

"What are you looking for?" Brian asks, nodding at the campus map on my monitor.

Dang! I've got to put a bell around his neck, or move my desk so he can't keep sneaking up on me.

I show him the Sigma house on River Road and the entrance to the cemetery further up. "I can't believe Lonnie or Adam just happened to see Tommy Martin walking along in front of the fraternity and decided he was on his way to a rendez-vous."

"Any luck with the sock?" he asks.

"Olsen says both Tommy's socks were there."

"Could it have been Lonnie's or Adam's?"

I shake my head. "Then how would Nate know about it?"

"Suppose Darrell found it and showed it to Charlotte. She gave it to Nate to run tests."

"How does a scenario like that even play out?" I ask.

"I don't know. I'm just thinking out loud."

I'm tempted to tell Brian to go think out loud someplace else but sometimes he comes up with a decent idea. I just need to get him to concentrate.

"Let's try a little experiment," I say.

I push Brian onto the daybed and then take the sash from my bathrobe and tie it around his head so he can't see.

"Okay, it's the party at the frat house," I say. "Adam has supposedly told Darrell about beating up Tommy."

Brian sits quietly. Is he thinking through the chain of events or wondering if we have any salami for a sandwich. I can't tell him to concentrate because then he'll get mad.

"Darrell starts worrying about the bad press for the fraternity and the football team," Brian says. "If there's an investigation, and the police come snooping around with suspicions, it could take a while."

"Okay."

"But if there's hard evidence—a bloody sock—with both Tommy's and Adam's DNA on it, the case is open and shut."

"I like it."

"So Darrell waits for Adam to pass out and then he sneaks into his room . . ."

"Uh-uh," I interrupt. "That won't work. Dawn Shipley said Darrell went home with Charlotte that night."

"Even better. Darrell and Charlotte have some pillow talk. He tells her about Tommy. With a brother like Nate, she'd be in tuned to all that forensic stuff. She tells Darrell to go back to the house and look for evidence."

"I love it!"

Well, I don't exactly love it. There's definitely some flaws. But it gets me thinking in another direction.

I say, "Dawn Shipley also said that after Charlotte and Darrell spent that night together, he decided to run for student body president that next year. Maybe she put the bug in his ear about doing something more with his life than being a football jock. And if he 'solved' the murder of Tommy Martin, that would be a win for Darrell. I doubt there was any real loyalty between Darrell and . . . anyone."

Now Brian's shaking his head. "But he never breaks the case. Why not?"

"Crap." I sit down next to Brian and tug on the blindfold to remove it. He stops me.

"This is kind of fun," he says. "Why don't you go get some food and see if I can guess what it is without seeing it?"

See? I knew he was thinking about food.

"I've got a better idea," I say.

I open my desk drawer and pull out the headphones I stashed there. I also have a ping-pong ball from Sarah. Brian can't see what I've got but he's definitely on the right track. By the time I turn back around to the daybed, he's stripped off his boxers.

Here's another advantage to not having kids. You can have sex anywhere, anytime. I clamp the headphones on him and he giggles like a kid who has seen a woman's breasts for the first time.

The ping-pong ball in the mouth gives him pause and he takes it back out.

"Hang on now," he says. "How am I supposed to give you a safe word?"

"This is an exercise in trust." I shove the ball back in and then tie my bathrobe belt around his mouth so he can't spit it out. Then the eye mask from the airline. The final step is binding his hands behind his back with a scarf. He's definitely worried now but I sit on his lap for a moment and kiss his face.

Once he relaxes, I drop to my knees. I pull his knees apart and tease him a bit with some tongue action, then stand and tickle my tongue behind his ear. He doesn't know what to expect next, or where.

Our sensory deprivation game goes great until he reaches his climax. I hear a pop but I don't think much about it because I'm in the throes of my own climax.

Brian is really adding to the sensation by jerking and thrashing around. Then I hear labored breathing that sounds like a barking seal. What the heck is he doing? And why is his face turning red?

I jump off his lap, and rip away the headphones, the blindfold, and the scarf around his mouth. Meanwhile, he's wrestling his hands free. He clutches his throat. His eyes are watering and his mouth is open but no sound is coming out. Dear God, where's the ping pong ball?

He crushed it in his mouth! That's the popping sound I heard. And now he's sucked it back into his throat.

I hop up on the bed behind him, wrap my arms around his chest, and squeeze, driving my fists into his ribcage. Nothing. He's making little moaning sounds like he's dying. I'm sure he will if I don't do something fast.

I jump off the bed and run around in front. Tears are streaming down his face.

"Open your mouth!"

He does, but now I'm afraid to reach in and get the ball. What if I push it in farther? We'll show up at the emergency room and the doctor will have to remove the ball with forceps. In the meantime, Brian is dead. It's back to the Heimlich.

I slam my fists into his chest two more times before the crushed ball goes flying across the room in a swirl of spit. He gasps for air then breaks into a racking cough. I keep my arms around him as I burst into tears.

"I'm so sorry," I wail, snuggling my face on his back. "I never expected that to happen."

He tumbles to his side on the bed and pulls me around to lie on his chest. I can hear his heart thudding at like 400 beats a minute.

I'm still crying while he strokes my hair.

"Damn, Babe," he says. "That was fantastic."

CHAPTER TWENTY-SEVEN

Brian is psyched to ride along to Lonnie's farm. He wants to meet a real-life hermit like Ted Kaczynski, the Unabomber. I should probably leave Sarah a note to feed Brian's fish in case we never return.

On the ride south, he tries to impress Cynthia with his knowledge of BBQ joints and who has the best Brunswick Stew in the state. Sure, he's flirting. Any man would, considering how beautiful she is.

Cynthia has concocted some story about us wanting to buy a goat farm. Brian is all for it. Interesting how when I make up wacky stuff, he shoots it down, but when a pretty woman does . . .

"Uh, we don't know anything about goats," I say.

"That's the whole point," she says. "I invited you to the farm to get an up-close look at what's involved in raising goats."

"And if he asks where we're buying this farm?"

"Don't worry about it," she says. "This is just a good way to ease into the real reason for the visit."

When we get to the farm, Cynthia tells us to stay in car. That's fine with me since the dogs are barking like mad. She gets out and yells at the dogs, calling them by name. They immediately stop barking and jump on the fence like boisterous puppies, whining and drooling and sniffing her scent.

Obviously, she comes here often enough that the dogs know her. On the drive down, she told us about living on this farm until Lonnie Junior was old enough to start school. But then she wanted her son to attend a more urban school and Lonnie wouldn't move. Their relationship wasn't going anywhere either. That's when she decided to cut her losses and move back with her parents in Atlanta but she still brought Lonnie Junior to the farm on a regular basis. From the way she talked, the son has a good relationship with his dad.

She opens the gate and the dogs nearly knock her down with their demands for affection. One by one, she kisses and pats before giving each the command to 'sit'. Once she has them all calmed down, she motions for us to come on in.

Good Rachel is in a hair-pulling brawl with bad Rachel, swearing up a storm at being dragged into a situation that will only end with a throat being ripped out. Brian decides to be a gentleman this morning and lets me go first, but I give him a shove through the open gate.

The dogs aren't really sitting; they're resting on their haunches, their muscles taut, waiting for Cynthia to blink so they can pounce.

"I'm going to let them come over one at a time so they can get your scent," she says.

If I wet my pants, will they leave me alone?

"Dante," she says and one of the Shepherds stands and trots over to Brian.

He sniffs Brian's shoes and then his hand. Once we both pass inspection, she calls him back and sends the next one. It's going well—although I'm sweating like a kick-boxer who drank too much last night—until the massive Rottweiler gets his turn. As soon as he comes up to me, he shoves his huge snout into my crotch. I'd love to push him away but I'm really attached to my hands.

"Lucifer!" Cynthia yells and he skulks back to her. "You behave or time out."

His ears lie back and he actually cowers.

She tells us to come along so we scuff through the dirt yard and around to the back. On the shady side of the house, I see food bowls and water pans, all with bite marks in them. I'm amazed any of these dogs still have their teeth.

I hear a loud motor running in the barn out back. Lonnie must be working on something. Cynthia goes in first. I stop at the door and the Rottweiler, who evidently was right on my heels, gooses me from behind. I yelp and turn. He at least has the decency to look guilty.

Lonnie is at a work bench on the far side of the barn, his back to us. The rattling noise comes from a rickety old gas generator. Cynthia cups her hands to her mouth and yells 'Hey!' He turns and I see sparks from a bench grinder. He's sharpening an axe. Brian backs up into me which pushes me back and onto Lucifer's muzzle once again. I swear when I glare at the dog, he smiles.

The generator sputters to a stop. Cynthia strides over and throws her arms around Lonnie. She pulls his face down for a kiss but his eyes stay on us. Does he ever go out to the woods and practice throwing that axe at trees? I really don't want to be decapitated today.

Cynthia talks quietly to him for a minute. I assume she's telling him about our goat farm aspirations. She motions us over for introductions.

The first thing he says is, "I've seen you before. You came by here a week ago. Was that your drone I shot down?"

Our jaws drop.

"I'm not an idiot," he says. "I just don't like people."

"I'm really sorry about that," I say. "We weren't sure we had the right house."

"And you thought if you stopped in, I'd tell you all about my goats."

Cynthia jumps in to save us. "I told them I'd meet them but something came up."

I don't think he's buying it, but he lets it go. "Where's this farm you're buying?"

See? I knew it would come up.

Again, Cynthia comes to our rescue. "They haven't made any decisions yet. Why don't you chill?"

She pats his pockets, then reaches in and pulls out one of those little wooden marijuana holders and grinds a metal pinch hitter into the hollow section that holds the pot. She actually puts the little pipe in his mouth and lights it. He takes a deep breath and holds it for a second before blowing out the smoke.

Cynthia packs it again and hands it to me. Swell. It's been years—decades—since I smoked. I'll probably end up choking and hacking.

I take just a little puff for starters. It tastes a lot different than pot did when I was in college. Brian goes next. By the time the little pipe is reloaded and handed to Cynthia, I'm feeling a little fuzzy. I hear them talking but I have no idea what the conversation is about. It's like in the Charlie Brown movies where the parents talk but the sound is just 'wa wa wa'.

I'm also a little unsteady on my feet. There are some bales of straw in the corner. Maybe I'll just sit down for a minute and get my bearings. I move in that direction but the bones in my legs liquefy. I try not to panic, reminding myself that I don't live on an alien planet where bad guys can disintegrate bones; there is no disease that spontaneously turns bone to jelly; I'm just high.

Without making a scene, I casually reach out for the nearest bale and have a seat. I'll just sit here a minute and pretend to be listening to their conversation while I collect myself. Only the talking seems to have stopped. I glance over at the group. They're all looking at me.

Two Brians walk toward me. I blink to get him pulled back together; when that doesn't work I wink one eye shut. That's better.

"Aaaarrrrreeeee yyyyyooooouuuuu ooooookkkkkaaaaayyyyy?" he says.

I nod but somehow I have acquired super-human abilities because Brian suddenly disappears. Even though I just convinced myself I'm not on an alien planet, I guess I am because I'm currently staring at a bird that is walking upside down. I think it's a pigeon. It's surrounded by a halo of light. Either that, or it has walked into a death ray. It doesn't explode in a burst of feathers so I guess it's a halo. Is this some intelligent being in disguise?

It is, and it is beaming me up to its perch. I'm flying! Soaring through the air, looking down on the farm, and green pastures, and a little pond.

"Jeez, she's snoring, Man," someone says.

My head lolls to one side and I see Brian looking down at me. Holy crap! He's flying too! He takes my arm and sits me up on the straw bale. I guess I laid down . . . and passed out. He sits on the bale next to me and I slump onto his shoulder for support.

A hand reaches out to my face; it's cool, and it's connected to Cynthia.

"You back with us?" she asks.

Wow, am I high.

Cynthia thinks maybe I need some fresh air but there's no way I can walk. Lonnie suggests I lie back down for a few minutes and he'll show Brian around the farm. I grip Brian's arm and plead with him not to leave me alone with the dogs.

The solution? Lonnie cuts open one of the bales, piles some straw into a wheelbarrow, and flops me onto the bedding. My arms and legs hang out over the edges but I'm still in a vegetative state so what can I do?

I'm moving. I'm out of the barn, and Brian is walking alongside the barrow so I assume Lonnie is carting me around. I'm afraid to look up and back to see.

Our first tour stop is the chicken coop. There's a white chicken, and two red ones. A brown chicken is off in the far corner with three little chicks. At the back is the classic wood plank that leads up into the coop where I assume they lay their eggs. My eyes are still free-ranging when I spot a black chicken that looks like it's wearing a feather hat. Okay, someone's playing with me. I lean my head up and focus harder. The chicken has feather boots on too! I can't even see its feet for all the feathers. Another chicken struts out of the coop with feathers swirled all around its body like it got caught in a clothes dryer.

I snort out a laugh. I'm not on an alien planet; I'm in the middle of a Dr. Seuss dream. Lonnie tells us the names of these odd birds but I instantly forget. The three of them talk about how many eggs per day, and when chickens molt. I'm busy staring at the swirly-feathered chicken. It's coming towards me and I swear it's spinning like it'll fly up into the air like a top.

Then suddenly, the wheelbarrow is moving again. This stop is a small field of baby goats. The kids find it highly amusing that Lonnie is hauling people. They frisk and hop and kick out their legs. One of them jumps up on top of me and smells my face before leaping back off. Within seconds, another kid hops up to bleat in my face and prance on my chest. I can't help laughing. Its little hooves poke me all over. Then a white and gray one steps on my cheek and launches off my forehead. A little black one leaps up and his hoof stomps me right in the throat. I hack out a cough.

"Hey!" Lonnie yells as he claps his hands. The last kid clamors off me and they all frolic away.

"This place is fantastic," Brian says. "When Reggie said you had a farm, I thought it was going to be cornfields and cows."

"Who's Reggie?" Lonnie asks.

I tip my head back to look up at him, a goofy grin on my face. "Reggie Riggs. He told us where you live."

Suddenly Lonnie's face doesn't look so friendly but then it's hard to tell with all that hair.

"And why were you talking to Reggie?" he asks.

The good-times haze I've been floating in whisks away. I don't think we have bonded enough with Lonnie to start talking about murder. Although, his eyes sort of look murderous at the moment. I glance over at Cynthia for a rescue but she just gives me a shrug, like I may as well get the conversation going.

"I'm looking into the death of Tommy Martin."

Lonnie raises the handles of the wheelbarrow and dumps me onto the ground. "Get out!" he bellows. The dogs jump to high-alert, barking and snarling at me. My high is gone.

CHAPTER TWENTY-EIGHT

Cynthia isn't at all intimidated by Lonnie's outburst.

"No!" she yells. Then for good measure, she slaps her hand onto his chest. "I want to know, too. All this time, I thought it was me and Little Lonnie. I think it's time you come clean."

Lonnie grabs her by the arm and tries to drag her away from us.

"We'll talk about this later," he says. "After they're gone."

She jerks her arm free. "Oh, no. I've heard that bullshit before. We're going to talk about it right now."

While they're arguing, Brian helps me up and brushes some of the dirt off my butt.

"Maybe we should go," he says quietly.

"No way," I whisper back.

"Look," Cynthia says, "let's all calm down. We'll go inside, get something to drink, and just talk."

Good idea. And make sure none of those dogs follow us.

LONNIE'S LIVING room is vintage farmer: an old quilt thrown over an even older sofa, towels covering the seats of two easy chairs, a boxy coffee table from the sixties, and a thread-bare Oriental rug. I'm guessing all this stuff belonged to the previous owner.

Cynthia scoots into the kitchen, hopefully to get us something cool and refreshing. My throat is so dry, every time I swallow, the sides stick together. Lonnie follows her and I hear them hissing at each other in hushed voices.

I plunk down on the sofa, relieved that I made it without being drawn and quartered by the dogs. Brian stays on his feet. I'm sure he wants to be ready to boogie out of here at a moment's notice, like if Lonnie comes back with his shotgun.

The women seem to have won the battle, however, because Lonnie skulks into the living room and flops down into one of the easy chairs. Brian takes his cue from Lonnie and sits next to me. Cynthia follows with a tray of drinks.

I take one. It looks pretty clear so I'm guessing it isn't lemonade. There's no ice, and when I get the glass closer to my nose I smell sulfur. Great. Tap water. At this point it doesn't matter. I'm so thirsty, I guzzle half of it down. I'm reminded of the Clint Eastwood movie where he's crawling through the desert, his face blistered, his lips cracked. The water revives me. The goop in my head is beginning to resemble a brain again.

Cynthia sits in the easy chair next to Lonnie and leans on the arm closer to him. "Tell us about the night in the cemetery."

Lonnie bows his head and stares at his knotted fingers in his lap. "What do you want to know?"

"It was you and Adam, wasn't it," she says.

He looks over at her with tears in his eyes. I can't believe it. Here's a guy who's probably six-four, and still looks like a linebacker—except for the long dirty hair and beard.

She hops up and drags a small stool over where she can sit at his feet. "Okay, let's go back a little earlier," she says as she rubs his knee. "The party at the Sigma House."

He startles like he's surprised she remembers. Then he puts his hand on top of hers. He shakes his head for so long that I'm sure he has clammed up for good.

But then he says, "It was the same old thing. The place was packed and we were running out of beer."

Brian and I look at each other. "Beer run," we say at the same time.

"Yeah. So Adam and I take his car to get more. We're passing the entrance to the cemetery when we see Tommy bopping along without a care in the world. Adam pulls over and gets out. I can either stay in the car or go with him." He chokes out a groan. "And I make the biggest mistake of my life. I go with him."

"It's okay," Cynthia says, giving him a moment to get it together. "Just get it out."

"Tommy walks way back to the river. We watch for a minute to see if he's meeting another guy. He unrolls this little rug he's carrying and puts it on the ground. Then he strips down to nothing and kneels on the rug, like he's gonna say a prayer.

"I'm so freaked out, I just stare at him. I mean, it was so bizarre. I think he must have heard someone coming but instead of jumping up and running away, he picks up a pair of handcuffs! He snaps one end on his wrist, and he's trying to get the other one on while holding his hands behind his back. Adam loses it.

"He yells 'You gotta be fuckin' kiddin' me' and charges Tommy. He just goes berserk, kicking Tommy, calling him a faggot. Tommy curls into a ball, but Adam just keeps kicking." Lonnie's voice cracks again. "He pulled him up by his hair and punched him in the face."

Cynthia pats his knee. "Take a breath. You can do it."

I remember Brian saying that sometimes the ones who protest the loudest are the ones trying to hide their true feelings. And Cynthia said she wondered if Adam was battling demons.

Lonnie breathes in and blows out a shaky sigh. "It took all my strength to pull Adam off. He was out of control. I think he would have killed Tommy if I hadn't been there."

He reaches into his pocket for the pinch hitter and takes another toke, probably hoping to numb all the feelings eating away at him. I can't say I blame him.

He blows out the smoke and continues. "Tommy scrambled over to this tomb where his clothes were. He was pulling himself up when Adam broke away from me and punched him on the side of the head. Tommy fell against the step and the next thing I see, there's blood coming out."

Lonnie sucks in a quivering breath, his chest heaving. I think Cynthia may be crying too.

His voice comes out broken as he continues. "I dragged Adam away again. He stood there panting . . . like some rabid animal. Then he saw the blood too, I guess, because he freaked out. He knew he was in trouble." Lonnie's voice turns exasperated. "So what does he do? He runs away!"

"What a prick," I say.

Lonnie's head whips up like he forgot we were there. Crap! When will I learn to keep my mouth shut? If he clams up now, it'll be all my fault.

But he just nods his head. I make eye contact with him but I don't see the anger like before. Just pain. I look past his gruff disguise and see a bewildered man who still can't quite fathom how he got himself into this mess.

"I couldn't believe it," he says. "I knelt down next to Tommy and checked for a pulse." He looks at Cynthia. "I swear he was still alive. But Adam is screaming at me to hurry up or he's going to leave me."

"Why doesn't that surprise me?" she say.

Lonnie swipes at his runny nose with his sleeve. "We made it back to the car without anyone driving by and seeing us. Then instead of going to the liquor store on Oak Street, Adam turned around and went to the store on Baxter. You know, like we'd have an alibi about where we were if Tommy reported us."

He hands the pinch hitter to Brian. I can't believe he can handle another toke. As he packs the pipe, he says, "So you buy beer and go back to the party."

"Adam went inside to buy the beer. I said I wanted to wait in the car. And once he went in, I slipped out and went to the phone booth at the front of the building. I was going to call 911. But the phone was busted."

Despair crawls over Lonnie like insects. He rubs his arms as though he can brush off the vermin. Then he places his hands on his legs. I'm afraid he's going to get up and walk away.

"You drive back to the fraternity. . ." I prompt him.

He just nods while he massages his thighs, digging into the muscle, trying to squeeze out his guilt.

Brian asks, "Was Adam feeling guilty too?" Then he lights the pinch hitter and takes a long toke.

"Hell no! He couldn't wait to tell Darrell all about beating the shit out of Tommy."

"Was this in front of everyone?" Cynthia asks.

"No. He pulled Darrell aside." Lonnie snorts out a laugh. "He thought Darrell would be so proud of him. But he was pissed. He called Adam an idiot. Dragged us both into the kitchen where he could really ream us out. He was saying stuff like 'don't expect me to come to your rescue if Tommy presses charges'. And Adam says 'Cool it, he couldn't see my face.' Then he tells Darrell we have an alibi with the liquor store, and Darrell calls him an idiot again."

Two seconds later, Brian chokes on the smoke in his lungs. It serves him right. I don't see how any of them is still conscious. He takes a long drink of water then tries to pass off the pinch hitter to me. I scoff and push his hand away. And now Lonnie has stopped talking again!

"Okay," I say to Lonnie, "you're in the kitchen arguing."

Lonnie nods. "I say 'I think we should call an ambulance', but Darrell says 'no way. What's done is done.' Then he tells us to get back out to the party and make sure lots of people see us."

"Do you remember Darrell leaving?" I ask.

Lonnie shakes his head.

"But he did," Cynthia says. "Amanda Bradley told me about it. Darrell was the drunkest she'd ever seen him. And he was hanging on Charlotte Wilkins of all people." She turns to me. "Don't get me wrong, Charlotte was sweet. She was one of those peppy, go-getters. But she was on the outside looking in. You know what I mean? She tried too hard to belong. She wasn't a real beauty. I mean, that didn't matter to most people, but it did to Darrell. And she certainly wasn't craven enough to suit Darrell's sexual tastes."

I turn to Lonnie. "You must have left the party first."

Lonnie's whole torso nods as he remembers back. 'I went to Cynthia's."

"And you were acting so strange," she says, "because you were afraid Tommy was dead."

His legs bob with agitation. "I thought about calling the police from your place, but then I got worried that they might trace the call back to you. What if they said you were part of it? I couldn't let that happen."

I really feel sorry for the poor guy. If anyone got caught in the wrong place at the wrong time, it was Lonnie Taggart.

"Every day I kick myself for letting those two talk me out of calling for help when I had the chance. Every fucking day."

Cynthia rises up off the stool to sit on his lap. She pulls his head to her chest and holds him tight. I know she wants to comfort him but the story isn't over quite yet.

I keep my voice low as I say, "The next morning, you go home for spring break. You don't really know what happened to Tommy."

"I kept lying to myself," Lonnie says. "Like 'Tommy's okay. He woke up with a bad headache and staggered home.' Shit like that."

"But then you came back to school after the break and the guys at the fraternity were talking about Tommy being dead."

"Yeah. And I'm still making up bullshit to ease my conscience. Like 'he was dead before we even got to Adam's car'."

Cynthia brushes his matted hair away from his face. He's sweating so much it's dripping out of the bottom of his beard.

"But then somebody showed me the newspaper story and I saw that Tommy drowned in the river. And I think, 'that bastard Adam went back and made sure he was dead'. That's when the guilt really grabbed me. If I'd called someone, Tommy would be alive today."

I'm trying desperately to think of something to say to make him feel better about what he did but the truth is, he screwed up. All I can do now is encourage him to get the whole story out.

"You confront Adam," I say.

"Yeah. I jumped him, accused him of murdering Tommy. I was as out of control as he was that Friday night in the cemetery. I think I might have wanted to kill him."

Lonnie pauses like he's trying to get something straight in his mind. "The crazy thing is, Adam was really whaling on me, too. You know what he said? He thought *I* went back and finished off Tommy!"

My head is clear enough that I stand. I've got to walk while I think through all this. Lonnie looks like he could use a break anyway. He's certainly purged his guilt this afternoon. Cynthia takes the pinch hitter and packs herself another bowl. They've both been through the wringer.

It's interesting that Adam and Lonnie each thought the other one rolled Tommy into the river. In a way, they cancel each other's guilt out. And it reinforces my suspicions of Darrell.

I'm pacing in front of Cynthia just as she blows out a cloud of smoke and I plow right through the noxious fumes. Oh, great, now I'm fogging up again.

CHAPTER TWENTY-NINE

"What about a sock?" I ask Lonnie. "Did you lose one that night? Or maybe Adam did?"

For the first time today, I see Lonnie smile. Well not really a smile I guess, but his cheek kind of crinkles; he thinks I'm bonkers.

"No, I didn't lose a sock," he says, and then he leans back in his chair. His eyebrows relax, and he's no longer grinding his teeth. He takes a deep breath and blows it out, like the proverbial boulder has been lifted off his shoulders; or at least a few chunks have been chiseled off.

Cynthia gets up and stretches her back. She twists at the waist a couple times before she turns on a portable radio sitting on a shelf. Country music fades in and out.

"You need new batteries," she says and drifts into the kitchen. This time Lonnie stays with us in the living room.

"So Reggie's still selling cars," he says.

"Yeah. BMWs," Brian tells him. "He seems to be doing pretty good."

The conversation dies before it even gets started. What do you talk about with a man who has cut himself off from the world? I doubt he wants to talk about his college football days. With only this crappy radio, he probably doesn't keep up with current events.

"You know," Cynthia says when comes back out with a pitcher of fresh lukewarm, sulfur-laced water and a plate of deviled eggs. "Reggie is the only guy from the team that makes an effort to keep in touch. Although for a while, Darrell and Adam would call me out of the blue, ask how Lonnie was doing."

Lonnie snarls his upper lip. "I'm sure they were checking up on me, to see if I'd told Cynthia what happened."

"Did you ever wonder if Darrell was the one who went back to the cemetery?" I ask.

"Nah," he says right away. But then I can see that he's thinking about it.

Cynthia's shoulders drop and she rolls her eyes. "It all makes sense now. Especially Darrell acting so valiant, looking out for his good buddy Lonnie."

The minute she sets the plate of eggs down, Brian pounces.

He shoves one into his mouth and has barely chewed it when he moans. "These are delicious."

It's not that I don't think men can cook, but I do wonder if Lonnie washed his hands before he peeled the eggs. Was there chicken shit under his fingernails? And how long ago did he make these? I don't think he has power, so I doubt if he has a refrigerator.

Everyone else takes one; I can't make up some BS like I'm allergic to eggs so I pick up one and take a tiny bite. It is delicious.

I reach for another. "I saw this chicken once. It had black floppy feathers on its head, just like a Hedda Hopper hat. And its feet were covered in black feathers too. It was weird."

Everyone is laughing but me.

"Babe," Brian says, throwing an arm over my shoulder. "We just saw it out back. It's one of Lonnie's."

Crap! I'm still high.

Cynthia perches on the stool in front of Lonnie again to show him pictures on her phone of Lonnie Junior and his new girlfriend.

"Yeah, he was up here last Saturday," Lonnie says. "Kept insisting they were just friends." They both chuckle.

For a moment he's almost forgotten what happened with Tommy, but then his grief circles around again. His shoulders slump, his mouth turns down. He's going to be stuck with this burden for the rest of his life.

Cynthia picks up on his mood swing.

"You know," she says, "if you count the years you've kept yourself prisoner here, I'd say you've paid for what you did."

* * *

WE DROP Cynthia off after pigging out on ribs at some local joint on the south side. It's dark when we get home. As our headlights sweep across the yard, I see a package on the front porch. It must be Jackson's used drone.

Brian texts him to arrange a rendez-vous to drop it off. I trot ahead to go to the bathroom. When I stand at the mirror, I see little goat hoof prints all over my shirt. Geez, I looked like this at the restaurant? Why didn't anyone tell me?

"You want to ride with me to meet Jackson?" Brian asks when I come out of the bathroom.

"Yeah. Let me change my shirt first." I pull it tight so Brian can see all the dirty prints.

"You look fine," he says.

Hmmm. The next time he tells me I'm beautiful, I'll probably have a black chunk of pepper in my teeth.

JACKSON IS waiting for us at the same kid's house where we borrowed the drone. We're all standing in the kid's driveway when a car drives by and screeches to a halt. Swell, it's Jake. And I was just about to remind Jackson that the Bat Shit Crazy concert is still a no-go.

"What's going on?" Jake growls as he stomps towards us.

Jackson takes a step back. Poor kid. No wonder Gwen's oldest son Sam never comes home to visit. I'm sure as soon as Allison and Jackson graduate, they'll get as far away from Jake as they can, too.

"Jackson was just showing us his drone," I say.

"Right. You drove all the way over here to see it," Jake says. He yanks it away and scrutinizes it, turning it over and back. "What happened to all the scratches on it?"

Urk! Isn't this just my luck? I replaced the drone with a better one.

I flounder for an excuse. "Brian found some polish that's supposed to—"

"Polish. To get rid of a gouge in plastic. Let me see it."

"Okay, fine!"

I confess to borrowing the drone. I don't really say it was shot out of the air; more that it was lost.

Instead of chewing us out for being irresponsible, Jake clamps a hairy paw on Jackson's shoulder and squeezes until the kid winces.

"When are you gonna learn not to trust people," Jake says, pressing harder. "They'll lie to your face and cheat you every chance they get."

"Screw you, Jake!" I yell. "How much do you think your intimidation and brow-beating will help Jackson? Probably as much as it did Sam."

"Mind your own business."

"My business includes my niece and nephews who are being abused by a bully," I snap back.

Jake bares his teeth at me. "You don't know the first thing about raising kids."

"Neither do you!"

Brian drags me back to the car before I can spit on the jerk.

249

A TALL glass of wine later, I've settled down. But the next time I'm alone with Gwen, I'm going to ask her if she's afraid of Jake, too. I think about the woman at the Fuller House who lost the use of her hand because her jackass husband slammed it in a door. Did Audrey start helping other women when she saw her sister in a miserable marriage?

That reminds me, I want to google River Mill Apartments. Cynthia was pretty sure Charlotte lived there when she was at school.

"Hey!" I yell down the hallway to our bedroom where Brian is watching some kind of sports. "You should come see this."

He wanders in quicker than usual. Must be commercials, or his team is losing.

"Look how close River Mill is to the cemetery," I say.

He leans in to the map on the screen. "It's right next door. If the party had been at the apartment complex, it would make a lot more sense."

"The beer run pulls it together." I scroll down the map and show Brian where the Sigma House is on River Road. "Adam saw Tommy and everything went to shit."

"So now all we have to do is figure out how Darrell finished the job."

"Yeah. That's all." I pick up my wine glass and drain the last drop.

"I need my own beer run," Brian says. He turns to leave and I tag along.

"So Darrell is at the party when Adam comes back all excited about beating up Tommy," I say as we head for the stairs. "He's pissed. He tells Adam he's on his own if this comes back to bite him."

"But then he starts thinking how great it will be if Tommy is dead. That whole payback for assuming Darrell was gay."

"Homophobia."

250

Brian is suspiciously quiet: either he's examining his life for tale-tell signs of paranoia or he's wondering if he can get away with popping popcorn after the huge meal he ate at the barbeque place.

"After the party," he says after he opens a beer, "he goes to the cemetery, drags Tommy down to the river and dumps his body. Then he heads over to Charlotte's apartment."

"No, no. They were seen leaving the party together. And they were both drunk."

"Oh, right."

I pour myself another glass of wine; not as tall this time. And I get some water, too. The whole hydrating thing. I even take a sip to prove I mean well. Although I'm probably still going to wake up with a headache tomorrow.

"So how does he bump off Tommy?" Brian says. "Ask Charlotte to hang on just a second, he has to duck into the cemetery for something?"

Good question. I ease down onto a kitchen chair feeling ever-so-slightly tipsy. Geez, I'm high all afternoon and clearly on my way to getting drunk tonight. Am I going to end up in rehab someday?

An idea thrashes its way through the muck in my brain until it surfaces. "How about this? They go to her apartment, all drunk and disorderly. They get it on, then he pretends to go to sleep." I give that a moment to percolate. "Once Charlotte is asleep, he gets dressed, sneaks out, goes to the cemetery and dumps Tommy."

"Then what?" Brian rummages through the cupboards. "He goes back to her apartment? Doesn't he need an alibi for the whole night?"

"Sure, he goes back, gets undressed, sneaks back in bed. Done."

Brian turns to look at me and squints his eyes. "So what about the sock? How does Charlotte know there's blood on it? Why would she save it? She doesn't know what he did."

"Good point. Even if she knows it's blood, she'd just figure Darrell stumbled and scraped his ankle. They were supposedly drunk."

Brian holds up a finger. "Unless she followed him."

"Why would she follow him? What if he was getting dressed and sneaking back to the fraternity like a dog? That would be totally humiliating to watch him skulk away."

Crap. None of this is making sense. And now I'm being distracted by the idea of popcorn, too. I can fight the craving but bad Rachel will just keep niggling at me until I relent. I push Brian aside and pull out the box I hid on the top shelf. At least while the corn is popping, I can think this through.

"Okay, let's go back to the party," he says. "That's where it all began. Why is Charlotte even at the party? Cynthia said she was sort of B level. Why would she be at an A level party?"

"Oh! I've got this. Dawn Ralston said Charlotte never joined a sorority. She was a little sister for the Sigma house. Spent all her time there. I'm guessing she had a major crush on Darrell from the beginning, but he always looked at her as a pal, a gopher. So she's at the party. The guys take care of the booze but she's probably playing hostess, putting out snacks, emptying ashtrays."

I futz around for a second, pretending to be Suzy Homemaker. "Maybe she's in the kitchen. Or better yet, in a pantry looking for more salsa or chips when Darrell drags Adam away from the party. Adam's all hyped about beating up Tommy. She hears the conversation."

"That would work," he says. He gets out two bowls while I pull apart the top of the popcorn bag.

"Darrell acts all pissed, but what if the more he drinks, the more he thinks he'd love to go over to the cemetery and gloat over Tommy."

"If he's even still there," Brian adds.

"Right! But how can he leave the party to go look? He needs an excuse. He knows where Charlotte lives."

"How?"

252

"I don't know." I wave my hand in annoyance. "He just does. So he puts the moves on her. Dawn isn't at the party. She left for spring break Friday morning." Even as I say it, I don't buy it. "How could Charlotte fall for that? She's seen him with a parade of women. Why would she think it was going to be anything but a drunken one-night stand?"

"Are you kidding?" Brian says. "She's been carrying a torch for the guy since she first laid eyes on him. This could be her big chance to win him over."

"Oh, my God. She might even have it in the back of her mind to get pregnant; or tell him she got pregnant that night."

Brian grabs a fistful of popcorn and attempts to shove it all into his mouth. He succeeds.

"Okay," he says between chomps, "for the moment let's say they stumble over to her apartment. As they pass the cemetery entrance, they both secretly glance that way to see if Tommy is staggering home."

"But they don't see anything. They get to her apartment, have sloppy sex, then they both pretend to go to sleep."

"Maybe she even passes out, but she hears him getting dressed—"

"Or hears him stumbling blindly through her apartment," I say. I know with 100% certainty that men are incapable of tiptoeing. "She thinks maybe he's going to sneak over to the cemetery. She decides to follow him."

"Right. If he's really just going home, she'll go back to her apartment, crying her eyes out."

"Oh!" I yell. "What if Darrell did go home but she went to the cemetery and dragged Tommy down the hill."

"Why?"

"She thinks she can somehow frame Darrell for the murder. What better way to keep him under her thumb."

"If she can find some evidence to link Darrell to the crime," Brian says as he reaches for another handful of popcorn.

"Yeah." I shake my head. "That's highly unlikely. It makes a lot more sense that Darrell wants revenge."

"Charlotte lags behind. She doesn't want Darrell to see her hiding behind a tree at the cemetery."

"Maybe she's not even sure where the fight took place."

Brian nods. "Did Darrell?"

"Adam must have told him it was near the bridge. At a mausoleum. She wanders back that way, maybe she sees the blood on the steps."

"But no body!"

I'm so excited I forget to eat any popcorn. "She hears rustling in the woods. Sounds like somebody huffing and puffing. She runs back to the entrance but waits to see if it's Darrell."

"Why wouldn't she just confront him right there. 'Aha! Caught 'ya'."

I shake my head. "Not if she's in love with him. She doesn't want to get him in trouble, she wants him to love her, too."

"I guess," Brian concedes. "So she books it back to her apartment, gets undressed, jumps back in the bed. Sure enough here comes Darrell. Takes his clothes off and hops back into bed with her. Now she's in seventh heaven. And he has an alibi that he spent the night with her."

"I like it," I say. "In the morning, she gets up early, wants to fix her hair, put on make-up whatever. She gathers up his clothes. Maybe she's going to wash them. That's always a good stall tactic in the movies, to keep someone from leaving. She notices one of his socks is wet. She touches it." I demonstrate by looking at my fingers. "It's blood. Is it Darrell's or Tommy's? She doesn't know what to do. Show him? Help him cover it up?"

"If she has the hots for him, it seems like she'd want to help him."

"Yeah," I say. Then I snap my fingers. "What if this is a little test. Was he just pulling her chain last night or does he really like her? She decides to get frisky and see if he's still lovey dovey this morning. If he wants to hightail it out of there, she's going to keep the sock. Maybe use it against him."

"I'd like to get lovey dovey," Brian says.

"I'm sure you would," I say, basically ignoring him. "We've got to see if Nate tested a sock. Then we'll see if it was Darrell's DNA."

"You know what I'd like to try?" he says. "Us in the bathtub, you on top. When I get close, you hold me under, like Ricco was saying at his sex shop."

Look at what I've done. It started with the ping-pong ball gag; who knows where it will end? With a belt around his neck like Michael Hutchence?

"I think I better take a CPR course before we try something like that," I say. "So do you think Nate ran an actual report of his findings? Could it be in a computer somewhere or printed out?"

Brian throws a kernel of popcorn at me and when I look over, he wags his eyebrows at me. Oh, Baby what a smooth move. How can I resist?

I try my best to ignore his advances. "I wonder if Charlotte got some of Darrell's DNA for comparison, like saliva or a hair follicle."

"I'd be glad to provide you with a DNA sample."

"Silence!" I yell. It's one of the things I read about being a dominatrix. Taking control. "You need to hook up with Nate again and I'm coming with you this time."

"No way," he says, but I can see my sudden attitude change has him confused. "You know he won't talk if you're there."

I jump up and grab the fly swatter off the top of the refrigerator. While glaring at him, I wave the swatter through the air, making it whistle.

"One more word . . ." I say through clenched teeth. Although I use a heavy German accent. So its, 'Vun more vurd'.)

The grin on his face is so lascivious it can only mean he's caught on. It's fun being Mistress Helga so I continue with the German motif.

"You vill go to the Old Fourth Ward Park and find Nate." I slap the fly swatter against my palm as I pace across the kitchen, my back ramrod straight. "Once he is located, you vill invite him to lunch at the Ponce City Market, vere I vill be waiting."

"He's not going to like that," he says.

When I lurch toward him, he rakes his chair back and jumps away. I chase him up the stairs, swatting the steps and threatening him with serious punishment for his insolence. And yes, he giggles like a little girl.

CHAPTER THIRTY

We can't really go to the park until Monday; it's way too crowded on the weekend. Nate would never subject himself to all those people. I spend Saturday and Sunday actually working on the book about our last adventure while Brian sits for torturous hours deleting hundreds of photos from his hard-drive.

Good thing we had that boisterous romp Friday night to carry us through. I'm just sorry I don't own leather pants or over-the-knee black boots. That would have really rocked the Helga scene. Wearing the rubber boots I wore at the river would not have been a turn on for either of us.

And now that the weather is getting nice, there's no point getting to the park Monday until after the office moles have returned to their cubbies and the restaurants are deserted again.

"Maybe I should try and disguise myself," I say. "So Nate doesn't freak out."

"Good idea," Brian says. "I've got that red spongy nose we got at the drug store last year for the charity event."

"Very funny."

"How about that red and green and yellow Rasta hat we got in Jamaica with the dreadlocks sewn in?"

"Even better," I say with what I call the 'smiling bitch face.'

I end up wearing a ball cap with my hair pulled through the back in a ponytail. Plus I've got an old pair of sunglasses that cover half my face. The plan is for me to get to the restaurant first and sit in a booth. Brian will come along with Nate, who hopefully won't recognize me right away.

The point is to get him seated before he screeches 'You!' at the top of his lungs, and either runs away or attacks me. Brian will sit on my side so Nate will sit across. Then I'll say something about Sarah coming to meet me and Brian will move over next to Nate. That way, we'll have him penned in so he can't escape. (At least that's the plan.)

* * *

I RUN A few last minute 'suggestions' by Brian before he drops me off at Ponce City Market. Then he'll head to the Old Fourth Ward Park.

"If he gets agitated, I promise I'll leave," I say. "But first let's try the good cop/bad cop routine. If he gets upset, you tell me to shut up."

Brian's pretty psyched with that possibility. As he drives away, I see his head bopping to some tune.

Inside the huge market, I have lots of time to kill. Brian's going to text me if he finds Nate and can talk him into lunch. I start at a women's clothing store and ogle all the Chloe and Prada I'll never be able to afford. I move next door to an accessories shop and mourn over a delicious Fendi handbag. Then it's on to a jewelry store . . . well you get the drift.

Finally, after I've saved us close to fifteen thousand dollars, Brian texts me. *Found him. On our way.*

I find a booth at Burt and Tillie's and wait. My plan goes off without a hitch. Brian acts all surprised to see me.

"I thought you were going to the Vortex," he says as he sits down beside me.

Once Nate has taken a seat across from us, I throw in the bit about Sarah coming and Brian moves over to 'secure' our guest.

Nate is quite chatty this afternoon. Of course, he's talking to Brian exclusively and it's about music—what a surprise.

I jump in after the waitress takes our order. "Brian says you went to University of Tennessee. And you saw Guns 'N Roses. That must have been awesome." (Okay, so Brian coached me on a good opening into the conversation.)

Then I add my own zinger by asking if they performed 'Knockin' on Heaven's Door'. I did my own research so I knew the playlist for the Knoxville concert that year. They did not perform that number, although that was the year they first added it to their shows.

Nate is impressed I guess because he actually looks at me for the first time and smiles. If he recognizes me, he doesn't seem to remember pushing me down at the pancake restaurant.

"Interesting," I say, "that Bob Dylan wrote the song for the movie *Pat Garrett and Billy the Kid*, and then GNR used it for their soundtrack of *Days of Thunder*." Boom! (In my head, I just dropped a microphone.)

Then before the geeks can get back into music talk, I throw in my own lead. "Brian says you studied forensic science?"

Nate gets a twitchy expression and looks down at his hands.

I keep things moving. "I've always wondered something about the OJ Trial and the bloody glove."

His head rises slightly from between his shoulders, like a turtle taking that tentative first move.

"Why didn't they turn the glove inside out," I ask, "and check for hair and skin samples?"

"Great question," Nate says as he shifts into Mr. Science mode. "The murder of Nicole Simpson was in 1994. The technology wasn't there at the time. But interestingly enough, just two years later, forensics experts mastered the technique now known as 'touch DNA' and used it to clear the Jon Benet Ramsey family of wrongdoing."

"You mean if they'd just hung on to the bloody glove for a couple more years, they could have gotten OJ on murder."

"Maybe," he says.

Brian asks him, "How long could the prosecution keep the bloody glove and still be able to test the blood? I mean, wouldn't it be worthless after a while?"

The question doesn't throw Nate into a fit of panic like I expect. He seems happy to be discussing his expertise again.

"The process of decomposition of DNA depends on certain things: Heat, water, sunlight, oxygen. Any of those will speed up the process. But if the glove was stored in a cool, dry place, the dried blood could last for years. They found King Richard III's skeletal remains in 2012 and successfully tested it for DNA."

I decide to test the waters. "It wasn't just a bloody glove. Wasn't there a bloody sock too?"

Nate's composure slips. The smile disappears, his upper lip twitches at one side. As he stares at me, I think the whole scenario in front of the pancake restaurant comes back to him. He turns toward Brian and calculates how he can get past him.

I figure, I've gone this far, I may as well spill the beans.

"Look, Nate. We know about the sock. And I think Charlotte put you in a terrible position, asking you to test it."

A low groan starts deep inside Nate. His eyes tumble around in his head as he looks for an escape: Over the table? Under the table? Across Brian?

"Nate . . ." Brian says.

"She killed that man," Nate screeches.

The few people in the restaurant glance our way. Two waiters tilt their heads together, wondering if we need to be tossed out or the police called.

Brian holds up his hands to calm Nate without actually touching him.

He speaks quietly. "I don't think she did. We think Darrell did it and she witnessed the murder. Weren't the hair follicles from a man?"

"Of course they were," Nate whines. "It was the victim's sock."

"No," I say. "It was the murderer's sock. Darrell Pressley."

I tell him the Limelight story, and how Adam and Lonnie followed Tommy into the cemetery. As I talk, Nate calms down. Conversations in the restaurant start up again. The two waiters are relieved they don't have to make a decision.

Once I'm finished giving Nate the details, I ask, "Who has the sock now?"

He's thinking about it all just like Cynthia did. How he'd thought one thing, but it was something entirely different.

At last he whispers, "I think Audrey has it."

"Audrey?"

"She said Darrell's been trying to find it for years." Nate shakes his head. "All this time, I thought he wanted Charlotte to get caught so he could leave her."

"You had it partly right," I say. "As long as she has that sock, he's at her mercy."

* * *

MY CAR is parked across from the Fuller House. I got here at seven this morning to stakeout the place. I'm hoping Audrey will show up sometime and I can confront her about the sock. I tried to get Brian to come along but he's pretty much over stakeouts since the last time when he got punched, a rental car was stolen, and then driven into a storefront window.

This probably isn't the best place to get into a conversation with Audrey about her brother, but I don't know where she lives, and I imagine a confrontation at Nordstrom's might be disruptive as well.

Two granola bars, a Yoo Hoo and a bag of pretzels later, she shows up at the women's center. I get out of my car and meet her on the sidewalk.

The scowl on her face would intimidate a less motivated person. There's no point in working up to the crux of the matter.

"You know," I say, "one of Nate's biggest problems is that he knows about Tommy Martin's murder. But he thinks Charlotte did it."

Audrey rears her head back like I've slapped her. I guess it does come as a shock that I know so much.

"He saw a simple dirty sock lying in the grass," I continue, aiming my hand at the ground, "and totally freaked out. This needs to be resolved and Nate needs professional help to get past it."

"You need to mind your own business," she says, jabbing a finger at me.

"Don't you care about your brother? Don't you realize how much this has been messing with his head?" My voice gets a bit high as I add emphasis. "It's been nearly thirty years!"

Finally, her prune face smooths out. "I had no idea he thought that."

"Yeah, well maybe you should spend some time with him now and then."

The cords in her neck stretch. "Now that I'm aware of the situation, I can take it from here. And you can go back to sticking your nose in your brother-in-law's business."

Time to go for broke. "I want the sock. I want Darrell Pressley prosecuted for the death of Tommy Martin."

"Absolutely not."

"I'll be the bad guy," I say. "I'll tell my friend in the police department I found the sock. They can do incredible things now. I can throw some dirt on it and say I found it in the woods. You won't be involved."

Audrey's mouth opens to argue but then she closes it. Is she thinking about it? Is she imagining Darrell Pressley in an orange jumpsuit?

I give her a little nudge. "I promise to keep you and Nate out of it."

"What about Charlotte?"

I shrug my shoulders. "I'll leave that up to you."

A good investigator knows when to back off. I say, "Just think about it." Then I hand her one of my cards from the magazine. "Call me and I'll come get it whenever you say."

I walk back to my car feeling confident that I've won her over.

* * *

I GIVE HER two days to call me. The wait is excruciating. In a moment of weakness, I even bought a box of Twinkies which I've been gorging on. Brian hasn't said a word. I think he's glad I've given up the fruit and vegetable crusade.

Thursday afternoon, I can't stand it any longer. I call the Fuller House and ask for Audrey but when Tanya comes back on the line, she tells me Audrey isn't interested in talking to me.

"And don't call here again," she adds.

In what is one of my dumber moves, I drive downtown and park in front of the Fuller House . . . again. I'm going to try one last appeal. My only fear is that Audrey will see me and send Tanya out to beat me to a pulp. Instead, the police show up.

An officer walks up to the driver's side window and taps on the glass. "We received a call that you are stalking a woman who works here. You are hereby ordered to cease and desist." He tosses a folded piece of paper onto my lap. "The victim has taken out a restraining order, so if I catch you here again, I'm taking you in."

CHAPTER THIRTY-ONE

I've been in my share of embarrassing situation throughout my life, but nothing compares to being slapped with a restraining order. I'm too ashamed to tell Sarah or Ellie. Somewhere down the road, I'm sure I'll think it was hilarious and recount the story to guffaws, but not yet. And I'm dreading the day Jake somehow finds out.

As far as investigating the death of Tommy Martin, Brian and I have exhausted our leads. Unless I decide to go undercover as a cleaning lady, get hired by Audrey, and then search her house while scrubbing her toilets, there's no way I'll get my hands on that sock. Darrell Pressley will no doubt win the election and I'll kick myself every day for somehow letting that happen.

The worst part of it all is that the mystery of why Deborah Wiley drove into that pond will remain just that.

At least I've been hammering away on my computer, writing the book about the capture of Farouk al Asad. It's been easy to get the nuts and bolts of the story down. Now I'm adding the fluff: the sounds of shattering glass, the humiliation of standing out on Mansell Road with my breasts exposed to passersby, the fear of dying in my own kitchen while wearing a bustier and fishnet stockings.

I take a break to pay some bills, and while I'm checking our credit card statement for bogus charges, I see over one hundred dollars to some company called BSC Enterprises. I meander down the hall to see if Brian knows what it's for.

"Oh, that," he says.

Talk about guilt; he even glances behind me like he might try and make a run for it. I cross my arms and wait.

"Well," he says, "remember when Jackson wanted me to take him to see that band?"

I nod. "I also recall that you told him no."

"Yeah, well, at the time, I thought it would be okay so I bought two tickets."

"Brian . . ." I whine.

"Hey! He wouldn't give me the drone until I proved I had them!"

"You bought them that night?"

He nods vigorously, like a kid who sees a way out of trouble. "But once you said it was a 'no-go' for Jackson, I invited Nate. At the time, it seemed like a perfect way to bond with him and maybe get some information."

I can't fault Brian's logic. It's just unfortunate that there's no more information to get from Nate.

"So when is this concert?'

Brian mumbles something that sounds like 'tomorrow night'.

My voice get shrill again. "And when were you going to tell me?"

"You know, I asked you first but you weren't interested," he says, all defensive.

"Yeah, well, I thought it was a hypothetical question."

"So have you changed your mind?" he asks. "Do you want to go?"

"No thanks. There's nothing about seeing a band called Bat Shit Crazy in some old warehouse that appeals to me."

"Good," he says. "Because when I told Nate about it, he was psyched."

* * *

LIKE MOST wives, I enjoy the occasional night alone. I can lounge around in tattered sweats, watch sappy romance movies, and eat a whole bag of popcorn without having to share.

While Brian and Nate were hanging out at the Old Fourth Ward park, they agreed to meet early at Pronto Taqueria to get something to eat and then go to the concert from there.

What a great plan. Eat a bunch of refried beans and jalapenos, then go stand at a concert for a couple hours while all that bubbles and boils in your stomach.

I'm lying in bed with a box of Kleenex, trying to decide what I should watch next: *A Walk to Remember* or *The Notebook*. The phone rings and I check the time. It's eleven o'clock. Too late for my mother to call unless they're on the West Coast again and she wants to tell me a funny story about a sea lion. I hope it's not Gwen warning me Jake knows about the restraining order.

I check caller ID. It's Brian.

"Hey!" he says all cheery. My Spidey senses are on high alert immediately. "We had a little trouble at the concert."

Oh, hell. The Jeep's been stolen, or the tires are gone and it's up on blocks. "What kind of trouble?"

"Nate got stabbed."

"Omigod!" I swing my legs off the bed like I can think better with my feet on the floor. "Is he alright?"

"Not really. They brought him in to Grady."

I stand. "Is that where you are?" I ask, heading to our closet. Already, I'm thinking about what to put on to drive to the hospital.

"Yeah. I kinda got nicked myself."

All of the blood drains from my head. There's a tingling in my lips and I can't feel my fingers. Either I'm going to puke or faint. I stagger back to the bed and sit.

"Rachel?"

My head is between my knees. "Are you hurt?" I whisper.

"I'm fine," he says. "The nurse cleaned up a scratch on my cheek and I'm just waiting for a doctor to decide if I need a couple stitches."

I burst into tears. "I knew you shouldn't go there. What if you'd gotten shot? What if you were dead right now?"

"Babe," he says. "I'm fine. If you want to feel bad about someone, it should be Nate. He got hurt pretty bad. I'm going to stick around here until he's out of surgery."

"Surgery?" I croak. Then I press my fist hard against my mouth to keep from howling.

"Rach?" he says, and he sounds like a little kid. "I think he's going to die."

I hop up. Brian needs me. "I'm on my way."

THE RECEPTIONIST in the emergency room tells me Brian is in one of the examination rooms. Once I prove I'm his wife, a nurse comes out and takes me to him. 'Examination room' is a bit of a misnomer. There's a long aisle of gurneys, each one divided by a privacy curtain.

Brian is lying on one such gurney, wearing a hospital gown. His legs are covered by a sheet. A small bandage on his face is the only sign of trouble I see. His eyes are closed, his lips are moving. If I didn't know any better, I'd say he was praying. He hears me and opens his eyes.

"Oh, Rach . . ." he says.

I rush over, throw my arms around him and pull him tight.

"Thank God you're okay," I say. "Have you heard anything more about Nate?"

His face is buried in my chest; all he does is shake his head 'no'. We sit clinging to each other for a moment, but then the curtain around the gurney parts and a doctor comes in.

"How's Nate?" Brian asks.

"Is that the other stabbing victim?"

Brian nods.

"We got him stabilized and he's gone to surgery."

"Is he going to be okay?"

"It's too soon to tell," the doctor says. "How's the leg?"

"Not too bad. The nurse numbed it a while ago."

I move out of the way so the doctor can remove the sheet. There's a huge gauze bandage taped to Brian's thigh. When the doctor pulls back the gauze, I gasp. There's a huge gash at least four inches long.

I reel back until my legs hit a chair and I slump into it. Now I know I'm going to puke.

"I think we can close this up without surgery," the doctor says. "When's the last time you had a tetanus shot."

I can't help it. I start to cry.

"Come on, Rach," Brian says. "Don't do this."

The doctor gives me the bug eye. If I make a scene, I'm sure he'll tell me to leave. I squeeze my trembling lips together and nod that I'm going to behave.

While the doctor stitches, he asks Brian what happened.

"We were at a concert in an old warehouse over on Lucky Street," Brian says.

The doctor snorts. "I wish I had a dime for every time something happened on Lucky Street."

"It was a pretty rowdy crowd," Brian says. "So Nate and I hung back. I'm not into all that body-slamming and head-banging. I didn't think Nate was either. We were just watching all the crazies in the mosh pit when suddenly Nate runs to the front and flings himself right into the middle of it. He's chest-bumping strangers, and swinging his fists. It's like he just snapped. Some guy didn't like it so he started pushing back. They threw a couple punches and the next thing I know, the guy's got a knife."

"I take it there wasn't much security," the doctor says.

"Nah. The guys at the door didn't even tear our tickets. We flashed them and they just waved us through."

"So the guy has a knife—" the doctor prompts.

"Yeah. I tried pushing through the crowd. I guess I thought I could stop it. But nobody was moving. I watch the guy stab Nate in the stomach but I can't get close. I rammed head first through the bodies just as the guy raises his arm to stab Nate again. The dudes nearby see what's happening and all of a sudden everyone steps back. I see the crazy guy on the floor, stabbing Nate. I jump on his back to pull him off and he swings his arm around to get me. That's when he got my face."

The doctor pauses in the stitching. "I'll look at it in a minute. Go on."

"I managed to roll him off Nate but then he was on top of me. And it was the weirdest thing. It was like slow-motion. I look around at all the faces staring down at us. Some of the kids are actually smiling, like they're enjoying the show. No one looks like they're going to pull this guy off me or take his knife away. I almost expected them to start chanting, you know like when some fool is up on a ledge and the people below yell, 'Jump! 'Jump!'"

"The mob mentality," the doctor says, shaking his head.

"The music stops and I hear some yelling. I hope it's the bouncers or somebody. And I guess the guy thinks that too because now he just wants to get away from me. But I've got my legs wrapped around him. That's when he stabbed me again." Brian nods at the slash in his thigh. "Some burly dude kicked knife guy in the face with his combat boot and it was lights out. The crowd cheered, a couple punks pulled him off me, and here I am."

"You were very lucky," the doctor says. "And so was your friend. I would never advise confronting an attacker with a knife, but then your buddy would probably be dead now if you hadn't."

Tears roll down my cheeks. I'm torn between being proud of Brian and wanting to throttle him for almost getting killed. My brain can't even compute what I would have done if he had. I think about times when I get mad over nothing, or harangued Brian over silly habits that don't mean a thing. And I think about the desperate women who show up at Fuller House every day, hoping to find a way out of their dire situation while I have a wonderful husband who loves me, and yes—puts up with all my crazy shit.

The doctor finishes up by putting a small butterfly closure on Brian's cheek. "That should do. I'll have a nurse come and explain how to clean and care for your wounds. And you'll have to stick around. The police want to talk to you."

"I'm not going anywhere until Nate's out of surgery."

The doctor pats Brian's good leg and turns to leave. A nurse pokes her head through the curtain. "The family of the stabbing victim is at the desk."

The doctor nods and walks out.

After the nurse goes through her spiel about not getting the wound wet for a few days, and keeping the bandage clean, she hands us a sheaf of papers. She also hands Brian a pair of men's sweats from their 'clothes closet' before disappearing.

He sits while I ease his wounded leg into the pants. Once he's ready, he leans on me and slides off the gurney so I can pull them up. They must be XXLs because by the time I have the drawstring tight enough to keep them from falling down, it looks like he's wearing balloon pants. I think about doing a little *Can't Touch This* foot shuffle but I don't think Brian's in the mood.

He glances down at his tee shirt. The sultry blonde on the front is now a ginger from blood that poured from his cheek. He groans. I hope the tee isn't worth a lot because there's not enough Spray and Wash in the world to get all that out.

I make a mental note to donate any of our clothing discards to area hospitals from now on. Everyone who walks out of here is probably in tatters.

Brian winces when he puts weight on his leg so I wrap his arm over my shoulders for support.

Out in the corridor, it's chaos as usual at Grady; and now that I'm not in a full-blown panic, I take a look around. Medical staff hustles from curtain to curtain pushing little carts and life-saving machines. On each gurney a person cusses, or wails, or shouts, or moans. As Atlanta's premier trauma center, they get everything from ghastly car wrecks to severe burn victims. But because it is located in the heart of downtown Atlanta, they also get the shootings and stabbings.

We round the corner and see the nurses' station ahead. The doctor who stitched up Brian has his back to us. Once we're closer, I see him talking to a couple.

I put on the brakes. "That's Charlotte and Darrell Pressley," I whisper.

Brian shakes his head and gets me moving again. "No Way. You are not going to harass either of them."

"But . . ."

"He could be dead, Rachel."

It's like a slap in the face.

"You're right," I say, ashamed of myself for even thinking about approaching them at a time like this. "Sorry."

I secure Brian again on my shoulders and we continue hobbling to the waiting room. As we pass by the Pressleys, the doctor sees us.

Then he glances over at a man in a suit and tilts his head in our direction.

"Mr. Sanders," the man in the suit says.

"Yeah."

"I'm Detective Peterson. I'd like to ask you a few questions."

I'm a bit surprised the detective didn't interview Brian in the examination area but then there's probably someone with a gunshot wound who needs the gurney. We follow Peterson to the waiting area and I'm shocked to see it's packed. At one in the morning? I guess crime never sleeps.

The detective spots some empty seats in a back corner. I get Brian settled in, with his leg propped up on an empty plastic chair that has *Die Mutherfucker* carved into the seat. Then I sit next to him and hold his hand. He tells the cop the same story he told the doctor.

"Any idea who the attacker is?"

Brian shakes his head. "Not a clue."

"He had no identification on him," Peterson says. "We've searched his pockets. He didn't have a ticket. My guess is he's a homeless guy who lives in the warehouse."

He asks a few more questions before closing his little notebook. He hands Brian a business card and walks away.

"You hungry?" I ask Brian.

"Starving."

"Let me find out if there's any food in the building," I say. I stand and then lean over and kiss him. "Be right back."

When I turn, I almost plow right into Charlotte Pressley. She looks a bit heftier than she did in the walk-a-thon pictures. And in most publicity shots, she's either wearing a long gown or a tasteful pantsuit. Her weight is probably another bone of contention for Darrell.

She gives me a weary smile. It looks like she's been crying. "I understand your husband saved my brother's life."

"As a matter of fact, he did." I step to the side so she can see his blood-soaked shirt and bandage on his cheek. She gasps just like I did. (She should see his leg.)

"I'm so so sorry," she says. "And grateful to you for coming to Nate's rescue. If there's anything we can do." She beacons Darrell and he inches his way forward. Not too close, though. He's probably wondering if Brian is one of Nate's street cronies.

"Thank you," I say, extending a hand. "I'm Rachel Sanders. This is my husband Brian."

Ever the gentleman, he struggles to get to his feet.

"Oh, no," she says, waving her hands at him to stay seated. Then she reaches down and shakes his hand. "According to the policeman, you're the only one who jumped in to save Nate."

"Well it was a young crowd," he says. "A lot of them weren't sure what to do."

He's being so valiant. I'm going to have to come up with a reward when we get home; either sex, or bacon and eggs *and* pancakes. Then I flash on the scene at home if Nate dies. It's a sobering thought.

CHAPTER THIRTY-TWO

We're all standing there, staring at each other. I'm sure Charlotte is wondering how to end this conversation and walk away. Darrell is texting, or pretending to text, on his phone.

"I was just going to see if there's a snack bar in here someplace," I say. Both Darrell and Charlotte look confused. I guess they figured we'd be going home.

I explain, "We don't know how long Nate's going to be in surgery."

"You're a friend of Nate's?" Charlotte asks.

"I guess you could say that," Brian says.

Charlotte whirls around to Darrell. "Why don't you call Patrick and see if the kitchen is still open. Ask him to send over something."

Darrell steps away as he taps on his phone.

"Let us get you something to eat," Charlotte says. "It's the least we can do."

Her head turns slowly as she surveys the dregs of society slumped in chairs watching an old Humphry Bogart movie in black and white. The sound is off so it impossible to know what he's saying since he usually talked through clenched teeth.

"Perhaps we can find someplace a little more quiet," Charlotte adds.

This has to be quite a quandary for the Pressleys. I'm sure they would much rather have Nate life-flighted to a nice white northern-suburbs hospital, but how would that read in the press? Besides, northern-suburbs hospitals are great for emergency appendectomies, but probably not so good with stabbings.

Charlotte whooshes off to the reception desk and ten minutes later, a woman who must be part of Grady's PR department comes out to shake hands with both Darrell and Charlotte. There's nodding and pointing at Brian and me, then more discussion. Something seems to be settled because all four of us are escorted down hallways and through PRIVATE doors. We end up in the doctors' dining area. The PR woman assures Charlotte she will send someone as soon as Nate is out of surgery. Darrell is still avoiding us by staring at his phone.

We've just gotten through the basics of who we are and where we work when a man in a chef's coat bursts into the room followed by two wait-staff in black trousers with white stripes, and black chef coats with black and white checked bandanas around their necks.

"Patrick!" Charlotte calls out and rushes to him, throwing her arms around him. "You are such a jewel to come to our rescue."

"Charlotte," he says, kissing both her cheeks. "I'm so sorry to hear about your brother. I wish I could do more."

The two staffers bustle about opening boxes. One throws a table cloth down on a round table while the other sets out real china for four. Lids are popped off containers and a meal of sautéed vegetables and veal medallions are dished up. Holy crap. It finally hits me. This is Patrick DuMonde, the chef at the latest trendy restaurant in Midtown.

While the two waiters serve dinner, Patrick opens one of those portable bar cases, places four wine glasses on the table, and pops the cork on a red wine that probably costs more than Brian and I make in a month.

"You shouldn't have done this," I say.

Secretly, I can't wait to tell Sarah all about tonight. I study the wine label so I can tell her what was served.

"Nonsense," Patrick says. He pulls the chair out for me since Darrell is already seating Charlotte.

Brian eases into the last seat with a sigh. "This smells great."

One of the staffers uses tongs to place tiny stuffed red potatoes on each plate. The other retrieves four perfect swirls of chocolate mousse in silver ruffled papers and places one in front of each of us.

"Bon appetit," Patrick says and with a bow and a wave of his hand they all disappear. There's no discussion about what to do with the plates when we're done. Darrell doesn't hand him a credit card to pay for the food. For the first time in my life, I understand what it's like to be really rich.

"Eat, please," Charlotte says. "Don't let it get cold."

Brian digs in. As I reach for my fork, my fingers touch the plate. It was warmed before being packed. I try to take small bites but it's the most delicious food I've ever had in my mouth. It's going to be hard to go back to tuna casserole.

Charlotte takes one bite of each item and then sets her fork down and picks up her wine. She takes a good belt of that.

"So how do you know Nate?" she asks Brian.

Gulp. I shovel a big bite of veal into my mouth in case Brian spills the beans and we get thrown out.

"We met at that pancake place on North Avenue," Brian says.

I ponder the idea of telling the truth. Maybe Brian's got something here.

"Do you live in Midtown?" Charlotte asks.

"No. I had some business in the area and we stopped in for coffee."

"And you met Nate?"

"Well, he had this Cranberries tee shirt on, from the *No Need to Argue* tour. We started talking about music and just hit it off."

"Brian's really into music," I say.

"So is Nate," Charlotte says. "He's always talking about bands I've never heard of."

"Welcome to my world," I say with a smile. I pick up my wine glass and take a healthy sip.

"He told me some of the local musicians hang out at the Old Fourth Ward Park," Brian says. "They've got that amphitheater and when you play on the stage, it really projects the music. So Nate and I have been hanging out down there."

"That's wonderful," Charlotte says, and I think she really means it. "I'm so glad Nate has found someone with similar tastes."

Darrell is busy reading on his phone, but he manages to get into the conversation for a quick comment. "Let's hope he pulls through."

All three of us turn in unison to glare at him. What a douche. I can understand why Charlotte keeps him on a short leash. He probably isn't allowed to say anything unscripted.

Brian says to Charlotte, "Nate's a great guy. I wish I'd met him years ago. Although I had to rib him about the UT orange."

Charlotte smiles. "I take it you're not a Tennessee fan."

"Let's just say our loss column would have looked better if we hadn't played them every year."

"Where did you go to school?" she asks.

But before he can answer, the door to the small dining room opens and we all look to see Audrey. She quickly scans the room until she spots Charlotte and hurries over. Charlotte stands, so Darrell stands. Brian tries to stand but I just pat his arm to stay seated. Then I shove the last bite of veal into my mouth and wash it down with wine. I'm going to make a concerted effort to eat at least some of my mousse before the shit hits the fan.

The sisters embrace and kiss cheeks. "How is he?" Audrey asks.

"We haven't heard anything since they took him into surgery."

"I understand the man who attacked him is in custody," Audrey says.

"That's right," Charlotte says. "And this gentleman is a friend of Nate's. They were at a concert together. If Brian hadn't come to the rescue, Nate would have been killed right there."

Audrey's mouth drops open as she glances over at Brian. Again, he tries to stand but this time Darrell clamps a hand on his other shoulder to keep him down.

"Brian was stabbed in the leg," Charlotte explains in a loud whisper, "and his face was cut in the altercation."

"Dear God!" Audrey says. "What is happening to this city?"

Darrell gets a haughty smirk on his face, like this sort of thing never happened when he was on the city council.

"And this is his wife, Rachel," Charlotte says, extending her hand to me.

My mouth is full of chocolate mousse. I'd give Audrey a sheepish grin but I'd have brown teeth so I go for the closed lip version.

I count the milliseconds until recognition hits. I get to three before she reels back.

"You!" She picks up a glass of wine on the table. Oh, no. She is *not* going to repeat one of the most tired and overused assaults ever created in the entertainment world.

Oh, yes. She is. The wine flies into my face. And it's red wine. Thank God I didn't wear a nice shirt.

"What are you doing?" Charlotte screeches.

"This is the reporter I told you about."

There's a bit of confusion but just the word 'reporter' is enough to produce a frown on Darrell's face. Charlotte is still struggling to get the connection.

"She was asking me about Tommy Martin," Audrey says.

Whoa! Curled lips, gritted teeth, flared nostrils. It's time to make our exit.

278

Darrell whips out his phone. I'm sure he's calling a bodyguard/thug to come and break my legs.

"She wanted me to give her the sock!" Audrey says. "That's when I got the restraining order."

Geez, she makes me sound so criminal. I told her I'd keep her and Nate out of it.

But the mention of the sock causes Darrell to stop texting. He looks at Audrey. "You *do* have the sock!"

Darrell looks so pissed, I swear if he had a gun, he'd use it on both women. And evidently Audrey sees the level of his anger, too, because she backs up, her hands out front defensively.

"No," she says, "I threw it away."

"You threw it away?" Charlotte and Brian and I all yell at the same time.

"That's right. I'm not going to jail over this mess." She keeps her distance, but she zeros in on Darrell. "So you can leave Nate and me alone."

"I don't know what you're talking about," Darrell says. But he's distracted because he's back on his phone.

"Oh, come on Darrell," Audrey says. Her bravado edges back as his anger wanes. "I know you had our house bugged—again."

"You bugged her house?" Charlotte says.

Darrell looks up from his phone and points a finger at Audrey. "You can't prove that."

"Just send your goons over to take it all out. The sock is gone."

The furrow in Darrell's brow relaxes. Evidently, he's finally computing the fact that there is no evidence anymore for his crime. As his face lightens up, mine darkens. My sleuthing days are over. Maybe I can at least find out what happened at the cemetery.

I prop my elbows on the table and lean towards him. "Why *did* you go back later that night?"

"You're a reporter," he says with a sneer. "Why would I tell you anything?"

"I'm not really a reporter. I write for a travel magazine."

"And anything you say is off the record," Brian throws in. (I'm not the only one who watches too much TV.)

Darrell glances over at Audrey. "The sock is really gone?"

"I threw it in the fireplace last night," she says. "And yes, I watched it burn."

He leans back and swirls his wine around in his glass, a faint smile on his face, then takes a sip. Does he think I'm going to let it go?

"Was it your intention to make sure Tommy was dead?" I ask.

"No!" He plunks his glass down with such force, I'm surprised it didn't break. "I did it for Lonnie. He was so upset, afraid Tommy was dead. So I figured I'd walk Charlotte home and stop at the cemetery on my way back to the house." He turns to Charlotte. "But you were so drunk, you were coming on to me like a hooker on Moreland Avenue."

"I was not!" Her back is ramrod straight.

"You couldn't keep your hands off me. Kissing me. Groping my crotch. When I tried to push you away, you grabbed my belt and started to unfasten my pants."

Charlotte flushes with embarrassment. "I did no such thing."

"Whatever," Darrell says.

"So you bedded Ms. Wilkins," Brian prods.

Darrell raises his hands in surrender. "Yeah, I screwed her. Then I got dressed and headed for the cemetery. I was hoping Tommy had already come to and stumbled home. But if he was still there, and alive, I was going to call 911 and get someone out there." He takes a breath and sighs. "But he was still lying on the mausoleum steps like Adam said. And it looked like he hadn't moved."

He takes another drink of wine. "I leaned down to check for a pulse and suddenly Tommy opens his eyes. He rolls onto his back and groans. And he looks right up at me and says my name!"

"Yikes!" I say.

"Yeah! Then he says, 'Why'd you do that, Man?' like *I'm* the one who beat him up. It was as if he didn't realized he'd been laying there for three hours." Darrell bows his head and shakes it. "That's what I get for trying to be the good guy. Now he was going to tell the police I did it instead of that asshole Adam."

He's still shaking his head and now he's wringing his hands, too.

"So," I say quietly. "You had to finish the job."

He nods without speaking. I hear Audrey gasp at the idea.

"And then you dragged him down the hill and rolled him into the river," Brian says. "Were you hoping he'd float downstream for a while?"

"I guess," Darrell says with a shrug. "I don't know what I was thinking."

"But you didn't go back to the Sigma House," I say. "You went back to Charlotte's. Did you think you might need an alibi?"

He nods again. But his remorse quickly fades. "Then she wakes me up in the morning, crawling all over me, wanting to get it on again." He looks Charlotte right in the eye. "I just didn't have the stomach for it."

Damn, that's cold! If Brian said something like that to me, I'd be a basket case. But Charlotte's eyes flare like she's about to come unhinged.

"You may have had those other girls fooled, but believe me, you were lousy in bed. It was all me, me, me."

Ha!" he says. "How would you know what a good lover was like?"

Oh, brother. This could go on forever. I decide to intervene. "And somewhere along the line, Charlotte let you know she had evidence. The sock."

"Christ!" Darrell presses his palms against his head like he's going to explode. "For years I've been playing her little lap dog." But then he just calms down, and raises one hand to make sure there's no confusion. "I want a divorce. I'm going to start proceedings today."

CHAPTER THIRTY-THREE

Charlotte teeters on her high heels; she reaches out a hand and lightly rests it on the table as she gracefully sinks into her chair. The moment she has always feared is here. She's getting the heave-ho.

"But why?" Audrey asks. "You wouldn't be where you are today without Charlotte's help. And she's been so accommodating with your trysts."

"Ha!" he bellows. "Sneaking around, always worrying someone's going to see me? I want to date beautiful, high-class women. I want to take them to the finest restaurants, get our picture in the paper at galas."

"In other words," Charlotte says to Audrey, "he's tired of settling for skanks."

That gets my dander up. "Like Deborah Wiley?" I say.

Charlotte wheels around to face me. "Yes, like Deborah Wiley. What a piece of work. A newspaper carrier with a GED who didn't have enough sense to get out of her car and wade to shore."

"She was afraid of the water," I say.

"Then why did she swerve and drive right into the pond?" Charlotte says, her voice rising to the same octave as Minnie Riperton's when she sang that song 'Loving You'.

"How do you know she swerved?" Darrell asks.

A pained expression ripples over Charlotte's face. Her eyes zoom around in her head as she searches for an answer.

"That's what it said in the paper," she mumbles, then grabs for her wine and tips up the glass.

"I don't think so," Darrell says. "Is that why you were in such a good mood when you got back from Lucy's? Because you saw Deborah drive into the pond?"

"No! I was just glad to be home."

Now I don't claim to be an expert on non-verbal communication, but even I can see that's total bullshit. And the drowning is finally making sense. Something did cause Deborah to swerve and drive into the pond. It was Charlotte Pressley.

Darrell comes to the same conclusion. Although, I'm absolutely gobsmacked when he lunges at Charlotte and wraps his hands around her neck. He's going to strangle her. Audrey grips his arm to pull him away, but he wings it up to shake her off. Instead, his elbow catches her in the jaw and she reels back. She grabs at a chair to keep her balance but it isn't enough. She falls to the floor and the chair tumbles on top of her.

How could a man who's running for the U.S. Senate turn psycho so quickly? Although I guess being stuck with Charlotte for 30 years has taken its toll.

Brian struggles to his feet and hollers, "Let her go!"

But Darrell's good sense has left the building. If this were a cartoon, his eyes would be red swirls, circling in his head.

Charlotte is quacking like a duck. He's really going to kill her.

Brian hobbles the few steps it takes to get to Darrell, grabs his suit lapels with one hand, and yanks him forward, then cocks back his fist. I'm glad we're in a hospital because Brian's probably going to break his hand. And he's going to do some serious damage to Darrell.

But Darrell is out of control. I expect him to let go of Charlotte to defend himself. Instead, he jerks back pulling Brian forward then drives his head into Brian's face. Geez! Is there a man left on this planet who *hasn't* seen the classic head butt and wanted to try it?

Of course, 'the butt' is edited in with a stunt double for TV and the movies. And I'm sure professional fighters have practiced the move many times to get it right. Darrell, on the other hand, does it all wrong. It's supposed to be forehead to forehead, but Darrell hits Brian on the cheek bone. And it isn't his forehead that makes contact, it's his nose. I can tell because blood immediately comes gushing out. Darrell staggers back in pain and finally releases Charlotte.

Even though Darrell screwed it up, the blow is still effective. Brian tumbles to the floor, writhing in pain.

I scream like a banshee and charge Darrell from behind. I leap onto his back and wrap an arm around his neck. He twists to throw me off so I wrap my legs around his thighs to hang on. Blood flies from his nose as he jerks and turns and claws at my arm.

Out of the corner of my eye, I see Audrey and Charlotte help each other to their feet. Then they back a safe distance away. I'm sure neither of them wants my sneaker in the face, or blood on an Armani jacket.

I also see some guy in scrubs standing in the doorway, his phone held out in front of him. Oh, boy. Another opportunity to make the six o'clock news.

Darrell takes advantage of my distraction to pry my arms from his neck. With nothing to grip, I tumble to the floor. But I'm not done with him yet. I grab the edge of the table to pull myself up. It tilts. I flop back down to the floor just in time to catch plates of veal with caper sauce and chocolate mousse in my lap.

The shattering of dishes seems to stop the action.

Darrell stands frozen, gasping for air, blood running down his chin and dripping onto his crisp white shirt. He finally sees the guy in the doorway and charges at him, no doubt hoping to rip that phone out of his hands. But the guy dashes away. And by the time Darrell gets to the door, he's rethought running through the hospital with a broken nose and bloody shirt.

Audrey and Charlotte cling to each other as they watch it all in horror.

I crawl over to Brian who has just managed to sit up. His cheek is already swelling.

"Are you okay?" I ask him. (Yeah, I know, dumb question.)

"Yeah," he says. "How about you?" (Please refer to the comment above.)

We help each other to our feet. I get him seated, then pick up chips of ice that have sluiced out of spilled water glasses, wrap them in an already wet napkin, and hold the cold compress to his face.

He smiles up at me, then swipes a finger through a blob of chocolate mousse on my shirt.

"Mmmm," he says as he tastes it.

Then he swipes another glob and sticks his finger in *my* mouth. It is indeed delicious.

Darrell wobbles over to a chair and sits, then gathers up ice for his own compress. Charlotte and Audrey are both still off to the side, but they've loosened their death grip on each other.

Sanity has evidently returned to Darrell. He stares down at the blood all over his shirt, and shakes his head. Is he wondering where all that anger came from? Did he really care for Deborah that much?

Finally, he looks up at Charlotte. "Why did you change your flight? You weren't supposed to be back until after ten that morning."

Charlotte rolls her eyes like she can't believe he still wants answers. "I knew I'd get stuck in traffic and I had things to do."

"No," Darrell says quietly. "You switched to the earlier flight because you thought you'd catch me and Deb in bed again."

"Okay, fine!" Charlotte says. "I wanted to catch you two. Happy?"

"After I told you it wouldn't happen."

"I can't believe a word that comes out of your mouth!" she yells.

But I believe Darrell. Why rock the boat when he's got a fantastic apartment where he can wrangle all night with Deborah and she has to wash the sheets. So what was Charlotte doing at their subdivision so early in the morning?

The scenario plays out in my head but because I don't have an on/off switch, it comes directly out of my mouth.

"You wanted to have a word with Deborah, about Darrell. But what were you going to tell her?"

Brian turns to me, his eyebrows furrowed. "Why wouldn't she just go to Deborah's apartment if she wanted to talk?"

"She didn't want to be seen," I say. "Or maybe she thought it would be more dramatic to catch Deborah right outside her house."

Brian screws up his face. He's not buying it. "What are the odds of driving back from the airport and catching your newspaper carrier at your driveway?"

"Astronomical," I say. Then I turn to Charlotte. "You sat and waited."

Charlotte tries to keep a neutral face, but she can't keep her head from quaking. It reminds me of Katherine Hepburn when she got old.

"Then she sees Deborah's car turn into the subdivision." Brian pretends to throw papers out the window. "It takes a few minutes for her to make the circuit around the neighborhood."

"Plenty of time for Charlotte to drive out of the subdivision, turn around and drive back in, like she just happened to be coming home."

"In case anyone remembers seeing you," Brian says as he turns toward Charlotte.

"But why the confrontation?" I say as I face her too. "Did you intend to get out of your car and flag her down? Tell her to stay away from your man?"

Brian wrinkles up one side of his nose. "That's pretty Tammy Wynette."

"And why now? After all these years?" I ask.

Charlotte's torso has joined in the shaking. If she doesn't sit down, she's going to fall down.

Brian pinches his lower lip for a second. "The guy at the gym said Deborah was talking about getting married."

"Did you ever snoop around the apartment?" I ask her. "Did you find Bride magazines on the coffee table?"

"I don't have to listen to this," Charlotte says with her last ounce of dignity.

But as she tries to walk away, Darrell jumps up and grabs her arm. "Yes, you do," he says, pulling her over to the table.

Charlotte reels around to Audrey while tugging her arm to get free. "For God's sake, call the police."

"Actually," Audrey says quietly. "I'd like to know myself."

Darrell forces her into a chair. She reaches up to rearrange a lock of hair that has shaken loose.

"I would never let myself into that tawdry apartment," she says, her nose raised above the legal limit. "And in case you've forgotten, it wasn't 'her place'. I had every right to check on a tenant."

"Did you have someone on retainer?" Brian asks. "Keeping an eye on Darrell's Babe de Jour?"

Charlotte's cheeks turn crimson.

"You did!" Darrell yells.

"Oh, for God's sake," Charlotte yells back. "You were bugging my sister's house. Don't act all indignant."

"So you see Deborah at the gate," I say. "You get out of the car and she sees you. Did you try to flag her down?"

"No."

"Yes!" Darrell says.

She gives him the best resting bitch face I've ever seen. "I just wanted to tell her that you were never getting a divorce. Why can't you ever see beyond the dick in your hand? If she was talking marriage, it was just a matter of time before she bragged to someone about who she was marrying. How do you think that would play out in the news?"

"She doesn't stop the car though," I say. "She recognizes you, panics and swerves. Right into the pond."

Charlotte's head is back to that shaking business. She looks like she could use a drink, but all the wine has spilled. She folds her hands in her lap and looks down. "I never dreamed she'd just sit in that car and die."

"So you laugh," Brian says. "Ha! Ha! Her car is ruined. And you drive on home. You're in a great mood because you've intimidated the poor woman."

Darrell picks up the narrative. "I come downstairs and you're in the kitchen making coffee. I asked when you got home and you said just now. You even kissed me."

His lips pucker as though he'd like to wipe away her germs.

"And then you heard the sirens?" I ask.

He shakes his head. "No. I didn't know anything had happened until my driver came to pick me up at nine."

Brian turns to Charlotte. "Is that when you found out, too?"

Charlotte surveys what's left of our gourmet dinner, strewn all over the floor. Is she wondering if this will be the last time Patrick hand-delivers a gourmet meal to her? Will she be eating lots more chicken in some Club Fed minimum-security prison soon?

"I saw it on the news at noon," she says.

"Oh, Charlotte," Audrey scolds. "How could you just leave her?"

'Well I didn't think she was going to drown!" she snaps back.

289

Darrell's phone buzzes and he glances at it. A smile creases his face. "As much as I'd love to stick around, I've got an appointment with my attorney to talk about a divorce."

Geez. He's got an attorney who takes his messages in the middle of the night? What other shenanigans has this scumbag pulled?

He stands and straightens his tie. "So if you bitches will excuse me . . ."

He has the nerve to look at me, too before he walks out. Not ten seconds later, two security guards come busting into the room. How does Pressley manage to escape unscathed yet again?

Although with Charlotte as his spokesperson, he could probably slit an old man's throat and get away with it. The security guys haven't taken two steps into the room when she strides across the room and stops them cold.

"Can I help you?" she asks.

I'm astonished. First of all, she's still protecting Darrell even though he gave her the boot not ten minutes ago. I'd be screaming bloody murder and giving them a full description of the jerk. She makes absolutely no mention of the broken dishes and food on the floor, doesn't apologize or offer restitution. And we're in the *hospital's* dining room so if they wanted to raise a stink, they'd have every right to toss us out.

But no, she just stands there until the guys give the room one last cursory scan, I guess looking for the perpetrator of this destruction, then leave.

Once they're gone, Charlotte turns and gushes her thanks to Brian and me for coming to her rescue. Wrong! She gives Audrey a little head jerk and they both exit without a backwards glance. (I guess that's another perk of being rich.)

Brian looks as stunned as me. I'd get into a good rant but I glance down and see blood seeping through the gray sweats the hospital loaned him. Looks like we're heading back to the emergency room. Do they bill patients for the second set of clothing if they can't even get out of the hospital before starting another ruckus?

As we drag down the hallway, I see a doctor in scrubs talking to Charlotte and Audrey. He looks exhausted. I sidle up a little closer to listen in.

"... vitals are stable for now," he's saying to them. "He should be moved to ICU in the next hour."

I hear things like 'peritoneal lavage' and 'laparoscopy', but the only thing that really sinks in is when he says, "We're cautiously optimistic."

CHAPTER THIRTY-FOUR

Remember that space movie where one of the astronauts accidently breaks the tether to the ship and just slowly floats away? That's how I feel today. Not only is my mission over, I have failed. The Tommy Martin case clung to one thread: the bloody sock. And because of my butting in, the sock is gone. Now there's no way to prove Darrell Pressley had anything to do with Tommy's death.

Do I feel guilty about being a part of this? Sure. But then Charlotte was never going to bring him to justice either. I realized that after her performance with security last night. She doesn't want to get dragged down by any hint of scandal even if it's her husband's behavior that dumps her in the mud. Too bad Darrell never realized that. He could have gotten out of his marriage a lot sooner.

Actually, I feel more guilty that because of my meddling, I was instrumental in unleashing another sexist louse into the world.

We got home around nine o'clock this morning, after stopping by to see Nate for ourselves in the ICU. We couldn't actually go into the room since Audrey and Charlotte were standing guard, but we're hopeful that he makes a full recovery.

It was interesting to see the sisters getting along after the 'sock incident' but then they've probably been snapping at each other for years. I know I lose my patience with Gwen sometimes but if she ever needed me, I'd be there in a flash. And after meeting some of those women at Fuller House, I'm thinking I might broach the subject of Jake and abuse when the time is right.

Brian tries to cheer me up as I sulk over coffee. I know I should have put him to bed and made him a nice breakfast but the doctor said he needs to keep moving his leg. (That is after he made Brian promise we would not get into any more brawls for 48 hours.)

If I start pampering him, who knows where it will end?

"It's just as well the sock is gone," he says. Then he edges a hand across the table to take one of the Twinkies I have stacked in a pyramid. (Yes, I was thinking of eating them all.)

I let him take it. I've already eaten three and my stomach feels queasy.

He takes a big bite before I can change my mind. "You don't know what Darrell would do if you got him in a corner," he says. "He might try and bring everyone else down with him. That means Lonnie, and Audrey, and Nate as accessories. And Adam as . . . I don't know what. A co-murderer?"

"I guess you're right," I say. "That's probably why Charlotte never did anything. She was afraid he'd accuse her of being an accessory."

"And what about Shannon? If Darrell went to jail he certainly wouldn't be paying her rent anymore. The only person you wanted to punish was Darrell."

"Yeah, well now I'd like to punish Charlotte, too. And that jerk Adam Winston."

"Let it go, Gladys." He takes away the sting of his tease by giving me a warm smile.

At least I'm vindicated on Deborah Wiley's death. Maybe it was an accident that she turned the wrong way and drove into the pond. But Charlotte certainly had a hand in that decision.

The minute I got home this morning, I called Tommy's mother. She was grateful for all the time we spent solving her son's murder, even though no one will ever go to jail for it.

I take another sip of coffee and check out my stack of Twinkies. Then I shove them all over to Brian's side of the table. I'm done binging.

"I wonder what Darrell *is* going to do about Shannon's apartment?"

"Good question," Brian says. "At least he paid ahead so she's got some time to find another place."

"Maybe he'll move in there and leave the house for Charlotte."

THE REST OF the day is a blur of naps and phone calls. First, I talk to Greg Olsen. He says they can't really close the case, but once he tells Athens police the details, he figures they'll file the case away.

I also call Bryce Shackleford. He's disappointed that the AJC won't be crucifying Darrell Pressley anytime soon. After that, I touched base with Detective Baker just to let him know the extenuating circumstances of Deborah Wiley's death.

I also get on Facebook to send Adam Winston a message. Something like: *Hey! Darrell says you're the one who beat Tommy Martin to death*, or something like that. But he's got me blocked so I can't even leave a private message.

* * *

In a very interesting turn of events, I get a call from Bryce Shackleford while I'm out walking with Sarah and Ellie.

"You're not going to believe this," he says. "I'm looking at a picture of you on Darrell Pressley's back. You've got him in a death grip and he's got blood all over his face."

I howl with delight. Maybe karma is going to bite Pressley in the butt after all. "Are you going to use it?" I ask.

"Hell yeah," he says. "Pressley would be crushed if he heard how many people saw this video before someone recognized him as a senator. Evidently, it's never a dull moment at Grady. When the guy brought his phone by to show me, he asked for money. But what the heck. It's a great picture. We're running it tomorrow."

"Holy crap! I'll bet he posted the video on YouTube. I've got to look for it."

Sarah and Ellie are both dying to hear who I'm talking to and what's going on. My neighborhood celebrity status has taken a giant step; I'm just not sure if it's up or down.

CHAPTER THIRTY-FIVE

It's been a fairly quiet spring at the Sanders household since Brian and I gave up on our latest investigation.

I finished another draft of the Farouk al Asad book and sent it on to my editor for a first look. She'll no doubt rip it apart and I'll have to go through it again from start to finish. Currently, I'm working on a short story for a crime magazine. It's about a female vigilante who seeks revenge on men who abuse women. The vigilante works at a women's shelter. Each time a woman relates how she was abused, our 'heroine' does the same thing to her husband or boyfriend. So, when a woman gets her hand slammed in a door, the vigilante catches the boyfriend unaware and slams his hand in a door. She doesn't kill anyone but she manages to wreak some havoc before she's arrested.

Brian's leg has healed nicely. He's got a nasty red scar on his thigh but he's walking without a limp—thanks to me badgering him every day to do his physical therapy—and he's back going to the gym. I think it's more about showing off his nasty red scar than about fitness, but whatever. He got a nice write up in the paper about saving Nate's life and he's going to milk it as long as he can.

Shannon is still living in the apartment. I guess neither of the Pressleys want the added publicity of having her evicted. I have a feeling she'll stick it out to the very end and then scramble to find a place to live. Maybe she'll go back to Eufala and live with granny.

Cynthia met Brian and me for lunch a couple weeks ago. She showed us a picture of Lonnie. He got all his hair cut off and shaved his face. I must admit he is quite handsome. I just hope I haven't been the cause of a rekindled romance between the two of them. That would break her husband's heart.

She said Lonnie took down all his signs too. And when he has a surplus of eggs, he sets them on a table outside the barbed wire fence for folks to take for free.

"He still won't leave the farm," she said. But it's a start.

I regret to report that Comet passed away. We're pretty sure he was devoured by a feral cat that showed up in our neighborhood recently. Undaunted, Brian bought a couple more fish to keep Pearly and the others company and he has covered the pond with some mesh like folks use to protect their pansies from deer.

You'd think that between the picture in the paper of our brawl with Pressley, and his very public divorce proceedings, his supporters would want to distance themselves from him. But that's not the case. Everyone loves dirt, and all the nasty comments coming from both Darrell and Charlotte are better than any daytime soap opera. (Yes, Charlotte has finally taken off the gloves and she's taking some scathing jabs at Darrell.) But his barbs are particularly cruel. I guess Charlotte is getting her comeuppance. And both of their lawyers are getting rich.

The primary is the first of June and Darrell is still leading the other candidates by a decent margin. Go figure.

He's gotten cocky enough with his invincibility that his picture has begun showing up on Facebook and Twitter with an assortment of babes. He's reveling in his 'eligible bachelor' status even though the divorce is not final. And it's another blow to Charlotte. I'll bet she can't even show her face at Bacchanalia. I'm sure she isn't dining at Patrick du Monde's restaurant.

Then a couple days ago, some pictures surfaced on Instagram. A couple are graphic enough to show that Darrell is having sex with some woman half his age. The official party line is that the pictures have been doctored in a desperate attempt to sabotage Darrell's campaign. Is it even Darrell? And if so, what does it matter? He's separated from his wife now. The problem is, she looks awfully young. Maybe too young?

The doorbell rings while I'm upstairs brushing my teeth. Who would come by this early? I'd let Brian answer it but he got up even earlier to take Nate to the park. I guess he figures if I'm badgering him, he needs to harangue Nate about his PT, too. So they take long, slow walks before it gets too hot.

I pull my robe tight and open the front door. It's Sarah, and from the way she's panting, she must have run all the way from her house. She's got this morning's paper in her hand.

"Check. This. Out."

The headline on the front page reads: **Candidate Accused of Sex with Under-aged Girl**. The subheading is even more of an eye-popper. *Russian ambassador taking Pressley to court for statutory rape.*

"Damn!" I shout. Then I throw my arms around Sarah for a big hug.

That's when I see Ellie bringing up the rear with her own newspaper. Across the street, I see Howard Jacobs in his driveway, reading the front page. His mouth drops open and he immediately glances at our house. 'Sorry Howard. Sarah beat you to it.'

Sarah and Ellie and I gather at my kitchen table to sip coffee and rehash all the reasons why Darrell Pressley deserves whatever he gets.

You know that saying 'Time Heals All Wounds', but then someone turned it around to 'Time Wounds All Heels'? It took a while, but Darrell Pressley is finally getting his comeuppance.

"It's obviously a set up," Sarah says.

"Who cares," Ellie replies. "That douche bag needs to be locked up for all the crimes he's gotten away with."

"Here, here," I say as I slap another round of pancakes on everyone's plate. Yes, even Sarah is eating non-gluten-free carbs with butter and real maple syrup. (Aldi's had it on sale.)

According to the article, the girl is only fifteen. And although one of the pictures on Instagram showed her riding Pressley like a bronco, now she's claiming she was drugged.

Even if he doesn't go to jail, I can't see him winning the primary now. And obviously, that's what this is all about. I guess the Russians want someone else in Congress.

After our breakfast binging, Sarah and Ellie and I walk a few of the calories off. At least three of my neighbors ask if I've heard the news and Sarah basks in the glory of being the first to break the story.

I finally head back to clean up the kitchen and wait for Brian to get home so we can go over it all again. That's when I get my idea.

Remember those rings I got at Cynthia's hardware store? I never got the chance to hang them on our bedroom wall. And of course, once the excitement of the case died, I wasn't in much of a frisky mood.

But I'm feeling frisky now. I rush upstairs with a hammer and other implements of destruction. It's been a while since Cynthia explained how to do this, but I know it had something to do with using these anchors to keep the screws nice and tight in the wall. I'm just finishing up when Brian gets home.

He's heard the news of course, but we still jabber away like magpies for a few minutes. When he says Pressley is 'going down', his right eyebrow jumps. And when I tell him Sarah gave us a 'blow-by-blow description' of an online article she read on Pressley, I shoot Brian a crooked smile.

We're upstairs in no time and I've got his wrists lashed to the rings I hung on the wall.

"In honor of Svetlana what's-her-name," I say, "I will be performing the bronco ride."

I don the kid's felt cowboy hat I bought at Stamps DIY and climb onto my one-trick pony. Who would have guessed it would be so appropriate? Brian looks up at me with adoration in his eyes. What man wouldn't?

I start out slow to get my legs warmed up. But soon we're galloping along with Brian throwing in some excellent bucks worthy of a class A rodeo rider. I cry out in ecstasy. It never fails that my excitement sends Brian over the edge. He bellows out his own primal cry and I see his neck muscles stretch, his biceps bulge.

The next thing I hear is a huge crack and both rings pop out of the drywall, anchors and all. One of the rings swings around and catches me on the ear. A cloud of dust from the crumbled plaster rains down onto Brian's face. He coughs and spits while I gape at the two big holes in our bedroom wall. This is going to be tough to explain to the repairman.

Thanks for reading *Into the Pond*. I hope you enjoyed it and will consider leaving a review on Amazon, Barnes & Noble, and Goodreads.

Why?

As novelist, journalist, and attorney Katie Rose Guest Pryal says:

"Your words are as important to an author as an author's words are to you." Those words may seem counterintuitive to you if you are a reader, but in our data-driven age, book reviews left by readers on Amazon.com and Goodreads can make a huge difference in the success of an author, especially emerging and mid-list authors who aren't getting their books reviewed in *The New York Times*.

So please take a minute to post a short review.

And if you'd like to contact me personally with your thoughts, you can find me on:

Twitter: https://twitter.com/marshacornelius

Facebook: https://www.facebook.com/marsha.r.cornelius

Goodreads: http://www.goodreads.com/author/show/4993738.M_R_Cornelius

Website: http://www.mrcornelius

You can find all of my books on Amazon.

https://www.amazon.com/M.-R.-Cornelius/e/B005HJP39W

Thanks so much,

Marsha Cornelius

CPSIA information can be obtained
at www.ICGtesting.com
Printed in the USA
FFOW03n1705301117
43843636-42800FF